THE CUTEST GIRL IN CLASS

QUENTIN S. CRISP was born in 1972, in North Devon, U.K. He studied Japanese at Durham University and graduated in 2000. He has had fiction published by Tartarus Press, PS Publishing, Eibonvale Press and others. He currently resides in Bexleyheath, and is editor for Chômu Press. His novella *Blue on Blue* was previously published by Snuggly Books.

JUSTIN ISIS was born at some point in the 1980s and has worked as a model, consultant, rapper and visual artist and currently heads the Tokyo Black Lodge occult group. His previous works include *I Wonder What Human Flesh Tastes Like* (ChômuPress, 2011) and *Welcome to the Arms Race* (Chômu Press, 2015), the poetry collection *Divorce Procedures for the Hairdressers of a Metallic and Inconstant Goddess* (Snuggly Books, 2016) and the anthologies *Dadaoism* (Chomu Press, 2012) and *Marked to Die: A Tribute to Mark Samuels* (Snuggly Books, 2016).

BRENDAN CONNELL was born in Santa Fe, New Mexico, in 1970. His works of fiction include *Unpleasant Tales* (Eibonvale Press, 2013), *The Architect* (PS Publishing, 2012), *Lives of Notorious Cooks* (Chômu Press, 2012), *Miss Homicide Plays the Flute* (Eibonvale Press, 2013), *Jottings from a Far Away Place* (Snuggly Books, 2015), and *Cannibals of West Papua* (Zagava, 2015).

QUENTIN S. CRISP
JUSTIN ISIS
BRENDAN CONNELL

THE CUTEST GIRL IN CLASS

THE CUTEST GIRL IN CLASS

Monday, 1ˢᵗ October, 9.47 p.m.

"I just feel more at ease around inorganic women."

Zak didn't look at Thad as he spoke, but inspected the fingernails of his left hand, the palm of which was resting on his right thigh.

"I thought you understood that, Thad, you know. That's why you're one of the only people I have round here. I don't want to hide Sooki away when anyone comes round. That would just be undignified, for her as well as for me."

Zak looked over to Sooki nervously. She sat in the opposite corner of the sofa, a presence as electric as she was demure. There was something about her of the shock of contrasts—the shiny black hair, almost vinyl, with a sheen like the grooves of a record, against the sculpted, void-like fog of her cheeks, ghostberry white, and the cherry-gloss gash of her mouth. She was not only a creature of contrasts in herself, but formed a contrast with her surroundings. Her perfect make-up and white summer dress seemed more suited to the catwalk than to lounging around in Zak's front room, and her stillness seemed to dominate the environment whenever Zak and Thad fell quiet.

Zak, in black T-shirt and jeans, despite his claim to feel at ease with her, seemed to be sitting at a distance almost as a mark of deference. His features were Caucasian, but his skin was mainly a dark coffee tone, with here and there a patch of pink suggesting skin disease or some anomaly in pigmentation. He looked, in fact, as if he had applied make-up badly to imitate someone of a different ethnic group. When he finished speaking, his mouth, in repose, remained open, his upper gums exposed, and he bore a general air of self-consciousness whose relation to his physical appearance, if it existed, was for some reason impossible to determine. If such a thing is feasible, it seemed a self-consciousness which, like his own skin, he was so used to that it had become *un*conscious.

"All I'm saying is, you've got a condo, you've got a good job—I'd be rolling in real live pussy. Hot, wet, organic pussy, you know, none of this inorganic bullshit."

"Thad, could you have a bit more respect, please? You know that Sooki's not like other girls. She's very easygoing, you know, she doesn't mind guy-talk so much, but frankly, you can go too far. It's embarrassing."

"Are you embarrassed?" Thad addressed Sooki directly.

There was silence. Zak and Thad both looked at her, waiting for a reply. None was forthcoming.

"See?" said Thad.

"See *what?* She's not saying anything 'cause she's embarrassed."

"Hey, Zak, I notice you said 'women' just now, as in like, more than one or something."

"I was talking in general. You use plurals when you're talking in general. Besides, Sooki knows she's not the first. We're okay with that."

"You ever had two together?"

"Come on, Thad."

"Sooki and maybe some blonde chick?"

"Thad, you're embarrassing me. Have some respect."

"Maybe you're not so stupid, eh? I mean, like, I know

you're a smart guy, Zak. What I mean is, you're not so dumb, are you, eh? You make, like what, 80K a year? Designing packages for M&Ms and shit. You know what you're doing. You know that chick I went on a date with—Angela—wouldn't sleep with me? She's a total slut."

"How is it, Thad, when some girl won't sleep with you she's a slut? You unpack that sentence, see, and it doesn't make sense. Does that mean she'd stop being a slut if she slept with you?"

"No. She'd still be a slut, alright. I just wouldn't mind so much, is all. Anyhoo, gotta take a leak."

Thad got up from his chair and walked across the room. As he passed the sofa he ruffled Sooki's hair.

"Hey, have some respect! I already told you!"

Thad entered the bathroom, looked at his teeth in the mirror, and took out his cellphone. He scrolled through the address book and pressed call.

"Mr Magister? Yeah, it's Thad."

From the other end of the line came a brief hum, then a deep voice, harsh but rich, like gravel stirred with treacle.

"Well? Does he have the Matsushima series?"

"I think so . . . it's definitely, I mean—it's definitely woman-shaped."

"Go on. Describe her to me."

"She has kind of black hair—definitely black. Red lips. If I saw her from far away I wouldn't be able to tell the difference."

"Did you take note of her vagina?"

"Um, no."

"Well, then tell me about her lips. Are they more of a rose colour? Or vermilion? What are the colour gradients on the hair like?"

Thad coughed.

"Yeah, see that's . . . I mean what does that shit even mean? I don't even know what you're talking about."

The voice shifted a register.

"Look. Did you get a picture?"

"Yeah, I took one with her and Zak right when I came in. I can send——"

"Do that," Mr Magister cut in. Thad thought he could hear another voice in the background. "Send it to the address I gave you."

"Okay, sure thing. So, anyway, about the payment . . ."

"It's already been wired to your account. But be sure you don't forget."

"Forget?"

"The bugging device dammit. In the choker. Switch. The. Choker."

"Yeah. It's as good as done. Just need Zak to take a dump or something."

"Don't leave there without making the switch. I need to be able to monitor the situation."

"Sure. Gotta go."

Mr Magister hung up and turned around. Hovering somewhere around the big five-o, he looked older than he was, or possibly younger—that is, only younger if one first guessed him to be older than he was because of the grey, the wattles, the creases, now mushrooming with a vigour that confounded even despair. His ageing was the premature ageing of the autodidact who has had to waste too much of his life force in trying to establish the good start that he never had, taking one detour after another, hoping each will turn out to be a short cut, and finally becoming so far lost that he has to pretend that this was his destination.

Regional manager of Fresh and Functioning (servicing American restrooms for more than thirty years), leading providers of all restroom hygienic services and facilities from here to the Western Seaboard, Mr Magister could certainly be proud of the solid respectability he had built, urinal screen by urinal screen, soap dispenser by soap dispenser. But that respectability was a pedestal only; there was as yet nothing to put on it, and already it felt like its foundations were giving way. A sensitive observer, brought in from another country and therefore not blinded by familiarity, might have read all this in his face in a few seconds.

His fourteen-year-old son Clive stood in the doorway, eyeing him from behind his glasses with a mixture of hesitation and curiosity.

"Shouldn't you be in bed?" Mr Magister said.

"What do you mean?" asked Clive, a slight edge of annoyance in his voice. It was almost as if his father had lost track of how old he was.

Clive sighed, letting and not-letting something go, shifted his position and leaned against the wall, holding his shoulders high and square. Appearance-wise, he took after his mother, Mr Magister thought: the same sandy-blond hair and pale skin, the same contorted frailty. Only his son's personality reminded him of himself, and even then it was a subtle resemblance. As Clive shifted and stared at the floor, Mr Magister sensed some of his own recklessness and secrecy, a kind of undercurrent visible at the edges, like the hazel rim of his green eyes.

"I was wondering if I could talk to you about something from school." Clive hesitated. "There's this girl . . ."

Mr Magister stepped forward and placed a hand on Clive's shoulder.

"We'll talk about this in the morning. I've got some business to take care of before I sleep. You don't want your dad to be tired in the morning, do you?"

He waited until Clive had closed the door, then turned and sank into his chair with a posture of mixed relief and exhaustion. After five minutes of rest he got up and went to the kitchen, taking the raisin bread from the table and the butter from the fridge. He toasted the bread, slathered on butter and made himself a cup of coffee. Then he pulled open the drawer that contained the frying pans and, digging beneath them, pulled out a slick catalogue and opened to the front page: a sleek baby-faced nude, her precision-moulded skin shining light pink. For months now, the kitchen table, the Real Doll catalogues, and the raisin toast had formed an inescapable triangle. Hunched over the pages in the aura of the Isla Clear Nickel 9 3/4" Wide Pendant Light, he took his time and stared at each full-colour photograph, a copy of the *Brynbach Daily Standard* near at hand to cover up the catalogue should Clive come in. It was so rare now to have any time to himself, any time to wander in that lacquered world of plastic beauty. Mr Magister closed his eyes and imagined the farmhouse where he kept his harem. Everyone would be waiting just where he'd left them. Elisabeth was in the kitchen, preparing him dinner. Maria was asleep on her side, her head resting on folded hands. Honey stood by the sofa, her left leg bent, leaning over to close the window. He imagined the moment when he would step through the door again and greet his brides by name.

Then there was Angelique, as he was thinking of calling her, though this Zak creature had opted for the ridiculous name of Sooki. He flipped to her picture. The last of the series . . . he had to have her. Since losing the online auction he'd returned to this picture night after night, unable to put it out of his mind. There was something different about her, something none of the other girls had. He swore to himself that he wouldn't rest until he'd made her his.

Tuesday 2ⁿᵈ October, 1.21 p.m.

Billy Glandzk took one last hit of the joint before extinguishing it with a little spit. He preferred Mexican weed because, aside from it being a quarter the price of the good stuff, he could smoke six or seven joints a day and keep going.

He put the roach in an Altoids container, amongst others of its kind, and then went into the bedroom, which, despite its name, he treated as an all-purpose storage facility. The boxes and packaging for his cameras lay beside empty plastic plates and cartons, the remains of last night's Indian take-out and last week's shrimp chow mien.

"Okay folks, time for me to head to work."

He had three dolls, Plock Plock, Sinthia and Darren.

He kissed Plock Plock on the mouth. A trim blonde, she was probably the cleanest, and newest of the three. Which wasn't very clean or very new. Passive, she took his mouth and stared at him, questioningly. He knew she wanted to be mastered, but he would wait to get back from work to do it. Sinthia, the brunette, he just hugged. She needed a good washing, but he had a pretty busy schedule and it would probably be a while before he got around to it. He also had been out of both shampoo and hand soap for days now. Darren didn't have a face. All the face plates were long since broken, but Billy still felt a lot of affection for him. And he had a really lovely body.

"Hey guy, take care of the ladies while I'm gone," he said, rubbing the doll's chest.

He picked up the bag with his Canon EOS 7D, flung it over his shoulder, went outside and got into his red Suzuki Jimny, turned the key in the ignition and pointed it towards Broad Street, where the *Idollatry* offices were.

As he approached the building front, he looked right and left for a parking space. He spotted one right in front of the building, but an old man in a Toyota Corolla was about to take it. Billy gassed his car and slipped in before the old man had the chance. The old man honked his horn.

"Take that horn and shove it up your ass!" Billy screamed from his window and then got out and trotted up to the office, his pony-tail bouncing behind him.

Carmen, the Puerto Rican secretary, greeted him.

"How goes it Billy?"

"Half baked."

"Right on."

She was a good-looking woman. Her breasts seemed like they were struggling to break out of her top and her mouth looked like it would be good for a lot of things besides eating.

Billy however, like all the men at *Idollatry*, had no interest in her. She talked too much and she was, well, a little too human.

He padded into the main office. It was a large room with a few desks scattered around it. Three or four doll posters were on the walls and there wasn't much else in the place but an empty water cooler and an old boombox resting on one of the deep window sills.

Billy waved at Sid—Sid Modimolle, a Tanzanian national on permanent resident status who wrote the magazine's few actual text pieces under various pseudonyms. He had previously run a small doll rag called *Dolly Viewz*, but it had folded after fourteen issues and Mr Mi-ti had lost no time in bringing him into the *Idollatry* fold. No one could write doll copy as well as Sid.

Bert Seidman was the copy editor. He always looked like he had been punched in the eyes a few times. He was in his mid-fifties and wore a black wig and dyed his thick moustache black to match.

"Billy," he said.

"Hey, Bert."

"Staying clean I hope?"

"Clean as a whistle."

"I had a goddamned pastrami sandwich for lunch and feel like crap."

"Yeah, yeah. But, um, what's shaking for me today?"

"Not sure. I think you have to go out to Long Island City to shoot a threesome, but not sure. Better ask the boss."

"Yeah, will do. Thanks Bert."

"Sure."

Billy went up to the door of Remy Mi-ti's office, knocked, and then opened it before waiting for an answer. Mr Mi-ti appeared to be squatting in the air with one hand on a touch screen tablet and the other on the keyboard of a bulky, outdated desktop computer. Both the desktop's tower and the plastic moulding of its monitor had been stained a dead-fingernail yellow by the editor's constant exhalation of smoke.

"Billy, how you going!" Mr Mi-ti asked with a smile.

"Pretty good boss, and you?"

"We got crazy work on, Billy. Big shoot up in Long Island City."

"Yeah, Bert told me."

"We got guy with two dolls Polish. Going all out."

"Polish?"

"Yes. Real sweetie Polish. You go up and do shoot. Take a lot of rolls, okay?"

"Um. I shoot digital."

"Okay, great. Lotta rolls then."

Remy Mi-ti was five feet two inches tall and wore tight discount slacks—ten dollars from Wal-Mart—and a light green Ermenegildo Zegna dress shirt with white pin-stripes—three hundred and fifty dollars from an online auction.

After handing Billy the shoot information, Mi-ti left his office, went down to the garage and got in his white Lexus Spider. Three cigarettes and twenty-five minutes later he was at his home in Rahway. There was a plum tree in his front yard, but the squirrels had already eaten most of the plums.

He walked between the two stone lions that flanked his door and opened it. His wife, Kiew Lan, a short, stout woman with permed and purple-tinted hair, greeted him in Hokkien.

There was a large brass peacock in the living room, but aside from this the place was decorated almost exclusively with AAA-grade dolls: reclining beauties with fully-articulated skeletons and medical grade platinum silicone flesh, their breasts and asses filled with the latest gel implants courtesy of Soft Chasm Products in California, the Echigen Studio in Japan, Sundown Dolls, and various private designers. Most had begun their existence as conventional models, but Remy had delved into his private treasury to bring them in line with his dreams, outfitting them with custom face-plates and heavily-modified vaginas in all the colours of the rainbow. Some of them were rimmed with knobs, spikes and metallic vestigial limbs, suggesting cybernetic implants from some grisly retrofuture; others were specimens of a deceptively chaste androgyny, nub-breasted, cherub-skinned. Still others had the barely human faces of newspaper caricatures and super-deformed anime heroines, all monstrous lips and eyes. A few, plugged into the software applications of nearby computers, were capable of recorded speech and rudimentary movement. Remy liked to set up a feedback loop between their voice recognition programs, stepping into the room and repeating a single word until a chorus of voices competed for his attention, the dolls cawing away at each other like electronic crows:

"My master——"

"My master!"

"MINE!"

"MINE!!"

"MINE!!!"

Sometimes at night the dolls responded to ambient sounds, picking up a drop of water from the faucet or a noise outside in the street; sometimes Remy and his wife were awakened by their escalating voices as one doll roused the rest. At these moments he was ecstatic. His wife, as ever, was patient.

After lighting a DJ Mix Apple Green cigarette, he got on one of his laptops while Kiew Lan fixed him a Banana Twist. He scrolled through the various doll auctions and checked a few items that he had book-marked to see what their status was.

"That real shit," he said after taking a sip of his drink, "They pay twenty-four thousand dollar for that real shit. These guys never taste real plastic pussy yet."

Kiew Lan asked him what he wanted for dinner.

"Three delicacies with garlic sauce," he replied without looking up.

He was just lighting another cigarette when the wind passion bamboo ringtone of his cell phone unfolded its blushes of ancient void electronic ambiance upon the air.

"Hello?"

"Mr Remy Mi-ti?"

"Yeah, this him."

"This is Fred Bergen."

"Ah, great, waiting long time hear from you. So you got it going on?"

"The pieces are being put in place. One of my, um, associates is working on it as we speak."

"That real sweet. I need Sooki bad."

"You'll get her."

"Yeah, she real fine model. All latest technology simulation structure polymer material selects the skin. I bet she got real soft handfeel. Plant hair relations with the vaginal reverse mould structure. Real very crunchistic strong. Great YiQing efficiency. All good vibration heating. She using the true feeling. Bring me and you get more dollar. Much more dollar."

Tuesday, 2nd October, 3.19 p.m.

Clive stopped by the trunk of the old cedar, and put his palm against the rough bark. Although there was something reassuring in its solidity, as if he could feel the hidden tree rings measuring the lost years of his life, and before his face was part of the world, it was also a reminder of his limitations. He would only touch this tree so many times in his life, and no more. And there were some things he would never touch. He took off his glasses and wiped them with the edge of his shirt, then put them back on.

He had often walked this way, through the woods, returning home from school. It was not a shortcut. On the contrary, he took this route when he was not in a hurry and had something to think about, and especially when he wanted just to be by himself. These woods were part of the world of quiet, perfect things that he somehow sensed was breaking up now, maybe never to come back together again. He tried to work out just what he meant by that— quiet, perfect things. Half of his mouth rose for a moment in a sad smile. Maybe the feeling he meant was something like being naked. Not just being naked. It wasn't exactly like the guys splashing around in the lake. This was like, just being naked, and still, and not saying anything, and not being ashamed. He thought about standing like that here, with Marybeth. Just standing here in the woods like that. In his imagination he was naked, but she was wearing a cotton party frock, beige with little brown flowers on it, and looking at him, and he was just looking back, not saying anything, waiting. He thought for a moment that Marybeth might begin to slip the dress off one of her shoulders, but her hand rose to her shoulder in his imagination only to brush away an insect, and then dropped back down again. He could see her neck, and where her neck became her shoulder, as delicate as a pink deer. But he could not imagine her taking the dress off. His mind hovered around the shoulder of her dress for a while before recoiling. He didn't even want to think of her naked. It would never happen anyway. If it did there would just be a kind of white light, like an explosion.

Actually, maybe he couldn't do better to explain what he meant by quiet, perfect things than just say Marybeth. Even if all the other quiet, perfect things broke up and floated away, he could not believe that Marybeth would ever stop being a quiet, perfect thing, deep down—the most quiet and perfect thing of all. Even her Little-House-on-the-Prairie name was perfect, and Clive had never been capable of laughing at it, or thinking about it in an ironic way. She had come to school as a new girl when they were eight, and, of course, she'd been teased a little at first, but after that it seemed like everyone forgot about her. She was too good-natured to react much to the teasing, but she wasn't loud enough to become really popular. She had made friends, of course, but not many, and had just got on with her schoolwork and her life. But to Clive she had been the most wonderful thing in the whole school, eclipsing all thoughts of schoolwork (though he did this studiously enough) and even dwarfing in significance his friendships with other boys. And he had never dared to tell anyone about her and the years passed. She was young for the school year (this year she was still thirteen), and somehow that made him feel vulnerable and tender about her, but it wasn't just that. She was too important to him, and he had known with the unerring instinct of a schoolboy what his peers thought of her, which was very little. He had supposed he even understood in a way why she had been considered plain, but he saw something in her that no one else seemed to see.

This unspoken obsession continued for some time. After a year or so, Clive's feelings became distant with a kind of hopelessness. He had entered a vast, silent winter, as if he were looking out at snowy wastes from an empty building in some far-off land he'd never been to, like Siberia. But he had never forgotten Marybeth, even when they were not in the same class.

At the beginning of this new school year, though, something had happened. For the first year of junior high, chance had largely separated them, but now he and Marybeth were in a lot of the same classes again, and, if possible, his feelings for her had become more acute than ever before. It had been five years of his life, all like one long year of Marybeth—the summer that was her arrival, the autumn that was the sweet, melancholy longing for her, the transcendent, icy-incandescent whiteness of a winter whose cold and loneliness no other human being would ever know, and now the aching, painful, flowering thaw of springtime. And it wasn't only Clive's feelings that had developed. What Clive had always seen in Marybeth was becoming more visible in her in a change of contours in both face and body, and a kind of radiance. She was also becoming more chatty, and people were noticing she had quite an eye for a wardrobe. Then, about two weeks ago, Clive had been hanging out with the guys between classes when Steve had asked who they all thought was the cutest girl in class. Because the whole gang had known each other since grade school, they were in the habit of thinking of junior high merely as an extension of their class. In fact, they were counting all the girls in the school in this conversational survey. Chris had said Natalie, and most people had agreed, then Miguel had said something that shocked Clive.

"I don't know. Everyone talks about Natalie, but if you stop to think about it, she's not anywhere near as cute as Marybeth. I guess people are just used to thinking that Natalie's hot or something, and they don't like, even look around at anyone else when Natalie's in class."

"I like Marybeth," said Clive immediately, as if he had to claim her for himself. "I think she's definitely the cutest girl in class."

His heart fluttered at the release of a five-year-long secret. He was aware that his use of the word "class" only failed to give away his secret completely because the others still mistakenly said class, and because they weren't always quick at picking up on such things. So, with the secret half-revealed, half-hidden, the fluttering was on the verge of becoming delight, before suddenly sinking into horror. The other boys were nodding. One of them laughed.

"You could be right," said Steve. "She's got a dumb name, but . . . what the hell! She's fine, all of a sudden, like, in the past semester. Actually, from right before summer break."

"Hey, I think Clive's into her," said Chris.

"No way."

"Yeah, he is."

"Are you?"

Clive remained silent. He shook his head vaguely and gave a wan smile.

There must have been something in the way he had made his brief confession that had stuck in the minds of the other boys. This had had three disastrous consequences for Clive. The first was that the guys began to talk about, and pay attention to Marybeth even more than to Natalie. The second was that they pestered Clive about him being in love with her, so that he had to deny this vehemently on more than one occasion, and even took back the words he had uttered about her: "I just meant she's not bad, you know, considering. I mean, she's better than Natalie, but Natalie's way flat."

Worst of all, however, was the moment when Clive was softly jostled by Christie in the school corridor. Christie was Marybeth's best friend, a tall girl with short, dark hair who always seemed to be smiling as if she had just thought of something funny. Clive never learnt whether Christie had jostled him accidentally or deliberately, but whatever the case might have been, she immediately said to him, with a particularly broad grin, "Hey, Clive, is it true that you said Marybeth is *definitely* the cutest girl in class?"

Clive felt as if he'd been stabbed with an icicle. The icicle was twisted in his wound by the fact that he'd childishly said "in class" when he meant "in school".

Secretly, he quite liked Christie. She was basically a good-hearted girl, if a little scatterbrained. He knew she was teasing him, but doubted she was intending to be hurtful. Surely, if he could tell the truth to anyone, it would be Christie.

"No, I never said that." He found himself lying. "Those guys are just trying to . . . I don't know."

"Too bad," said Christie, and disappeared.

One thing he was sure about was that Christie could not keep a secret. He could guarantee now that Marybeth knew both the fact that he had apparently said she was the cutest girl in class (*class, dammit—he meant school, anyway*), and the fact that he had denied this. How he wished he had kept quiet when the guys had been talking about her. Everything now was ruined.

It had been better, after all, when Clive had been able to think about quiet, perfect things. The guys had never really understood him, though they let him hang out with them. It had been Chris, a couple of years back, who had first called Clive a "dark horse". Steve had found this exquisitely funny.

"A dark horse? What the fuck is that? You're saying Clive is like some kind of animal or something?"

Chris had explained the phrase, but the hilarity surrounding it had ensured that it stuck in relation to Clive, with numerous variations, such as Horse, Darky, the Dark Rider, DH, Black Beauty, and so on.

Somehow this nickname had encouraged the guys—and it was hard to tell how much they were joking in this—to believe that Clive had some secret girlfriend somewhere, more than one, in fact, on the downlow. When he protested, they thought—or pretended to think—he was just being mysterious, and he did not protest too much, because to get them to see the truth would involve confessing exactly the kind of idiot he was around girls. Maybe they thought he really wasn't interested in Marybeth, that was the irony.

Ironic or not, nothing had changed the fact he was helpless to do anything but look on as the guys in class took more and more interest in Marybeth, and she began to get more and more chatty as she warmed to the attention. Nothing, that is, until, perhaps—*perhaps*—yesterday, Monday, after school. But that was possibly the most difficult thing of all, and the reason he was particularly lingering in the woods today. Well, maybe it didn't matter about himself, or what she thought of him. Maybe it didn't matter about the other guys. The strange thing was, however chatty Marybeth became—and this did irk him, somehow—he could still see, with a kind of piercing, aching clarity, the quiet, perfect essence of Marybeth underneath. He was sure *that* would never change. He was the only one who saw it, just like he was the only one who remembered that dark freckle on the left side of her neck from when she first arrived. It was so oddly placed, as if to emphasise the little eddy of milky down where her jaw met her neck. That down was finer and less fluffy now than it had been then. The freckle was one mark of the years that Marybeth had been in Clive's heart, one measurement of all that had changed and stayed the same, like the rings inside this tree.

With this thought he came back to his present location and looked at the trunk of the tree like an old friend. He walked around to the other side of the tree and crouched down. There, low in the bark of the tree, was carved a loveheart with an arrow through it and the initials 'MC' inside. Marybeth Cuthberts. This was something real and objective. Like this tree, it existed even when he was not looking. It had been there all these years like the quiet, perfect proof that the most sentimental of all feelings are the greatest physical reality.

Tuesday, 2nd October, 4.28 p.m.

Although popular with students and occasional out-of-town visitors, Mr Song's Korean Palace was regarded with suspicion and even hostility by most of the downtown Korean community. It was said that the restaurant was Korean in name only, and that its proprietors—Mr Song, a grinning geriatric, and his single surly waitress—were not Korean at all; depending on the account, they changed from Burmese dissidents to illegal Iranian immigrants to an elderly Japanese war criminal and his granddaughter, who was said to perform disreputable acts in back alleys for mere pocket change.

Thad had heard the rumours, but hadn't credited them until now. Stepping through the entrance, which was inexplicably flanked by an old-fashioned revolving barber's pole, he was greeted by the waitress, who stared at him with evident disdain. She looked Asian, he decided, applying the term in its broadest, pornographic sense. She was also old enough to be his mother, or at least his vastly older sister.

"Table for ONE?"

The question seemed irrelevant; at present there was no one else in the restaurant. Which served his purposes well, Thad thought: no chance of anyone eavesdropping. Mr Song was nowhere to be seen, although Thad detected movement behind the black plastic curtain that hid the kitchen.

"Uh, two . . . the other one's coming soon."

He was shown to a booth at the back of the restaurant and handed a glass of tea that tasted like jasmine-scented mothballs. He looked at the menu, where under the heading **AUTHENTIC KOREAN FOOD** he was confronted with the following:

```
HAMBURGER PLATER - SERVED WITH FRIED CHIPS
DELICIOUS CHEESE WAFFLE - SIDE OF "GRAVY"
KOREAN POTATOES SALAD - THE "SPICY" SALAD
"THE PICKLED BACON" - KOREAN BACON WITH SPROUTS
ASSORTED NUGGETS - "MEAT" OR "FISH"
MR. SONG SPECIAL - DELECTABLE EEL
SOUP OF THE DAY - SERVED HOT
```

On the table were several copies of *The Ivy-League Christ*, which looked to be either a religious pamphlet or a fashion brochure. Perhaps it was both: there was no text, only images of a bearded Caucasian Jesus in a variety of lush campus settings, posing with blonde teenagers in white robes and sheepskin boots. Thad ordered a Rheingold, the only available beer, and used one of the pamphlets as a coaster. The waitress hovered around the table for a while but he ignored her until she retreated behind the plastic curtain.

As he glanced again at the menu, Thad heard the door swinging open. He looked up to see a man in an elegant but obviously well-worn grey double-breasted Brooks Brothers suit entering the restaurant. The man looked weedy, aristocratic and offended all at once; he scanned the bare, faded walls and glanced at the waitress before meeting Thad's gaze. This was Fred Bergen.

"Thaddeus," the man said. "No trouble finding this place?"

"Nah, I'm strictly local," Thad said. "Brynbach has everything you need. And . . . my friend Ryan's been here before."

"I heard about this place from our employer," Bergen said. "Apparently he owns a stake in it. It doesn't seem like much, but who knows? The college kids love this ironic racism thing now, anything that isn't 'correct' is raking it in. Apparently there's a fake Ethiopian restaurant in Trenton that's just a glorified hot dog stand . . ."

The waitress walked over and Bergen waved her away.

"Hot dogs, fuck . . ." Thad said. "I wish I had one now. What is this shit . . . bacon with sprouts?" He closed the menu and pushed it aside.

"Let's get down to business." Bergen took a folded sheet of paper from an inside pocket and handed it to Thad. "Here's a map from the city centre to St. Mary's Church, along with a layout of the church grounds. The plan is to leave the doll in an open grave I've had dug. That's where I'll make the pickup. How you get her there is up to you."

"Yeah, no problem," Thad said. "I've got a few, let's say, strategies in mind. Misdirection, so it doesn't seem like, you know, an inside job. I was even thinking we could get Zak to think he's in some kind of conspiracy, X-Files style. Like the government is trying to take his doll. Or there's a gang that's going to kidnap her."

Bergen gave a brief, sceptical smile. "As I said, that's up to you. And if you perform well, there could be other opportunities . . ." He glanced away suggestively. "I have a variety of contacts. Because of my . . . well, I have certain talents that command a price. And certain trusted clients. They're always on the lookout for reliable help. If you complete this one on time, I could make some introductions. Just remember your deadline."

Thad nodded. "And they're going to use her for some kind of ritual? The magazine people, I mean."

"Best not to ask," Bergen said. "The client's business is their own. The less you know the better, really." He leaned back in his seat. "Now, is there anything worth ordering? Doesn't look like it. If that's all, I have another appointment to make."

"Yeah, me too, actually," Thad said.

"I almost forgot," Bergen said, producing an envelope from another pocket and flicking it across the table, "Don't spend it all at once."

Thad caught the envelope and pocketed it. The two of them got to their feet, ignoring the waitress's livid stare, and left the restaurant. Outside, Bergen incongruously departed to wait at the bus stop across the road, while Thad hopped onto the back of his black Kawasaki Vulcan 900. After a ten-minute drive through the city, he caught sight of his destination and pulled into the parking lot.

He removed his helmet, shook his sandy hair, got off the motorbike, and then strode with a perceptible swagger into the roadside diner. Immediately, despite the fact that the premises were nearly empty of customers, he approached a table in the corner where an older man was reading a newspaper and drinking coffee.

"I normally take the corner table," said Thad. "Do you mind if I sit here?"

The newspaper lowered.

"Be my guest," said Mr Magister.

The waitress came and Thad ordered waffles with double syrup.

"Double syrup?" she asked.

"Yeah."

"They come with plenty of syrup already. A little pitcher of it."

"Yeah, well, like, whatever they normally come with, I want double."

"Something to drink, honey?"

"No."

"You sure?"

"Yeah, I'm sure."

When she had left, Thad passed a small plastic box across the table. Mr Magister looked up with one eye, palmed the box, slipped it into his pocket and folded his newspaper.

"It works," said Thad. "I checked."

"Good. You've done well."

"See, the thing that concerns me, Mr . . . ?"

"Brooks."

"The thing that concerns me, Mr Brooks, is that, if things go missing, I'm going to be the first one blamed."

"You think he doesn't trust you? You're afraid of him?"

"No! I'm not afraid of that pussy. Only, between you and me, I think he could go a bit nuts. You know, a guy like that, whose girlfriend is like, a toy doll. I mean, Hello! No offence, Mr . . . er . . . Brooks."

"None taken."

The waitress slipped a plate of waffles in front of Thad and two small pitchers of Pinnacle Log Cabin Regular Syrup.

"I just don't want it to look like an inside job," he said as he poured the contents of one of the pitchers over the waffles. "You see what mean?"

"I see exactly what you mean, Brian, with crystal clarity."

"Er . . . My name's not Brian."

Mr Magister stared at him for a moment.

"I know that."

"Okay, yeah, I see."

Thad stuffed a forkful of syrupy waffle in his mouth. The older man looked at him for a moment and blinked—blinked in a manner either weary or self-confident.

"Let me assure you, Brian, the use of the thing you've just given me will be purely for the purposes of reconnaissance. This will not look like an inside job. It would not even help me if it did."

"Okay, well, I appreciate that. And I appreciate the money and all, but, there's something that's been bugging me, and I hope you don't mind if I ask."

"Go ahead. What is it?"

"Well, first of all I guessed that maybe there was some kind of smuggling thing going on, like, dolls full of diamonds or something."

Mr Magister gave a shallow laugh.

"Hardly."

"Yeah, well, I realised that didn't seem to fit. Pretty soon I figured you're just a collector, right? But what I don't get is, you got bread, you got a lot to lose, so why don't you just have whatever doll you want custom made? You don't actually need to steal some other guy's doll. You can buy your own."

"Brian, there's a lot that you don't understand. If you stick around, my guess is that you will. Now, you said I'm a collector. Right enough. And what does a collector want? I'll tell you. Something unique. Now, unique comes in two forms, nature and nurture; pedigree and biography. So, you have unique dolls made at the factory, and that's good. But even this kind of unique is half-blank. We all try to bring our she-homunculi to life by injecting them with our . . . essential desires. This is good, too. But for something to truly come alive, it needs two parents, and a history. Are you beginning to get the picture?"

"Er . . . yeah. I guess. Like how it's always better fucking some other guy's girlfriend than your own."

"Very succinctly put. Anyway, have you thought what you want to do with the money?"

Thad smiled, his lips glistening with artificial maple syrup.

"Yeah, you might say I've got a few ideas."

He pushed away the half-eaten plate of waffles and got to his feet.

"But yeah, I've got some shit to do now. I'll catch you later, Mr, uh, Mr Brooks."

Mr Magister turned back to his newspaper.

"Be seeing you."

Tuesday, 2nd October, 5.32 p.m.

Outside, Thad took out his cell phone and dialled Zak's number. After five rings Zak picked up. Thad began speaking at once.

"Zak? Yeah, what's up? Listen, there's something you might want to know about. No, relax, it's nothing big. Listen, you care about Sooki, right? Want to protect her and all? Yeah, of course. All I'm saying is there's been some shit going around about a possible kidnapping. Dollnapping, whatever. No, just wait, hold on. It's nothing like that. Look, calm down. I can't talk to you right now. Meet me at McDonald's in half an hour okay?"

He hung up, put the phone back in his pocket and took out his keys. As he hopped back on the bike, he felt more excited than he had in months. Starting up the engine, he imagined himself as a kind of spy, a double-crossing double agent. It was easy enough for him to run missions, bouncing from Zak to Bergen to Mr Magister, and before long all of them would be coughing up even more cash. He thought back to his days selling pot and fake exstasy out of the garage—that had been small time compared to this doll game. Who'd have thought there'd be this kind of money in moving around a bunch of mannequins?

He pulled off the kerb, onto the road. As he passed a new Mercedes, its chrome grill shining in the sun, he imagined himself behind the wheel, the future stretching before him. Lately, all he could think of was money and girls. And the more you had of one, he knew, the more you had of the other. With the last payment from Mr Magister alone, he'd be able to get himself a new pair of shoes, a new helmet, and enough liquor for a party on Friday. Craig, his room-mate, was away visiting his brother, so he had the place to himself. He knew he'd be able to get Tommy, Ed Chiang, and the usual gang from Rise to come. And there were a few prospects for hookups: Debbie, who he hadn't talked to for a few weeks; Mariah, who was fat but usually put out; Jacyn, whose number he'd gotten at Wendy's on the week-end. He'd try inviting them all, he thought—it was always best to stack the deck.

Once an older guy he had met in a park and smoked a joint with had told him that if a male, any male, asks ten chicks to go to bed with him, one of them will.

"It's called the law of probability," the man had said.

It was some of the sagest advice Thad had ever heard.

But to make probability more probable, he'd need more girls.

So there was Angela—he thought of calling her again, even though the last time he'd tried, she'd brushed him off. Completely retarded. And it was all her fault, anyway. Who brought their little sister along on a date? Didn't that kind of shit stop in grade school? But she'd been strange from the start, he remembered. High-maintenance-looking, for one: not his usual type. At first he'd taken her as a challenge, and hadn't gotten his hopes up. But then he'd made the mis-take of drinking the night before he'd gone out with her. The hangover had been bad enough that he hadn't wanted to talk to anyone, much less try to break through a bitch shield. And the kid had just pushed it over the edge.

"So you're what, like, twelve?"

"Thirteen," Marybeth had said.

He looked at her. She wasn't bad, he thought—if you gave her a few more years, maybe. She was wearing a white sleeveless dress, her hair held in place with a clip in the shape of a dragonfly. Thad figured Angela's style was rubbing off on her.

"She's just started eighth grade," Angela said. "I'm so completely jealous. I wish I was still that age."

"Yeah, well . . . I guess we all got to get older."

He thought about where to take them. The usual diners and bars seemed out of the question. Finally he decided on a movie. He'd have to pay out, but if he could get rid of Marybeth before the end of the evening, it might be worth the investment.

They had arrived at the theatre about twenty minutes before the film was to begin. When Angela excused herself to go to the bathroom, he moved into her seat, next to Marybeth.

"So, you like school?"

Marybeth thought for a bit, slanting her eyes to the side and twining a strand of her hair around her finger. She looked attentive but slightly confused, as if she'd just been asked a question in class. Thad was a little surprised. He wasn't used to people taking anything he said seriously. For him, any form of conversation with a girl was just an all-purpose noise—a diversionary tactic. He never listened to the words, only the signals behind them: this meant stop; this meant go; this meant I'm tired; you don't have a chance; I'm sad now; I want to dance; I'm expensive; it's okay to touch me. But Marybeth's answer didn't seem to signal anything. She spoke quickly, unselfconsciously, with brief pauses interspersed, as if her own words were surprising her.

"Yeah, I guess so. I like the classes I have this year more than last year, which is good. Not that I didn't like any of the classes last year, I mean—they were good, but I hated math. Oh, and Christie is in my PE class, which is cool—she's my best friend. She's so much more athletic than me! What else, um . . . I feel like everything's a lot more exciting. It's a lot of the same people from last year, but there's some new girls—" she stopped, "—some new boys, too. I mean, I still have all my old friends and everyone I grew up with. It just feels a bit bigger."

She was about to continue when Thad broke in.

"That's cool, yeah. Hey, I don't know how to say this, but . . . could you fuck off for a bit? I want to be alone with your sister. You know how it is, right?"

He took out his wallet and reached for a ten.

"Go get something to eat. Or smoke. Do you smoke yet? No, you don't seem like a smoker. When I was your age, shit . . ."

He stopped, realising what he'd just said. His head was still throbbing as he offered her the note. If only Craig hadn't brought back that 151 from the Canadian trip . . .

A hand snatched the note from his. He looked up and saw Angela standing next to the seat. He hadn't even noticed her coming over, he realised: that's how fucked he was.

"Are you paying her off? Oh my God, I can't believe this . . ."

He shrugged.

"I just figured she'd be bored. Don't you think it's, you know, kind of unfair? Third wheel and all?"

Angela took Marybeth's hand and dragged her out of the seat.

"Come on, we're leaving."

"It's okay," Marybeth said, clearly embarrassed. "We don't have to go . . ."

But Angela was already pulling her towards the exit. Thad watched them go. As Angela opened the door, he called out:

"Yeah, well you can call me when you're ready to stop being such a bitch!"

The usher came over and warned him. Shaking his head, he sank into the seat and watched as the lights dimmed and credits started. It was one of those awful CGI cartoons, he realised: all bright colours and loud noises. The worst thing for a hangover. He wished he at least had a joint he could smoke in the toilets.

Thinking back to it now, it didn't seem worth the effort. But he hated to let anything get away from him. He wanted to see her one more time, he told himself as he pulled into the parking lot and waited for Zak. One more time, just to see where everything stood. You never knew who the one in ten might be.

Friday, 24th May, 1940, 11.49 p.m.

369 Sutter Street. San Francisco. Forbidden City night club. Noel Toy had just finished doing her fan dance routine and Larry Ching was up on stage singing a number called 'Embraceable You'.

Toy went to her dressing room and started putting cold cream on her face. There was a knock at the door; she invited the knocker to come in and, looking in the mirror saw a man, probably in his mid-30's, holding his hat in his hands. His only distinguishing feature was his nose, which was rather large.

"My name's Carl French," he said.

"So."

"You might have heard of me."

"I never heard of you."

"I'm a sculptor. I do the human figure—and baby, you got a figure!"

Noel Toy turned around.

"This your pick-up line?" she asked.

"No. I am making a sculpture of Venus. In immortal bronze."

Toy lit a Pall Mall cigarette. She was listening.

"Yes, I am making a statue of the great goddess Venus and—can I be frank with you, Miss Toy?"

"You can be anyone you want to be."

"Well, to be *frank* with you, you have a little bit of Venus between your legs."

"Between my what?"

"Your legs, Miss Toy. Your, how shall I put it—your *VAGINA* is that of my Venus."

"Boy, you crazy!"

"Yes, crazy enough to offer you $700 to let me take a plaster mould of it!"

His voice had risen up to a frenzied pitch. Noel Toy looked down, crossed one leg over the next, and took a deep drag of her cigarette.

Tuesday, 2ⁿᵈ October, 5.38 p.m.

After leaving the diner, Mr Magister walked back to his car and sat for a while in the passenger's seat, thinking. He was about to take a trip to a place he had not been to for months. Caught up with recent events, he had had little time to think of the lower ground at the edge of the town of Brynbach, past the great steeple of St. Mary's. But now, the sprawl of the cemetery filled his mind with its neatly trimmed grass and faded headstones. He thought of the little quartz obelisk and the inscription at the bottom. Shaking his head, he started the car.

She had already been gone for five years. When Marie had showed him the first hospital reports, he hadn't believed her. Surely there were treatments, new advances in drugs, surgery, chemotherapy? But as the year went by, all of his hopes were dismantled with a thoroughness that seemed to mirror the precise, systematic movements of the hospital staff. That year, he had grown to hate nurses and doctors. He thought back to the final day by the bedside, Clive at his side. No, he told himself—it was best not to think of it.

After he pulled past the cemetery gates, he reached to the back seat for the little bouquet of blue flowers. With them in hand, he stepped outside and strolled through the rows of headstones until he found Marie's obelisk. He leaned down and read her name carved in quartz. Then, after smoothing down the grass and kissing the tombstone, he placed the flowers on the grave. For a while he stood, thinking of the recent past. The first year alone with Clive had forced both of them to retreat inside themselves. For a while he had considered moving the two of them in with his spinster sister, but he valued his privacy too much. And as for remarrying—well, when he thought of that, something in him gave out. He had gone after women his own age for a while, but each of them had come with her own tedious history, a carefully tended catalogue of wounds. And most of them hadn't seemed very fond of sex.

No, he thought, it wasn't worth the trouble.

And younger girls? He could probably afford them, but a part of him resisted it. It just felt silly, as if he were escorting around a daughter.

He recalled when had met one, a twenty-four year old named Anusia. They had met online and had set up a rendezvous in Nat Turner Park in Newark, a good thirty-minute drive away from his actual home.

"You're really forty-six?" she had asked.

"Yes, I am."

"You look older."

"You don't like older men?"

"Well, it depends."

"Of course it does."

"Age doesn't matter if the guy is my type."

"Am I your type?"

"You look older than forty-six. But yeah, I guess you're nice."

"So, you would, um?"

"What?"

When he had told her she had started yelling at him right there in public, calling him very undignified names.

People had begun to stare and so he had got up and walked away. He hadn't done anything wrong of course—but it had been embarrassing.

After a few such ill-advised adventures, he had given up on the whole thing.

Then he had found the first Real Doll catalogue. At first, he had treated it as a joke, a grotesque curiosity. What kind of people would pay so much for such a thing? It seemed impossible to believe that anyone could attach themselves to a doll. And the first one he saw, the first one he bought— she hadn't changed his mind. Not for a while, anyway. After getting her home, he had kept her in the attic, taking her out only late at night, when Clive was asleep. Those had been strange, tentative nights of infatuation, and he had made excuses to himself for the entire first year. He was a collector of art objects, he told himself; exquisite simulacra, the modern equivalent of classical sculpture. To arrange, to tend, to curate them—that was his only interest. He be- came a photographer, an aesthetician, experimenting with lighting, position, cosmetics. He even managed to sell six of his photographs to a German website who had paid him with a ninety-euro First Androids coupon that he had never used. But before long, the pretence gave way. It wasn't just the sex—the girls had crept up on him, surprising him with the subtlety of their emotions, their delicate moods and un- failing discretion. There were, after all, other forms of love besides the purely physical. No, it was their constancy, he told himself: that nearly catlike quality, how they expressed themselves without saying a word. Thinking back now, he knew that he had made the right choice.

It would be sunset soon. After reading the inscription a final time, Mr Magister walked away from the grave and back down the path leading to the parking lot. Already he was imagining the Matsushima series and the joys he would have with her in his harem, tucked away from the rest of the world. Only one thought troubled him: what would Marie think of him now? As he walked back to the car, reaching for the box in his pocket, he made a silent prayer to no one in particular: that if there was a God, He wouldn't let her watch.

Tuesday, 2nd October, 6.04 p.m.

"Why McDonald's, Thad?"

"Hey, you agreed."

"I wish I hadn't."

"I forgot you don't like the food here."

"It's not the food. People stare at me in McDonald's. Why do they do that?"

"Maybe they're just being friendly. You ever thought of that?"

Thad smiled and waved to a couple of girls at the adjacent table who appeared to have overheard some of their conversation.

"Anyway, Zak, I wanted, like, to tell you about this, um . . . thing."

"Okay."

"Yeah?"

"Yeah, I'm listening."

Thad stuck a straw in his mouth, sucked hard at his soda, and then began.

"It was real weird, right. First of all, this guy with shades and a scar right across his face, and, like, a real weird . . . er . . . ear, a real weird ear—"

"A weird *ear*?"

"Yeah, you know, like gangrene or some shit like that, you know—made me want to puke. Anyway, he says to me,

'Do you know Zak Landers?' I'm like, 'Maybe. Who wants to know?' And he starts coming out with all this weird, fucked-up shit. I can't remember it all now, but he's offering me money, and asking about Sooki. So I say, 'Whoa, bro, you got the wrong guy. Did you say Zak Landers? Sorry, I thought you said Jack Landis. Well, gotta go.'"

"Hey, that's creepy."

"Yeah. Right. That's what I thought. I thought, that's some creepy shit."

"So how come you didn't tell me?"

"Hey, I'm telling you now, aren't I? Besides, I didn't want to scare you. I thought it was just some creepshow dude asking weird questions. But then, right, I started getting phone calls. I don't quite get it, but it seems like there's some kind of, like, dollnapping Mafia or something. They know where I work, where I live. They're offering money for information on Sooki. They say they're collectors, see?"

Zak had a fish fillet sandwich in front of him but wasn't eating it.

"Maybe we should go to the police?" he said.

"And say what? Someone's planning to steal your doll? Besides, these guys are scary."

"You said on the phone it was nothing to worry about."

"Yeah. Right. If we play it cool. I mean, unless we get these guys angry, the worst that can happen is you lose Sooki to some secret society of sickos."

"Oh, that's all is it?"

"Right. It doesn't have to be life and death for you. So, I figure if we're smart about it there'll be no problems. So, how d'you feel about selling Sooki?"

"*Selling* her? SELLING HER? Jesus, Thad, are you crazy?"

"Okay, okay. Keep it down, dude. We're in McDonalds, remember? Christ, don't want people to stare."

He waved and smiled at the girls again.

"It's all right," he said as the girls gave him disdainful, bewildered looks. "He just means his bitch. You know, his poodle bitch. He doesn't want to sell her."

The girls said nothing and looked away. One of them began timidly to eat her French-fried potatoes.

"Yeah, Zak, so I guessed you might feel that way, but I thought, hey, we gotta look at all the options, right?"

"So, what are the other options?"

"Er . . . I guess that's the only one I thought of."

"Jesus. Thanks, Thad. That's a lot of help."

"Hey, hey! What's that meant to mean? I just thought you oughta know. Christ, that's all the thanks I get. How can I help you? Tell me."

"Well, I don't know. Maybe you could keep Sooki for a while."

Thad smirked.

"Hey, nice to know you trust me with your girl, but I already told you, they know where I live. They're probably watching both of us. If they break in at your place and don't find her, my place is the first place they'll check out."

"Yeah. You're right. Maybe that's not such a good idea."

For a while they sat in silence.

"Hey," said Thad thoughtfully, "I got it."

"What?"

"It's—No, I guess it's too crazy."

"Tell me. What is it?"

"No, you won't like it," he said, stirring the ice in his soda with his straw.

"Well, how can I know if I like it if you don't tell me?"

"Okay, it's just an idea . . ."

"Okay, so tell me."

"You know my buddy, Ralph?"

"Ralph? Ralph the gravedigger?"

"I knew you wouldn't like it. Okay, forget it."

"No. Go on. Tell me." Zak took a bite of his fish fillet sandwich.

"Okay, this is my idea. If we hide Sooki in a garage these guys are going to find her, right? Or if they don't, they'll just wait till you bring her back or something. So, what we've got to do is make them think she's gone for good. We've got to fake her death."

Tuesday, 2nd October, 7.26 p.m.

Zak locked the door behind him, and then leant against it, breathless. He was usually glad to be back inside, especially knowing that Sooki was waiting for him and that the hours were theirs to beguile together with no thought for the outside world. This time he was probably more relieved than usual, but he had not left the outside world behind. He locked the door because the outside world had come in with him, as a gnawing at his heart.

"Honey," he called out, impatient to know that she was still there.

There was no answer, but he felt somehow reassured. He sensed her presence. Walking through the living room to the bedroom, he opened the door and leaned inside.

"Oh, I left you asleep."

Very softly, he crept into the room and sat side-saddle on the bed next to her, where she lay half-propped up with pillows. She was wearing a white cotton dress with red polka dots. The whiteness of the dress was somehow sad in contrast to the fresh blue-black dark of night that slicked the window. Zak drew the curtains. The light of the vanished day seemed trapped in the polkadot folds of that dress, creating a blurred, peaceful hush as of the gentlest, most refreshing kind of sleep. With the curtains closed, this soft lingering light was no longer drained, but released to glow unreally. Zak looked at Sooki's face, the eyelids closed, seeming to invite the touch of his lips, and smiled fondly to himself. As lightly as he could, he brushed his fingertips along the smoothness of her cheek. Then he leaned forward and kissed both eyelids. Her body moved, but only because the mattress had dipped as Zak leaned. Her eyes remained firmly closed, as if she were under a spell, and her dreams were so mild that she neither murmured nor stirred. There was only the silence of the lost day's fading glow in her sleep. Zak simply sat and looked at her for a while. Then his hand crept mischievously and mouse-like towards the hem of her dress. It paused where the hem rested lightly against the vagueness of her leg. Then it crept under the hem into the night that gathered there, more intimate than that outside the window. His fingers began to caress and tickle her thigh. He laughed a little to himself then stopped. A thoughtful expression came over his face, and then he nodded solemnly.

"I guess I'll let you sleep a while longer. No use waking you now. I've just got a little work to do and then I'll be right with you."

Getting up from the bed, he went over to the computer on the desk against the wall and sat down in the swivel chair. For the next hour or so he visited all the doll-related chatrooms he knew and made enquiries. Usually he didn't like to visit these places; he didn't like the way some of the people there talked about their dolls. But this was a matter of urgency. He had to make sure he knew where he stood and what his options were.

He went to www.idollized.com and logged into his account. The site prided itself on being the world wide hub for Real Doll enthusiasts and was replete with photo galleries depicting teddy-babes, advertisements for cyber realistic

mouths and senso lips, intim toy clean spray and love torsos. There was a newsroom, a chronicle database, links to
other Real Doll websites, and a hall of fame. Zak went to
the chatroom section and clicked into the New Jersey room.
As usual, very little was happening in the main room, so he
private messaged a few people to see if he could figure out
if the dollnapping situation was in fact real.

Online Chat Transcription 1.

\<zaktastik\> hey

\<Panch006\> Hi

\<zaktastik\> asl plz?

\<Panch006\> No.

\<zaktastik\> WTF?

\<Panch006\> Fine. Jersey. Male. Don't worry about
my age. I'll just say that I got a fender and it
IS NOT a bender. The wang supreme.

\<zaktastik\> Okay

\<Panch006\> got pix?

\<zaktastik\> not really. Just looking for some
info.

\<Panch006\> newbie?

<zaktastik> No. Real owner.

<Panch006> Cool beanz. I'm a three doll a night man myself. What u need?

<zaktastik> Dollnappings. You heard about em?

<Panch006> Who hasn't. It's all the buzz. A lot of guys are having to go back to humping shoes.

<zaktastik> So what's the story?

<Panch006> Hellz if I know. Some kind of ring maybe. Hard to say. My amigo Tom was in his house and went down to the corner store to get a submarine sandwich. Door locked and everything. Wasn't gone ten minutes and when he got back Krissy, his 87 pound platinum body 7 was taken. They busted through the window and took her. He'd had had her since 2000 and she had become really soft and flexible. A fun girl. A fucking gem.

<zaktastik> Holy crap!

<Panch006> Holy crap is right. That's why I keep an AR-15 hot and ready to roll at all times. Someone wants to put their hands on my fucking lady friends it'll be over my dead fucking body.

<zaktastik> Um. Okay

<Panch006> Hell yes okay. You some kind of doll cop?

<zaktastik> No.

<Panch006> Who the fuck are you?

<zaktastik> Bye

<Panch006> FUCK YOU!

Online Chat Transcription 2.

<zaktastik> hey

<__Mi_ti> hello

<zaktastik> nj?

<__Mi_ti> Choucha! U got incretion?

<zaktastik> ??

<__Mi_ti> radiant beauty of windfall. See her u
pick jaw out of basement.

<zaktastik> yeah right

<__Mi_ti> u no lookin?

<zaktastik> I got buddy

<__Mi_ti> ok. what kind doll?
<zaktastik> Full silicone semi-solid with gel im-
plants. Don't really want to go into too much
detail.

<__Mi_ti> :P

<zaktastik> you?

<__Mi_ti> all kind. Looking buy sell trade. So as
to achieve physiological balance. 3sum good up
4 swapping pic. It made according to the meci-
cal principles. Polymer of synthetic resin, make
artificial joint limbs free Stretch bending arbi-
trarily regulate, and the different position, make
sex sex more fun.

<zaktastik> ok

<__Mi_ti> u want I sent pic?

<zaktastik> I'm just looking for information

<__Mi_ti> shoot

<zaktastik> Have you heard of any dollnappings in
the area?

<__Mi_ti> U must be crasy

<zaktastik> So that's a no?

<__Mi_ti> Fuck off

<zaktastik> Same to you

<__Mi_ti> male impotence premature ejaculation has
asignificant effect

Online Chat Transcription 3.

<zaktastik> hi

<crocodilestreet> Yo

<zaktastik> hey just asking around about the doll-nappings to see who knows what.

<crocodilestreet> I know what alright. Damned.

<zaktastik> What happened?

<crocodilestreet> napped.

<zaktastik> Who?

<crocodilestreet> Adela. Redhead. Four foot eleven. Seventy pounds. Size 6 shoe. She had a damned ten year warranty and I'd only had her for a little over a year. Our first anniversary was just a month ago. She was numero uno.

<zaktastik> Shit.

<crocodilestreet> Yeah. I remember when she arrived. A hot but windy day toward the end of August. When I unpacked her she took my breath away. She was equipped with an orgasm groan and everything. She was a really good girl and we had some super sweet moments. During our first six months together I hardly came up for air. She never complained and she brought so much peace into my life.

<zaktastik> Did you call the cops?

<crocodilestreet> I shouldn't have, but I was so pissed, that yeah.

<zaktastik> What did they say?

<crocodilestreet> They just smirked. Acted like there was something wrong with me. Then a week later.

<zaktastik> They found her?

<crocodilestreet> No. I found an envelope in my mail box containing some disturbing photographs of Adela. There was a message warning me not to talk to the police again if I wanted her back in one piece. But that's it. Nothing else has happened since. Zero contact. I've been trolling all the doll sights hoping she shows up or something. But it really makes me think.

<zaktastik> How you mean?

<crocodilestreet> About what's important in life. Basically the only things that matter to me are God and my woman. And my woman is gone. I was pretty heavy in the pints for a while but I think I'm starting to come out the other side.
<zaktastik> Geez. Sorry man.

<crocodilestreet> Yeah

<zaktastik> Yeah

<crocodilestreet> Hey

<zaktastik> ?

<crocodilestreet> Do you ever go to church?

<zaktastik> No. Not really. Why?

<crocodilestreet> Well, they say sin has a price that must be paid. The plan of God for Salvation.

<zaktastik> yeah?

<crocodilestreet> Yeah. Sometimes I think about Adela and pray, seeking God's will. I know every person is sinful and under condemnation to eternal judgement and I'm just trying to figure things out.

<zaktastik> Hey, I gotta go. Good luck finding Adela.

<crocodilestreet> Thanks. Bye.

<zaktastik> Bye.

Something about these chatroom exchanges unnerved Zak, and for a while he could not say why. Then he began to remember the episode that had confirmed to him his position as loner, and determined him in a policy of distance from the Real Doll community.

There had been something called 'Dollfest' advertised on the idollized website some time back, and he had gathered it was some kind of convention, "strictly for Real Doll lovers". It looked like a state rather than a national congregation, an ad hoc affair, but he thought it might help him to be among others like himself, no longer to feel himself in a desperate minority, but, instead, among supportive peers.

He had regretted his decision soon after his arrival. The building where the meeting was held appeared to be some kind of low-class strip joint that the organisers had hired for the purpose. Really, the unfavourable impression had begun from the exterior of this building. The website had given a photo of the entrance, at which something like a Real Doll (not a real Real Doll) had been mounted on an animatronics motor. What the website photo did not show was the off-putting way this poor creature moved—like the last dying flails and twitches of a Japanese dancing prawn. Also, at the actual location, Zak was sure this was merely the strip joint's usual lure for customers.

Things only got worse inside. There were two or three speakers, including an older guy by the name of Remy something, whose English was not always easy to understand. This Remy, however, was clearly a respected figure, whom Dollfest was apparently "honoured to welcome". In his turn, before giving a truly bizarre lecture on the tantric method as used with Real Dolls, he affirmed with an unsettling gleam in his eye that he always "like to attend these event—even small one".

Knowing references were made throughout the talks, and in general conversation, to "the main event" when the dolls—the presence of at least one doll per person was a condition of entry—would "take centre stage".

Zak didn't like the way the other attendees inspected each other's dolls, and he definitely did not like the kind of attention that Sooki was having to put up with.

Soon Zak understood what was going on, and as the main event approached, he almost wept with panic. At the very nadir of this misery, as he was contemplating his meagre options for escaping unnoticed, the bewhiskered Remy for some reason approached, producing in Zak such a confusion of different expectations that he almost spluttered, not knowing whether he should prepare himself to repel or importune this interloper.

"Interesting in this doll," said Remy as he rolled some strands of her hair appraisingly between thumb and fingers. He looked straight in Zak's eyes, seeming to hesitate or judge.

"May I see vaginal?"

"You mean . . ."

"First one. Vaginal she come with."

"Well, that's kind of personal."

"I understand. Collector must be careful. But I think maybe you got Toy hole one—I mean funny game toy ha ha hole buddy happy!"

At the word "collector" something had clicked in Zak's head.

"Oh, yeah, sure, the first one. That's in the van with the other accessories. Hey, you know what, I'll just go and fit that now. For the . . . er . . . for the main event."

And he fumbled to put Sooki in a fireman's lift.

"No need. No need. Leave her here, and bring."

He had an excited, almost desperate tone in his voice.

"Ah, it's okay," Zak replied. "It's better this way. I'll be right back."

And so he had fled.

As he drove the night roads home, he thought of some of the skin-crawling compliments that had been paid to Sooki that evening. Many of the attendees had not tried, or had been unable to hide the fact they considered Sooki very special. Zak had not questioned this, since he knew very well that she was. But Remy's words had aroused his suspicions.

The next day he had done some background research. Eventually, he'd spoken to someone in the chatroom who knew a little more than the usual syndicated publicity and the popular mythology. There had been a nano-brief period, it seemed, when the Real Doll manufacturers had advertised some of the dolls as having vulvas modelled on the bona fide genitalia of various celebrities. It was true, as well, said his source. Some flaky L.A. artist had a side-line in making plaster casts of famous pudenda. Some of these casts were legendary now. Soft Chasm Products had paid a lot of money for access to these casts, and had fitted out a number of their dolls with the moulds duplicated from these. But they had hardly got the publicity started when law suits began flying, and, panicking, Soft Chasm had removed all direct references to famous pussy. But word had got out here and there, perhaps assisted by deliberate leaks. Prices on some models had been discreetly raised, and winking hints given in advertising copy. This was just one dimension among many in the collectability of Real Dolls—a concrete and representative example of the spooks and spirits that animated this almost pathless erotic forest.

Remembering all this now, Zak realised it should have come as no surprise there were dollnappers about. Any of the attendees of Dollfest could be a suspect where Sooki was concerned, and god knows they had all been suspicious enough in one way or another.

Finally logging off and turning his attention back to Sooki, Zak's face was now a gulch of sober concern.

"Sooki," he said gently, and then he moved over to the bed once more, like a concerned parent tending a child with fever.

He began to stroke her cheek again, but her eyes remained closed, as if she would never wake.

"Sleeping beauty," Zak murmured to himself.

His fingers curled behind her jaw as if to get a grip there, and he brought his other hand forward to the other side of her face. He made some manipulations, like someone tackling a difficult-to-open lid. Then he was lifting the peaceful face away in both hands.

"Time to wake up," he said, placing the eternally-sleeping mask on a shelf at the back of the room and picking up another mask with its eyes wide open. Soon he was fitting this second mask carefully into place, making sure that it was on properly, and stroking the hair that had become disarranged.

"There. Does that feel better? Do you feel better after your sleep now, honey?"

His eyes were fixed on her face.

"Uh-huh? Well, I'm sorry to bring down the mood, but, well, there's something I really need to tell you about."

He picked up her right hand and held it in both of his as he continued.

"It looks like . . . I'll just come out and say it. It looks like there have been some dollnappings recently, and you're probably next on the list. Why? Well, because you're beautiful, of course and have qualities no other woman has. I know it's upsetting, but—Hey, listen, it's going to be alright. I'm not going to let them take you, okay? Okay. Good.

Now, the thing is . . . the problem is . . . Look, I've been talking to Thad. Yeah, I know what you think of Thad. I can understand that. But maybe this time he knows what he's talking about. Well, if you'll let me explain. His idea— oh boy, you're not going to like this, but hear me out—his idea is to fake your death . . . Well, yes, it might involve burial. We don't know yet. Thad's going to discuss it with his friend Ralph. Thad says that Ralph says that some of these places—funeral parlours and so on—are willing to do some unconventional things sometimes for a price. Think of it like when I sent you back to the workshop to get fixed that time. You had to go in a crate then. Gee, that was hard. For me, too. All I'm saying is we have to consider it. Honey, you know I wouldn't make you do anything you don't want to. I'm doing this for you. For us. You do know that, don't you? And maybe we won't even have to actually bury you. We'll see. I . . . Honey, this isn't easy for me either. You do believe me, don't you? What's that? Your tongue? Of course! Oh honey, I knew you'd understand. Just a moment. Just let me get it."

Zak returned to the shelves and took, from a plastic container resembling a letter-rack, a pinkish, rubbery object like some little-known sea creature. Back at the bedside, he put his fingers between Sooki's lips and opened her mouth. Then he slid the pinkish object in. This done, he shifted Sooki a little to one side and lay down next to her on the bed. His head was about level with her breasts, and he put his arms around her stomach. She stared straight ahead while he tried to get comfortable.

"Honey," he said. "Darling, I've never known anyone like you, anyone so sweet and wise and understanding. I just want to stay here and snuggle close to you. I wish we were already through with this terrible business, but it'll pass.

And the only thing that will keep on going is me and you. Till the day I die. There's everything I want right here in my arms. Sometimes I feel so strange holding you like this. I know you're quiet and demure, and I guess some people wouldn't see your personality, but sometimes, just holding you like this, I feel like I'm getting to know you more and more. It's like . . . I can see stars. And it's just going to go on forever, getting better and better. Oh, Sooki, I love you."

Zak sat up and moved awkwardly towards Sooki's face. He kissed her neck, just above her choker. His right hand, now void of furtiveness, swooped up beneath her dress so that her upper thighs and lower belly were exposed. She was wearing white panties, delicate as butterfly wings, with creases in the fabric that somehow managed to convey that the most delicate and most subtle of all things was a flower whose root was a hairy, drooling madness. Zak's fingers found the edge of the gusset and he pulled it aside.

"I love you. I love you so much."

Tuesday, 2nd October, 8.13 p.m.

Clive took his ear away from the door as the words sounded again. In the dark of the corridor, they seemed to echo like the sound of a distant radio.

"I love you. I love you so much."

But if it was a radio, it was not any kind he had seen before. Positioning his eye to the keyhole, he watched as his father took it from the table and slid it inside a small plastic box. Before the lid closed Clive glimpsed a metal cube with a single speaker and no knobs or dials. Then his father placed the case on the table and took a magazine from the other side. The angle prevented Clive from seeing the cover, but he had some idea of its contents. He looked away. Then, stepping carefully so that the floor wouldn't creak, he turned from the door and walked back towards the stairs, stopping only to notice a ray from the newly risen moon steal through the windows of the corridor and catch the constellations of dust there in its light.

It had occurred to Clive before that there was something wrong with his father. At first he had assumed it was his mother's death, but as the months went on and his father became more and more secretive, spending more and more time in that third-floor room of his, Clive wondered if it was not something else. In his spare time the boy had taken to reading horror novels, which provided him with an endless series of possible explanations. Was his father a serial killer? A vampire? Possessed by malevolent gods? Even if Clive ruled out supernatural influence, the fact was that Mr Magister spent far too much time alone. Clive had some idea of his father's work schedule, and he knew that it had not changed considerably in the past year. So what was he doing by himself? Wasn't it supposed to be the other way around—the father scolding the son for spending too much time in his room? And then there was the time he had gotten up to go to the bathroom in the middle of the night and seen his father pushing a human-sized object up the steps to the attic. He had dismissed it the next day as a dream, but he kept finding strange flyers and catalogues in the mail. More than once, in the garage, he had noticed the remains of mysterious crates, with nothing on them to indicate what they had contained. But even apart from all these bizarre details, it was hard to ignore the fact that in some large, general sense, something in his father had changed. Or perhaps it was better to say something had changed him.

But then, as curious as Clive was, a part of him wanted to forget his suspicions and his taciturnity and rush back to his father's room. There was so much he wanted to tell him— well, not his father necessarily, but *anyone*. It was all right messing around with Steve and everyone from class, but he couldn't talk to them seriously. He sometimes wondered if they all felt like this; if they all had secrets they kept from each other. He tried to imagine Chris or Miguel sitting alone in his room and wondering about the future—no, it was too stupid. Only he felt like this, he told himself. If only he had an older brother, or cousins his own age . . . then at least there would be someone to compare experiences with, someone to understand. But now, as he had always been, he was alone.

He stepped into his room and turned on the light. He supposed he should be studying, but all he could think about was what had happened to him yesterday afternoon, the thing he'd wanted to talk to his father about (they hadn't spoken in the morning, after all), the thing that might be about to take all that was perfect and quiet beyond Clive's reach forever.

Monday, 1st October, 3.09 p.m.

Not wanting to be alone in the house, Clive had taken to hanging out at the track after school, sitting outside on the grass and reading, finishing his homework, listening to music. The school hours ending at three, at three-thirty the track team came out and he watched them run laps in their red uniforms. By five-thirty they cleared off, and he had the area to himself. At the time he had been lying on his back, using a fat spiral notebook as a pillow, the earbuds of his mp3 player hanging around his neck.

"All by yourself?" he heard someone say. Looking up, he saw that it was Christie. She was wearing a white T-shirt and blue gym shorts bearing the school logo.

"Uh? Yeah . . ." he said, a little startled.

"You're not doing track?"

"No. I just like to come here and hang out."

"By yourself?"

He looked at her.

"Yeah."

She sat down next to him.

"Well, that's kind of weird. But I come out here sometimes too. Cassandra Connelly is doing track and I usually meet her on Mondays and Thursdays 'cause her house is so close. I can't believe she lives like two minutes away. It's really unfair."

"I usually ride my bike," Clive said. "It only takes me ten minutes."

"Lame. I have to ride with my brother and he starts work at seven-thirty, so I have to get up at six, and then when I get dropped off I just have to wait around for an hour until school starts."

"So what do you do?"

"Just my homework. I go to the library and draw sometimes too."

"Yeah? What sort of stuff?"

She unzipped her bag and took out a small sketchbook. Clive took it and flipped through the pages. Most of them contained heavily shaded sketches of horses, several of them filled in with coloured pencil.

"Pretty good," he said. "I didn't know you were into this kind of thing."

"Yeah. I just do it when I have spare time, but it's not serious or anything."

They fell silent. Clive looked over at her. The sun was declining towards close of day and he realised they were alone. There was no awkwardness, but perhaps it was this lack of awkwardness that made him feel . . . well, awkward. Although he had always liked Christie's personality, it seemed strange to him that he might speak to a girl without either making fun of her or wanting to go out with her. Nothing in his experience had suggested this could happen. For his friends, girls were either someone to kid around about, or they were girlfriends. To be alone with a girl, to talk to her in the same way he talked with his friends, all without trying to get anywhere with her—there was something strange about it. Without knowing why, he felt as if the other guys would make fun of him for it. But they didn't have to know, he told himself.

He was still turning it over in his mind when she said, quite plainly:

"So you think Marybeth is cute, right? Don't lie."

And without realising what was happening, he found himself answering:

"Yeah . . . well, I guess I like her, yeah . . ."

At once an enormous smile lit up Christie's face. Looking at it, Clive felt a sudden, terrible joy; a kind of obliteration. He felt as if these careless words had condemned him somehow, but there was freedom in it as well, the release that comes with complete hopelessness.

"I knew it! I knew you liked her. It's soooo obvious, you look at her *all* the time. And the one time we were in the library and she asked to borrow a pen you like ran back to your locker to get one even though it was on the second floor."

Clive shifted his position and leaned back, feeling the grass beneath him. Already the excitement was leaving, and he felt reality closing around him like a suffocating plastic bag.

"Yeah, but there's no point to it. There's no point, I mean I know she's not going to go out with me . . ." He picked a blade of grass and began to peel it, tearing it into thin strips. "The thing is everyone is getting into her now but I liked her from way back . . ."

Now he was just making himself look stupid, he thought. How was he saying these things, how had this happened? He felt as if Christie had gutted him.

"You mean you liked her from before junior high?"

"Yeah."

"That's sweet. Well, I'm not *completely* sure, but I know she doesn't have a boyfriend and she *did* say something about you the other day. . . ."

He looked at her.

"What did she say?"

Christie smiled.

"No, I can't tell you."

His emotions were rising and falling as she spoke each word, but Christie seemed perfectly calm.

"I really can't tell you, but . . . I'll give you her phone number, okay? You can call her by yourself."

She took a cell phone out of her bag and handed it to him.

"What, like . . . call her now? Right now?"

She laughed a little.

"No, just get her number. Call her when you get home. Haven't you ever called a girl before?"

"Yeah, but I mean . . . well . . ."

"Clive, it's not that hard. You just pick up the phone, dial the number, and start talking."

Too ashamed to say anything else, he looked down at the phone and scrolled through the list until he came to Marybeth`s number. Even looking at it on the screen filled him with longing and terror. His hands shaking, he took out his phone and added her to his address book. When he had finished Christie said:

"So you have to call her when you get home, okay?"

He mumbled something inconclusive and excused himself, and as he walked back to the parking lot to unlock his bike he felt Christie staring at him.

On the way home he went over the conversation in his mind, analysing her tone of voice and the nuance of every word. Was it possible that Christie was deliberately deceiving him? It seemed unlikely, but there was no way for him to be sure if she was telling the truth. Perhaps she and Marybeth had come up with the whole thing; perhaps they were joking about it even now.

He pushed the thoughts from his mind. It was already too late, he told himself—even if he did nothing. Yes, Christie was sure to tell Marybeth what he had said. But she was nice, wasn't she? They wouldn't make fun of him. Maybe not, but he would still seem even more of a fool and a coward. And the news would spread—he imagined all the girls in the class staring at him with mocking eyes, his shame not even worthy of open laughter. No, there was no escape now. No matter what he did, his life was over.

"You know Clive Magister?"

"You mean that ugly boy who looks like his clothes come from Goodwill?"

"Yeah. He has a crush on you."

"Yuck!"

"Ha ha!"

"Yuck! Yuck! Yuck!"

He imagined a gleaming black scythe coming down and cutting off his head, which, rolling along and settling at Marybeth's feet, looked up at her pathetically and pleadingly with the last dying light in its eyes.

"Fine," he thought. "If she wants to spit on me, let her."

He knew it was too late to turn back.

Sitting on the edge of his bed, he took out his phone, selected Marybeth's number, and held his finger poised over the button. Each passing moment seemed to harden into an eternity. At the thought of Marybeth knowing anything of his existence, he felt an even greater contempt for himself. Looking back, he saw that it was all his fault—if he had been able to control himself, none of this would have happened. Now there was nothing left but to finish himself off. He was about to throw away the one quiet, perfect thing he had ever known. A single moment of pressure from his thumb, and the world would collapse.

He pressed call.

Wednesday, 3rd October, 3.57 p.m.

Wreathed in that ozone feeling of freshness that comes with emerging from a well-timed shower, Angela, wrapped in a blueberry-purple towel, trod with heavy bounce along the deep-pile carpet of the landing and returned to a room not quite as fresh as she was. She was about to throw back the curtains, but thought better of it. Instead, she clicked play on an old portable stereo with her toe, and knelt down in front of the mirror, next to the bed, where her hairdryer lay, still plugged in.

"American boy . . . American girl . . . Most beautiful people . . . in the world . . ."

She sang along in snatches as she finessed, with hairdryer and fingers, the damp tresses of her strawberry-blonde mane into feathery, almost Farrah Fawcetty, layers.

Restless, she left off before completing this task, let her towel fall, and pulled open the drawer containing panties. After thirty minutes or so of dressing, undressing, drying hair, brushing hair, applying foundation, and so on, she rolled onto her bed, where her Apple, hood open, was on standby mode. Lying on her stomach, she tapped and stroked the touchpad with her fingertip, checking her Facebook and e-mail accounts. There was nothing of interest there. Her Facebook page had begun to make her sad since she took this year off college; it now either reminded her what she was missing or gave her the feeling she was swiftly being forgotten as everything except the most perfunctory electronic presence. She had been trying to lure her Facebook friends into writing e-mails, but with little success. All traffic in electronic communication seemed to be from the particular, one-on-one, to the general social network. Her main e-mail in-box, today, had only received newsletters and so on she'd subscribed to—PETA, Cute Custom Clothing, the latest featured article from *Delilah* under the title 'Fuck You, Menstruation!', and one or two others.

Angela turned on her back and heaved a sigh, or maybe just gave an exhalation of exhaustion. Her feeling of ozone freshness, sadly, was dispersing. Listening to a mix-CD in her bedroom on a mild October afternoon (an Indian summer this year, as she reminded herself) should have been happiness as carefree as bubblegum, except that the (real) summer for listening to mix-CDs was maybe even ten years ago now, when she was a girl. It didn't seem possible so much time had passed.

But this was stupid. She had a lot of free time right now; she should be making the most of it, not moping.

She turned back onto her stomach and clicked on the menstruation article, snickering to herself through her nose here and there as she read, and then, hearing herself snicker, making fun of herself with a fake snicker. Finishing the article, she had a sudden thought, and clicked on a special folder under the title, 'Journo stuff'. She next clicked on one or two of the e-mails in this folder and began reading through.

Just then she felt a bouncing weight on the bed beside her.

"Oh, it's you."

"Were you hoping for someone else?" asked Marybeth.

"No. Who else would I want bouncing on my bed except my silly little sister?"

"What are you reading?"

"Nothing. Haven't you heard of privacy?"

"Yeah . . . I guess I did hear about that. Wasn't that something they abolished in the nineties?"

"Ha ha. Take a look, if you're really interested."

On the screen was an e-mail with the subject heading, 'Re: Just a background question'. The e-mail contained, at the top, a brief reply, and below it, the original message:

Uh . . . duh . . . No?

From: Angela Cuthberts [mailto:angelcuts@yahoo.com]
Sent: 03 Dec 2011 13:50
To: Julia Westbrook
Subject: A background question

Hi Julia.

I'm just writing again with a question about Delilah's background as I think this may help me in pitching future articles to you. One thing I always wondered about was the thinking behind the name of the magazine. I don't think I really guessed the kind of magazine you are from the name. So I wanted to ask, was there some specific meaning behind the name? I mean, I get that it's the Biblical lady who Samson was kind of soft on, but don't you think there are more obvious strong Biblical women to choose from? I'd really like to hear your views on this.

Yrs,
Angela.

"Why does it have a question mark after 'no'?" said Marybeth after a while.

"That's . . . Maybe you're too young to understand. It's kind of an ironic thing, I guess. You've got to understand the *Delilah* schtick."

"Schtick?"

"Yeah. Right. They kind of have a . . . schtick."

"Hmmm. Anyway, I'm going to hang out with Christie. Can I borrow your butterfly scrunchie?"

"Give it back tomorrow."

"Sure, I will."

Marybeth was almost out the door.

"Hey, I had a message for you."

"Tell me later."

Then she was gone.

Angela maximised the older e-mail from Julia Westbrook that, for some reason, she had just hidden before Marybeth could see it. The subject heading was, 'Re: A Year of Observant Chastity'.

Angela had started reading *Delilah* in the first year of her Media Studies degree at Vassar. The magazine had the distinct mix of feminism, pop culture and niche, up-to-date modes of communication that was most relevant to her course. It hadn't taken her long to decide that getting an article in *Delilah* could be a significant step for her post-graduate career. Before her first year was out, after two complicated and humiliating romances, she had an idea—deliberately remain chaste for her whole sophomore year, keep a diary, and write an article on male attitudes toward the single coed. Then, near the end of her sophomore year, the Churg Strauss Syndrome had set in, and it was decided she would take a year off, resting, having treatment, and so on. Maybe even because of this detour in her life's plan, she didn't miss a beat; as soon as she got home again she wrote up the main points of her chastity diary into an article and sent it to *Delilah* with a 'covering e-mail' over which she had agonised for some time. She was not kept long in suspense, but the reply was disappointing. It was encouraging that Julia Westbrook, the magazine's editor, was this accessible, but she found the content of the reply slightly cold. Julia explained that the article was off the mark, as it was mainly about things that didn't happen. She said snippily, in passing, that the "observe/observant" wordplay in the title was forced, and, like the article itself, didn't work, and advised Angela that any prospective writer for *Delilah* needed to understand exactly where *Delilah* was coming from. "We're all about that guys shouldn't be creeps not that women should be nuns," she had written in conclusion. Angela wondered if Julia Westbrook, or anyone at Delilah, ever felt as confused as she did.

Disheartened at first, she had decided to bounce back with the kind of enthusiastic follow up e-mails that she had heard were supposed to impress editors and bosses in general, but, if anything, Julia had grown less encouraging, not more. Secretly, Angela had become so furious that she'd more or less agreed to a date with some lobotomised douchebag out of sheer spite. To be fair, when she had first met Thad (that was his name) at the Brynbach Mall, he had also seemed half-cute, in a weird kind of way. Ugh, and look at how that had turned out, too!

She rolled on her back once more, and once more sighed. Listlessly, she checked the time on her phone. Recently there was a radio show she'd been tuning in to when she was on her own in the daytime. It would be just starting now. With nothing else to do, and craving distraction, she got up and switched her stereo function to radio.

". . . promised last week, we're taking calls all this week for Uncle Reasonable, otherwise known as Doctor Graham Clegg, who's come to us all the way from sleepy Oxford, England, the city of dreaming spires, or so I hear. Uncle Reasonable, hello again."

"Hello, Doctor Mockjock."

"And you'll be answering questions from any callers on just about any kind of problem. Is that right?"

"Yes. That's correct."

"Are there any problems you won't be able to answer?"

"Er . . ." Here Uncle Reasonable gave a throaty chuckle indicating humorous modesty. "Well, yes. Probably. If I . . . er . . . Don't ask me what's going on under the bonnet of your car. The hood, I mean. Other than that, I'll do my best to answer anything that's thrown at me."

"And we are going to throw the lines open now."

Soon the first caller was describing with barely coherent rapidity the catalogue of grievances with which his life was cursed.

". . . and so, you see, Doctor Clegg, that after everything's already failed, now I find the one person left in my life I trusted, my therapist, is actually trying to drive me out of my mind."

"Oh, I think that's pretty unlikely."

"I'm sorry, Doctor?"

"I said, I think that's pretty unlikely. I think you're feeling a bit wound up. Could you tell me, please, Roger, do you have any cocoa in your household?"

"Cocoa?"

"Yes."

"I believe I have some, but——"

"Splendid. I would suggest that tonight, at about eight o'clock, you make yourself a nice mug of cocoa, listen to some Peter, Paul and Mary, and get a good night's rest. Sleep is really the best medicine."

"You think so, Doctor?"

"Believe me, I've been telling people this for years now."

"I see. Thank you, Doctor."

The calls continued in this manner, and Angela noticed with something between consternation and bemusement that Uncle Reasonable appeared to give disconcertingly similar advice to each person he spoke to. Cocoa was mentioned often, as if it were something incidental he had just thought of, and getting a good night's sleep was mentioned invariably, and often with a strong note of insistence. One or two of the callers, who had been listening to the show from the start, even began to lose their temper, at which they were told a good night's sleep would calm them down. Finally, there came a caller suffering with insomnia.

"But that's the problem, Doc, don't you see that, I cannot sleep."

"Yes. I suggest you have a nice mug of cocoa, turn in early, and get a good night's sleep."

"You know, I'd really like to do that, but I'm telling you, if I 'turn in' early or late, I still can't get any sleep."

"Shelley—may I call you that?—I think you're worrying unnecessarily. Get an early start in the morning, go to bed early, and once you're nice and tired you'll soon find yourself drifting off."

"Is that all you've got to say?"

"I think you'll probably find that's all you need, believe me. It doesn't hurt, though, sometimes, also to have a nice mug of cocoa before you go to———"

And at this point the caller hung up.

"Dude is nuts," said Angela to herself. "I could help people better than that."

Reaching out, she flicked the stereo function from radio back to CD and pressed play.

'Chariots of Fire' by Vangelis began to hum out from the speakers.

She pursed her lips then, thinking.

Rolling onto her stomach once more, she opened a new browser and selected a video she had favourited on YouTube. It featured celebrated male feminist, Brad Spritzer, at a microphone on a podium, at some kind of outdoor event. He spoke as if spontaneously vocalising an epiphany.

"I was that man," he said. "I was that predatory, unreconstructed male. But I'm here with a message of hope for all you beautiful sisters and brothers. Men can change. Sisters, you can change your brothers. Brothers, you can also change your brothers. And I want to give a special message of hope for you brothers out there, who've been living wrong, just like I was—I want to tell you it's possible: you can see a beautiful, young woman, in lingerie, or with nothing on, and be so aroused you're like granite, and you can still be filled with respect from the tip of your toes right to the top of your head."

These final words were half-obscured by applause.

"Hm," said Angela, and closed the browser. Maybe, she thought, there was an article that *Delilah* would not be able to resist.

As the next song on the CD started, she sang along to it.

"I'm a spy . . . in the House of Love . . . I know the dream . . . you're dreaming of . . ."

Wednesday, 3ʳᵈ October, 4.14 p.m.

Thad stood in the living room silently for a few minutes. He knew Zak wasn't there, but it felt strange being in the house without him. There was a painting of an elk on the wall that he had never noticed before and he guessed it must have been a new addition. He kept looking at it, wondering if it had any value.

"Fucking art," he said.

It was around a quarter to four in the afternoon, so he had plenty of time before Zak would be back.

He wasn't really too clear on his plans, but the main thing was to get Sooki out of the place. Then he could figure out how to generate the most profit from the heist. Both Bergen and Mr Magister wanted her, and both had given deposits. Bergen seemed to have the deeper pockets, but Mr Magister seemed somehow more trustworthy. Bergen's thing with the cemetery also vaguely bothered Thad. But it was really a matter of who would fork over the most money. And maybe, in the end, Zak would pay more just to have her back.

"After all," Thad thought, "the fucker's, like, in love with her."

He entered the bedroom and put his helmet down on the desk. Sooki was supine on the bed.

He licked his lips, seeing stars and profanity some chasm of wonder because surely it was more than just profit that compelled him.

If I could just like um get her out of the house her hair's sort of cool isn't it black forest spread it out Christ I gotta get this done real live um yeah. But I'm not like an um vegetarian give you my domesticated fresh texture.

"Hey," he said tentatively.

She didn't answer. Why should she? After all, she was just some big doll.

He glanced at the choker around her throat and wondered if by some chance Magister were listening. Probably not, since he would be at work too, but with that guy it was always hard to be sure.

"Hey baby," Thad said in a loud voice, "I got a guy who likes you a lot and wants me to bring you to him. His name is Mr Brooks and he's good looking and in love with you. GEE I SURE WISH I COULD TAKE YOU TO HIM NOW BUT ZAK'S IN THE NEXT ROOM FRYING EGGS!"

He walked over and grabbed her right ankle and pulled her halfway off the bed.

He looked at the rigid outline of her breasts and licked his lips which felt like straw ready to be lit on fire and then sat down next to her. He didn't really look at her face. For some reason it seemed like she was staring at him with disapproval.

He lay back and gazed at the ceiling.

"So this is where it all happens," he said aloud and then found his hand straying over to Sooki feeling her hand and he didn't let go hand out of reach for the mother an opaque white the ceiling was.

I'll just like um get her and get the hell out of here Christ more real than the just one like um kiss for the fuck of it the joy of life remembering the heavy breathing if he could just get that and can it and kick it because like it wasn't about her after all was it an um volcano? Your old man what does he do? Will you come to the party?

We can like melt together in organic fun so crazy just feeling a jet of steam superficially attractive slut and hereby you shall know the full body binder sack and ye shall know. And ye shall know the plastic gates of hell. I can't hear his steps. I can't hear his steps so don't struggle baby or are you like an um bitch you rubber wolf dame de voyage it would be like ha ha. Are you goneoclinic? Am I still holding her? Dude get moving. Some fucking Korean meatball not just some inflatable like balloon. I wonder if embracing a doll can like make her happy the fucking psychic process. Christ like I gotta get her on my bike and get out of here just dig into her pot. Wait like I, I like, um, better get up.

He opened his eyes. He was lying on the bed. Sooki was staring at him.

"Did I just fall asleep?" he asked himself.

He looked at his wristwatch. It was 5.47.

He heard the sound of a door opening.

"I'm home, dear!"

It was Zak's voice.

Thad bounced up off the bed, went to the window, opened it—then, suddenly remembering his helmet, grabbed it. He flung himself out the window and closed it behind him. As he sped away on his Kawasaki he wondered if he had done anything with Sooki. He didn't really think so, but wasn't sure. He sort of wished he had.

> *Ngun Yee*
> *That fan dance covered in moss*
> *Reverie orgasm guaranteed coated with an appropriate amount*
>   *of lubricant select their favourite sex mouth*
> *All things for love*
> *Forget about Carol Doda and Tura Satana fold structure*
>   *thorns and the structure tail added the uterus*
> *Love keepeth them Ngun Yee the great Miss Toy*
> *That destiny your vagina on a doll*

Monday, 1st October, 6.07 p.m.

"Hello?" the girl's voice said.

Clive felt something hot and sick flooding his guts: bile, or maybe adrenaline, he couldn't tell: possibly some rancid combination of both that his body had prepared just for the occasion.

"Um, Marybeth?"

"No, I'm sorry, this is Angela. Marybeth's out right now."

He paused, unsure of what to say.

"She left her cell phone?"

"Yeah. She's just gone next door, she should be back soon. Do you want to leave a message?"

"Just . . . just tell her Clive called."

She hung up, and he pocketed his phone and fell back on the bed, feeling equal parts relief, disappointment and dread. Somehow, impossibly, he had managed to call her, but chance had prevented him from making contact. Whether this was a success or a failure, he couldn't tell. He hadn't embarrassed himself *too* much, he decided . . . and yet, this opened up a fresh set of worries. What if Marybeth never responded, never acknowledged the call in any way? He couldn't imagine seeing her face every day and knowing she had chosen to ignore him. And if he tried to call her again too soon, he would only come off as desperate. No, he decided, it would have been better to have caught her, better to have failed outright. Nothing was worse than uncertainty.

Eosphorus, Woven with Flowers, ▲

You want to know what time it is? Because you can see dawn's steely blade disembowelling the night you thought was endless? I'll tell you the time. It's time to decide whether to sleep or to vote for manic hope and take more MDMA. It's time to decide whether to hunch shoulders home all bleary in a pale day of commuter panic, or stay at the party, even though the rest of the world refuses to believe.

It's time for the story of Noel Toy's vagina.

After Ryan Gosling starred in *Lars and the Real Girl*, he kept his, shall we say, co-star as a memento and developed a taste for inorganic pussy. That's how I got to know him. He'd always be calling up the shop: Have you got Siamese twin dolls? Have you got dolls that bleed?

"Look, Ryan," I'd say (I hated that the bastard had my name), "they're conjoined twins—not Siamese."

"Yeah, well, if I'm gonna be fucking them," he'd come back, witty as a switchblade, "they'll be any damn thing I say they are."

But even I have to be grateful to this luckier-than-thou hunk of humanity for hire. See, I learnt from him about all kinds of things much sought after in Hollywood. Such as Noel Toy's vagina.

You don't get sex symbols like you used to. She got to the top the old way—with live crowds. No need for special effects and Photoshop. Word of mouth, too—her fan dance drew them like the Sermon on the Mount. Made it into movies after a while, though her act was cleaned up by then. Well, so, she almost missed her chance for immortality. This wasn't pre-code anymore; her talents were stifled. And today, when the restraints have gone, no one knows what sexual immortality is, anyway. Or only a few.

Who knew that some nobody sculptor would offend those with the deep pockets at the California Palace of the Legion of Honour. No, they did not want his *Venus* placed beside Rodin's *Thinker*.

The wax model was rejected.

And the plaster mould of Noel Toy's vagina?

He couldn't keep it secret, of course. It got stolen, lost. Picked up again.

I understand it fell into the hands of the boys at Soft Chasm, the world's greatest manufacturers of love dolls. They only made a few dolls with it when the mould disappeared. Stolen, probably. But not before a few of those dolls got into circulation.

They say the mould itself could do something to you if you just stood in the same room for a while. The Internal Orgasm, they call it. You don't lose anything. It's more like you're gaining something—this squirming glow inside you don't have to work for. Some heavens are not for virgins. But if you've strayed far enough to hear this story, keep going. Rumours. Word of mouth. People talking to people. Little by little, you might find your way there.

Thursday, 4th October, 4.12 p.m.

Three days of it—and all the different tactics he had employed in that time to make the waiting and uncertainty bearable. His father had been no help, of course. His now habitual horror novels had been the best he could manage—a kind of 'hair of the dog' for the fear that simmered in his gut. And now, again, returning home from school, he still had nothing to tell him what ripples his conversations with Christie and (briefly) with Angela were spreading in the world. After returning from school today without anything he could possibly interpret as 'the signs' from Marybeth, he fell again into his routines of attempted distraction. He tried reading for a while, but his thoughts kept wandering back to Monday's phone call, and before long he placed the book aside. He couldn't eat, he had no e-mail, and nothing on TV interested him. The only thing now was to go for a walk and clear his mind. He took his jacket from the chair beside the bed and headed out the door. But as soon as he entered the hall, for some reason, a different impulse unfolded in him. He padded stealthily up the stairs to the third floor and saw that the door to his father's study was open. He walked closer, wondering if his father was still at the table, in front of the strange speaker. But as he approached, he saw that the room was empty. A vague curiosity pushed him forward: although it was never openly stated, his father's room was usually off limits. Clive had always gotten the impression that he was to stay away from it unless invited in, and it was rare for his father to leave without closing the door. And a man that meticulous about privacy was not likely to change his routine unless something had distracted him. But what could that be?

He made his way to the door, stepping lightly to avoid the creak of the floorboards. The plastic box, he saw, was still on the table where his father had left it. Other than that the room was bare: most of the books and papers must have been stuffed away in drawers. The box, when he picked it up, was lighter than he had expected. He opened the lid and removed the speaker. There was a switch on the side which he flicked, and then placed the speaker against his ear. The only sound at first was a low, droning static, as distant as the sound of the ocean in a shell. Then there were faint murmurs, distorted snatches of conversation. He found a small dial on the back of the speaker and fiddled with it, adjusting the volume nervously, afraid to make it too loud in case his father was still in the vicinity. There was crackle and whistling, as from a badly-tuned radio station, but then some words cut with distinctness through the aural blizzard.

". . . know something happened while I was out. I just don't understand why you won't . . ."

Then the crackling obscured the voice again, as if the rent in the curtain had been closed. The voice didn't sound like a radio presenter, or an actor. It seemed to Clive to have the unmistakable quality to it of real life, which is always hopelessly unrehearsed and unpolished. And there in the empty house—if it was empty—the sound of that anonymous voice somehow made a direct appeal to Clive's loneliness, as if nothing could be more important than to listen to the lives of people who did not know there was an audience, as if only this could provide him with the secret cure for his loneliness.

He began holding the box at different heights and angles to see if this would help it to get a clearer signal. He could still hear the voice a little through the fuzz of interference, but could not quite hold the box so that the reception remained good. He began to worry. What would he say if his father returned? If his father had gone out then he should be able to hear the front door when he came back. He wished his father's hours weren't so irregular recently. Suddenly a voice jumped out of the speaker.

"I love you!"

Clive swallowed hard, licked his lips and listened.

". . . And that's how I can tell. You've changed. In like, a day. Even apart from the other stuff. You think I don't know you well enough to notice when something's wrong? God, of course I love you—still love you and always will. I'm not the one with the problem . . . Well, yes, I know you say you're not, either, but you know what, I don't believe you. I never thought I'd say this, but I don't believe you."

Clive noticed that although he had at first thought this to be a conversation of more than one voice, it was, in fact, a monologue, or, more accurately, only one half of a dialogue. There was a slightly nasal, whiny voice that sounded like it belonged to a man in his twenties, but that was all. Whoever it was, he must have been talking on the telephone to someone. Now he seemed close to tears.

"Oh, what are we going to do, Sooki? I'm not going back to the way I was before. Never! I need you. Do you understand? I will do anything. Any-fucking-thing. You'll see. You'll realise that no one's going to love you like I do. No one can. No one ever can. Nothing's going to stop me, you understand? Is it the dollnappers? Just tell me what's going on. I don't want to do it with things this way between us, but if you don't tell me . . . I swear . . . I swear I'll have to bury you, just like Thad said. I'm sorry, baby, but I swear I'll——"

"DO WHAT YOU LIKE!"

Clive had tilted the box a little and suddenly the whole device had vibrated with a different voice, a voice buzzing with static, a woman's voice whose living heat he seemed to hold in his palm. He jumped as at an electric shock and sent the box flying across the room to clatter on the floor. He heard the man's voice again, wailing as if in agony, and then the signal seemed to cut out.

For some moments Clive stood where he was, stunned. He felt a vindication of his hunch that his father was mixed up in something terrible, unspeakable even. It was as if, with that female voice, his entire body had been filled with a radio signal telling him the exact nature of the evil in which his father was secretly involved. It was far worse than he had imagined. And yet the information in the crackle, buzz and purr of that weird radio signal had been entirely emotional. He could not say now in words just what it was he had understood.

The crackling seemed to turn into a kind of tingling pins-and-needles, and then began to dissipate, and with this dissipation he began to recover his thought processes. What had the man been talking about? Sooki must have been the name of the woman he was talking to. Sooki? More like 'Spooky'. And he had used a strange word. What was it? "Dollnappers". And right at the end he had said something like—Clive was quite sure of this—"I'll have to bury you". For all the images these fragments conjured to his imagina- tion, he could not put them together into a coherent story. They remained a kind of phantasmagoria, forming shapes here and there out of the ectoplasm of obscuring white noise.

Dollnapping. Dolls. What was it about dolls? All kinds of scenarios now began to flicker behind that ectoplasmic veil, lent a sketchy form by the horror stories that had come to preoccupy him. He thought of the films *House of Wax* and *The Body Snatcher*, with Vincent Price and Boris Karloff. Surely this couldn't be anything like that? And yet, if not, what was it?

Suddenly he felt the need to try and tune in to those voices again, to find out more. He walked over to where the speaker device had fallen and crouched down to pick it up. Twisting the dial behind the speaker seemed to produce no effect. Perhaps he had broken it. He placed it back on the desk, trying to remember exactly how it had been positioned. When he was satisfied, or as close as he could get to satisfaction, he stopped adjusting its position and looked around the room.

Would the drawers of the desk be locked, he wondered idly. He tugged with unnecessary force—the drawer shot open with ease. Inside, amongst letters, papers, a staple-gun and so on, was a small stack of magazines, the topmost of which bore the title, *Guys and Dolls*. The photograph showed an uncannily realistic mannequin in a bikini and tie-dyed sari on what appeared to be the deck of a private yacht. In her hand was a flute of champagne. Opposite her, a man in white shirt and trousers was pouring himself a glass from the bottle. Clive reached into the drawer to pick this up. Doing so, however, he discovered that he had inadvertently taken hold of the front cover of the next magazine, too, and, with the weight of gravity brought to bear by the rest of the magazine on this single sheet of glossy paper, it tore from top to bottom, about an inch from the staples. Clive swore in frustration and put the copy of *Guys and Dolls* on top of the desk. Then he took out the next magazine and tried to fit the torn section of the cover back in place. This magazine was called *Idollatry* and seemed to be more mysterious in tone than the one that Clive had just laid aside. Even that one was not the kind of magazine you might expect to find on the shelves next to *Vanity Fair,* but if that was specialist then this was positively hermetic. The cover photograph seemed to have been taken in some damp and crumbling ruined temple somewhere. The cover model was a doll with long and shockingly pink hair, dressed in a skimpy and exotic outfit that made Clive think of certain kinds of fantasy and hentai anime. In fact, that must have been the intention, because the eyes of this model were unnaturally large, creating an unsettling contrast with the realistic nature of the rest of her body. She had been placed upon a stone pedestal set in an alcove where there had presumably once stood a statue of some kind. The scene had been expertly lit with a combination of coloured lights to enhance the lurid and provocative nature of the picture. Several different species of spider crawled over her skin, and before her there knelt two men in business suits making peculiar signs of obeisance. Between them, in a box, was an object that appeared to be some kind of blasphemous offering . . . or perhaps an accessory.

The first time Clive had seen hardcore pornographic pictures, when he was nine, they had made his stomach turn in a way it had never turned before, as if he were witnessing a scene of violent brutality through the eyes of the perpetrator. It was the discovery of that open secret, lust, like a boot in the guts. This, he felt, was another such discovery. He felt sick and dry-mouthed at an occult mystery whose textures were those of plastic, rubber and wax.

He placed this magazine on the desk, too. Part of the nervous trembling that had come upon him was to do with the fact that he knew he could not repair the cover in such a way that the tear would go unnoticed. Perhaps he would stand a better chance of covering his trespass by simply stealing the whole magazine.

It was while he agonised with this terrible, slack-limbed indecision that there came, unexpectedly, the sound that dread should have taught him to expect—the sound of the door. Quickly he stuffed the copy of *Guys and Dolls* back in the drawer. But what to do with *Idollatry*? Whatever he did, his father would guess he had been here. Why not take the magazine, then? At least then he would learn a little more about the weird influences that now prevailed in his father's life. Perhaps his father would not dare to ask him about the theft. Perhaps he wanted his father to ask him. He would take it.

Now he could hear his father's tread on the stairs. He did not want to be discovered like this, anyway. He slid the drawer closed and pushed the copy of *Idollatry* down the front of his jeans, covering it with his T-shirt and shirt. All this was done too late, however. There was no longer any way that he could leave this room without being seen by his father. But perhaps there was one thing he could do. He could hide until his father had gone again. He looked desperately around the room for something to serve as a priest's hole.

Thursday, 4ᵗʰ October, 5.59 p.m.

"Zak? Zak, are you there?"

The signal had gone. Thad tried phoning again, but the dial tone was cut without Zak picking up.

"Fuckin' Zak."

He let out a sound between a sigh and a raspberry, and decided to phone again later. Apart from phone Zak, he'd done nothing the whole day, and now he felt the peculiar tiredness that comes from doing nothing—not a genuine exhaustion, but only a faint sluggishness, an inability to move. He couldn't even get comfortable on the couch, which was too small for him anyway. A relic of the 70's, its sickly pea-green covering had begun to harden with age, turning almost black in places. Thad had found it abandoned near a dumpster on the way home from drinking at Rise one night, and the next day he'd returned for it, loading it onto the bed of Ed Chiang's Tacoma PreRunner. Apart from the table, a few cheap plastic chairs and a flatscreen TV, it was the only piece of furniture in the living room.

He propped himself up on his elbows, trying to find a different angle. As he shifted his weight, his foot knocked over a half-filled bottle of Corona that had been resting against the table leg.

"Ah, shit . . ."

Warm beer spilled across the carpet and under the couch, forming a faint brown stain. A stray rivulet connected it with a mosaic of several other hard, crusted patches of carpet. For a moment he considered getting a towel and wiping it up, but then thought better of it. He leaned back in the chair, lit a Camel cigarette and gazed at the ceiling, drifting into a kind of trance. Then, after a moment, he remembered: the party. He still needed to invite everyone. He should have done it earlier, but since yesterday he'd been feeling as if he'd slipped into another world. He realised he'd forgotten all about Angela and everyone else. Instead, he'd been thinking of Sooki and the way—he remembered now, not for the first time, but as if for the first time—her eyes had seemed to change, the dream-landscape unfolding inside her . . . it was like the time he'd masturbated to transsexual porn when he was sixteen. Hand in pants, he'd sat on the floor of his room, his back pressed firmly against the locked door, the magazine propped open in front of him. He'd shoplifted it on a whim along with a few others, but as he flipped through it all kinds of horrible dreams flooded into his mind until he had had no choice but to give in. Afterwards he felt slightly ashamed and vaguely sick, but the next night he found himself in the same position, crouched against the door. He kept the magazine for a week before he was able to break its hold on him.

Still, he told himself, he was more mature now. No need to feel guilty—there was nothing wrong with experimentation. He wasn't going soft, just branching out. No matter what he did, he'd never be a total creep like Zak.

He crushed his cigarette out against the table and took another from the pack. He'd have to go back to Zak's apartment soon, he knew. But apart from getting Sooki away from him and Mr Magister, Thad had no real plan—he'd never been one for thinking ahead. No, it was always best to improvise. And all he had to guide him now was the desire for more money and a vague but growing sense of possession—why, he wondered, should he let either of them have Sooki? Didn't he have as much right to her as they did? He could hold her for ransom, and give her to whoever paid the most—or not, depending on his mood.

He picked up his phone again and scrolled through the address book, sending a mass-mail to everyone to let them know the date. Then he called his closest friends individually.

"So you're in for tomorrow, right?" he said as he heard Ralph's voice on the other end of the line.

"The party?"

"Yeah. You can bring your own booze if you want, but I'm going to be pretty stocked. Going on a little expedition tomorrow."

"Beautiful."

"Hey Ralph, you know that song 'Mo Money, Mo Problems'?"

"Yeah?"

"That song," Thad finished his cigarette, "is full of shit."

He pressed the 'end call' button immediately after delivering this line, as if he were in a film and didn't have time for irrelevant filler like, "See you later".

Just then his Salt-n-Pepa 'Push It' ringtone sounded. It was Zak.

"Hello?"

"Zak? What happened? Where in the fuck are you?"

"I'll be there soon. Just wait."

The called ended. Thad flipped his phone closed, held it in both his hands, almost as if in prayer, and nodded thoughtfully to himself. Then he flipped it open and dialled up a number from the memory.

He held the phone to his ear almost absently. He heard the ringtone a number of times, an electronic purr that told him his existence was now throwing dice to see if it would be able to interrupt another existence. While his expectation was still ambiguous, the ringtone abruptly ceased and was replaced by a female voice.

"Hello?"

"Hey! Angela!"

"Yeah. What's up?"

Thad sensed something in the voice, as if he were being mocked. It intrigued him. Angela had not seemed this playful before.

"I was, like, wondering if you felt like coming round for a party."

"Sure. I'll come to your party. Who is this?"

"Thad. You remember, right?"

"Oh, of course I do, Thad. How could I forget?"

Thad found himself confused. There was an entire tone of suggestion in the voice that he couldn't trace to its meaning, as if he were meant to understand something unspoken, but didn't. Then he heard another voice in the background, and realisation dawned on him.

"Give me that, you little brat."

And then came the voice that had first answered, now at a little distance from the mouthpiece.

"You always answer *my* phone."

"Give me that phone! I'll spank your little white ass!"

"You'll have to catch me first."

"Who is it?"

"It's your sexy boyfriend."

"Shut *up*! . . . Hello! Whoever's on the phone, if you

can hear me, that wasn't Angela who answered, that was Angela's dumbass little sister."

There followed a number of shrieks and thuds and some hysterical gurgling giggles. These giggles continued for some time, punctuated by more thuds and squeals, and a number of sounds of more obscure causation.

Quite suddenly and unexpectedly there came the sound of the phone being picked up, and another voice. This time it was definitely Angela. Thad had had time to observe the difference between their voices now.

"Hello? Who is it?"

"Your boyfriend, right?"

"Yeah, right. I don't have a boyfriend."

"Sounds like a good start."

"It's Thad, right?"

"Yeah. Doesn't your phone say?"

"I accidentally deleted your number."

"Yeah, right."

"Whadda you want?"

"I . . . er . . . I just wanted to apologise for the other night, you know, with your sister. What's she called again? Marylou?"

"Marybeth."

"Hey, what're you guys saying about me?"

He could hear Marybeth's voice in the background.

"Yeah, right. Marybeth. I never forget a name. Anyway, I wanted to make it up to you. I'm having a sort of party."

"A party?"

"Well, I call it a party, I mean like a . . . you know, a gathering, just a few close friends and relatives. Kinda like a funeral. But not as serious. You know, you can dress casual and everything."

"Relatives, eh? What is it, like a family occasion?"

"Yeah. That's it. Like, you know, a family occasion kind of thing. Well, but without the family, but . . . yeah. We're all like family. Hey, why don't you bring your sister, too, right? Like a . . . family thing."

"Is it going to be safe?"

"Safe? As long as none of the guys bring nunchaku, I guess."

"I'm thinking of Marybeth, not me."

"Oh yeah. Safe. Sure it is. It'll be like, you know, Euro theme and all that. A little music, a little cheese, some chilled drinks . . ."

"Thad, if there's any sign of . . . of adult things at this party——"

"Adult?"

"You know what I'm talking about."

"Hey, don't sweat it. I'll tell the guys to smoke out back and shit."

"Well, I might come. We'll see."

"Sure. It's up to you. It'd be great to see you. You're like, um, one of the great conversationalists."

"Thanks."

"Yeah."

"Oh, when is it?"

"Yeah. It's Friday. Mañana."

Thad gave the time and the address. All the while, in the background, he heard Marybeth asking questions, eager, it seemed, to learn how she was involved in the plans being made by Thad and her big sister.

Angela seemed to adopt a warning tone towards Thad, but he sensed from the care with which she listened to what he said that she was interested. At the very end of the conversation her tone changed abruptly in a way that inflamed expectation in him like a warm waft of perfume.

"Hey. Thad. It was really sweet of you—was, um, nice of you to think of me."

"Really, don't mention it. I just thought we'd started on the wrong foot, you know."

"Yeah. Okay. Well, goodnight then."

"G'night."

Thad pressed the 'end call' button and raised his eyebrows to no one in particular with an almost whistling exhalation of breath. The situation had turned out a little different to what he had expected. It certainly had not been part of his original plan to invite Marybeth—that had just tripped off his tongue somehow. He had a feeling of unusual precariousness when he thought about it. Of course, it would be immediately obvious to Angela that he had not exactly been straight with her about the nature of the party. What the hell! He'd just make up some stupid excuse. If she fell for his bullshit on the phone she'd probably fall for more bullshit, and improvisation had always been his style. Just get a few drinks in her and she would be wiggling out of her clothes like a worm around a hook. Things always got more interesting when you were winging it, and it meant you were ready to take chances you might have let pass otherwise.

Thad was almost satisfied with this line of thought when suddenly, quite from nowhere, something else reared up in him. That wasn't the way to nail Angela, by being a half-assed loser. And he meant to nail her. No, he should think of this like robbing a bank or something—like a real job. What this called for was to go all out on some kind of stealth and surprise operation. What he needed first of all was to tidy the place up a bit and make sure that when Angela and Marybeth arrived, at least, the party looked halfway civilised.

He'd buy some olives. Maybe some cheese and olives and wine. Hell, he had the money for it.

He then recalled hearing somewhere that Julia Roberts always served fondue at her parties.

He flipped his phone open again.

"Yeah, Ralph, it's me again. What? Oh yeah, we must've got cut off. Anyway, I was just thinking, do you know anyone with a fondue set?"

When he had completed this call, too, he sat back in the sofa. It looked like the next twenty-four hours were going to be busy. At least he'd made a start and set things in motion. Hopefully that would force him into action later tonight. In any case, there was going to be a party soon. He checked the time on his phone. It was almost time for his favourite TV show, *Spider-Eating Sluts*. His friend and mentor, Ryan, had been hired as some kind of consultant on it. There would still be some shit on before it started, but he felt like vegetating for a while anyway. He went to get a beer from the fridge.

Monday, 1ˢᵗ October, 7.38 p.m.

They stood at the edge of the warehouse studio while the crew checked the cameras and lights and the audience began to file in. Dan was blond and muscular, with a skin-tight pink T-shirt and bleached jeans. Ryan wore a high-collared designer shirt and Pierre Cardin trousers. His prominent cheekbones made him look vaguely aristocratic.

"So, since that work with Girlicious, things have been pretty slack, really," said Ryan. "I am interested, though, in this whole celebrity/porn-star crossover thing. I can't help thinking there's something in that. I mean, you see, like, Cicciolina or Aria Giovanni on a celebrity site along with the likes of Alyson Hannigan. It's really postmodern, if you want to look at it that way. They are porn-stars who have become celebrities who are on a porn site for celebrities. What about yourself? You said you might have something to interest me?"

"Yeah, the magazine I mentioned. The idea for the magazine is . . . Well, it comes down to flags."

"Flags?"

"Yeah," said Dan. He sipped at his coffee. "Flag panties are always quite popular. It's psychological. It's like, the stranger always seems demure and unknown, right? Especially the exotic stranger. So, with the flag panties you got the whole psychological-cultural tension right there over the girl's pussy. It's like that, you know, 'Do they really have sex in, say, Germany?' I mean, that's what people think, not what we think. We know better."

"Even so, I've never seen panties with the German flag."

"You're right. That would look strange. But you know what I'm talking about, right? Do Norwegians really take a shit like the rest of us? Do Mongolians really do facials? Those kind of things that people are curious about."

"I think I can see what you're getting at. It's already there, actually, but no one's really monopolised on it. I mean, you have the Indian porn, Oriental porn, Brit porn, Latino porn. The fact is, it reflects an historical trend. If you look back at the development of the sex industry and erotica, you find that it was rife all over the world, of course, but the rule was you could do whatever you wanted as long as you were discreet, as is exemplified in the works of Rosa Coote or Etonensis. So the competition was in appearing modest and upright. If you read *Lady Gay Spanker's Tales of Fun and Flagellation*, this becomes pretty clear. Now everything's coming out in the open and you've got a different social direction. You're right, this could be a big thing. I mean, we've got girls from all over the world competing to see who's the biggest slut—it's a new branch of the industry waiting to happen."

"Right. And we have a website, that goes without saying, but also live events and other tie-ins. Maybe we really could make it a competition, like, er, Miss World Slut."

"Or Miss Slut-of-the-Universe. Yeah. We need to work on this. Who d'you think would win?"

"Which country, you mean?"

"Yeah."

"My money would be on Japan."

"Hmmm. You could have something there."

"That's right. No girls are dirtier than the Japanese, right?"

"Except the British, maybe."

"Oh yeah, that's true. I was forgetting about Britain."

"Or Italy?"

"No, Italian chicks don't put out. Just a lot of carrot in the ass bullshit."

"So, would the Japanese flag work?"

"Of course."

"Wouldn't it just look like a patch of blood?"

"That's the beauty of it. The kind of guy who likes Japanese girls loves that kind of shit."

"Oh, hang on, the floor manager's come out now. Looks like you'll be on in a minute."

"All right. Anyway, we'll talk about it later. I've already got the format copyrighted."

"Okay, Dan, talk to you later. Oh, I've just had a thought. You ready? Japanese war flag!"

Dan nodded slowly.

"I like it. You should check some of those flags out, man. Like the Welsh one, for instance. Or the Islamic Conference flag."

To emphasise the raw, dynamic nature of the show, the audience, all of whom seemed as if hand-picked for a meat market, were not seated, but standing, the line on the floor past which they were forbidden to stray making it look as if they were crushed in excitement against some invisible barrier.

Dan stood in front of the roulette table that was the show's centrepiece and the two main cameras were adjusted to focus on him as if he were about to have some state-of-the-art medical procedure. The floor manager was giving a pep-speech to the audience and Dan could feel something tightening around his chest. He hoped that the sweat wouldn't show on camera and wished to hell that he had had his body depilated the day before like he had meant to. He had called Dyanna Best Brazilian Wax on East 21st St. but hadn't been able to get an appointment.

He checked the image on the main screen, trying to be discreet and professional. Although the show was not broadcast live, when the cameras rolled in front of a live audience, the adrenaline hit was still so nasty for Dan he sometimes wondered if it would get him arrested. And the private jokes—the kind he had shared only with his sickest buddies at school—that he managed to sneak in under the cover of professional entertainment had progressed to such a point that he was surprised his backing had not been withdrawn by the studio. The fact was, after the first of these failed to cause outrage among the studio executives or the audience, he felt, for a while, very small, and began to question the very foundation of his existence. He soon got past this, however, perceiving how ridiculous it was to dwell upon his own identity when he had just pushed at the door to freedom and success and found it open. It was all the better if he was not hindered in his fulfilment by the bulk of his own ego, all the better if no one noticed the guy in the pink T-shirt who facilitated the spectacle. It did not matter, in short, whether or not anyone was outraged; all that mattered was whether someone was degraded.

He braced himself like a sprinter at the starting line, waiting for the sound of the pistol. The lights came on to indicate that the cameras were recording, and Dan felt himself catapulted into a very different species of time than that in which he normally existed. He had to adjust himself to this time, to its exhilaration, as a skydiver has to adjust himself to freefall.

CLOSE UP OF DAN

"Hello. This is Dan Carter, and if you've tuned in by accident, you're about to discover what television was invented for. It's another sick and sophisticated edition of . . . *Slut-Eating Spiders!*"

INSERT THEME MELODY BLAST (0:03) RIGHT BRAIN CUE

The audience cheered. Dan made a cutting motion and they were silent.

"No. Just testing you there. You've got to be on your toes for this game. It's . . . Spider . . . Eating . . . SLLLU-UUUUUTTTTTTSSSS!"

INSERT THEME MELODY SUPER BLAST (0:05) CAMERA PANS OVER AUDIENCE AS IT CHEERS AGAIN

Now Dan made encouraging, fanning motions with his hands, as if conducting this din to ever greater cacophony.

He had found a crystalline equilibrium in the freefall of the audience's roar. He knew with a loaded and point-blank certainty that it was going to be a great show tonight.

He got through his introductory routine in a state of flow, as if he had become a spectator to his own actions. Everything was expertly punctuated by the drumming and impact-whoompf of the show's incidental music, and the video-game flashing of lights, designed to arouse in the audience a state of nervous tension conducive to aggression.

"And now," said Dan, addressing his co-presenter, Juan, "could you bring on our first contender?"

Juan brought a curly-headed blonde girl, wearing cut-off denim jeans and a T-shirt, from the audience, and led her to a spot behind the roulette table. The girl, who looked as if she could easily have been a swimsuited extra in a surf film, introduced herself as Amanda, a manicurist.

CAMERA DOLLIES IN ON AMANDA'S TENSILE YET SILKY BREASTS. CUT TO MEDIUM SHOT OF DAN AND AMANDA

"And what brings you on the show, Amanda? You're not going to tell me you like spiders, right?"

"No, I hate 'em. Ugh!"

"Right. So I'm gonna guess it's the twenty thousand dollar prize. Right?"

"Er. Well, I guess so."

"You guess so? You know something, Amanda, I know so. But that's good. Where would the fun be if you liked spiders? We *want* you to hate them. We want this to be hard. We're not going to just give twenty thousand dollars away, are we?"

"I guess not."

"Well, I'm glad we got that understood, 'cause this is for real, Amanda. We're not nice guys here. We're going to treat you real mean, 'cause you're a greedy little girl and you deserve it. Understand?"

"Uh-huh."

"Good. Okay, Juan, release the spiders."

CLOSE UP OF JUAN'S ULTRA-CLEAN SMILE

"Coming right up," he said, and, stepping forward, pressed a switch on the side of the roulette table.

As soon as he did so, six holes, like those around the edge of a pool table, shot open, and from within were ejected a number of scuttling grey things the sight of which caused Amanda to put her hands to her face and let out a shriek.

The audience cheered and laughed and made juvenile sounds.

For a while the camera focused on the creatures as Dan talked. As if they had just been forced into a gladiatorial arena, they turned about, crawled back and forth and stood their ground with a jerky, inhuman alertness. They were a little larger than most spiders, their bodies being about the size of a small cockroach. They were unusual, too, in other respects. They did not have, for instance, the soft, mushy appearance of many spiders, but seemed, instead, like hard lumps of calcified hostility, so hideous in the genius of their animating spirit, that they had grown into the form of shrivelled, prickly devils in which all parts seemed to point to and emphasise the evil, barren craters of eyes and mandibles. They looked, in fact, like the theoretical offspring of a spider and a crab.

MED. CLOSE SHOT OF DAN

"Regular viewers," he said, "will know it's been a while since we had the actual spider challenge on the show. Last time we did, it was a nasty little species by the name of Dysdera crocata. This time we thought we'd try and go one better. We located this species in Africa, and we think you'll agree, it's quite a find. Now, this creature doesn't have a deadly bite, but, as usual, in case of emergencies, we have a medical crew standing by. Amanda, how are you feeling? Are you ready for this?"

LONG SHOT

"Oh, my God!"

CAMERA TRACKS IN TO AMANDA

She still held her hands to her face. Her expression had taken on that delicate, serious quality sometimes seen in people on the verge of tears. She had grown very pale and looked as if all capacity for humour had been drained out of her.

"Amanda? Hello, Amanda? Are you still with us?"

"Yes," said Amanda in an unsteady voice. "They . . . they have little claws."

"Hey, they're probably more afraid of you than you are of them."

Amanda shivered and danced on the spot from toe to toe and made a low, disgusted sobbing sound, almost like laughter, as if unable to endure the anticipation of what was to come.

"I don't think so," she managed at the end in a breathless, pitiful voice.

"Amanda, you know what the name of this show is, don't you?"

She nodded.

"What is it? Tell me."

"Spider-Eating Sluts." Her voice had a questioning, rising tone.

INSERT THEME MELODY EXTREME BLAST (0:03)

"Right. Spider-Eating Sluts. So that's what you've got to be if you want that cash prize. First we're going to get that T-shirt of yours nice and wet—Juan, bring the bucket—and then you've got one minute to eat and swallow as many of those ugly mothers as you can. If you've got nothing in your mouth within thirty seconds, you're disqualified. Got it?"

She nodded.

"Okay, one minute starting from when Juan throws the bucket of water over you . . . Now!"

There was a splash. Amanda's T-shirt turned dark and clung to her torso.

CAMERA ZOOMS IN ON AMANDA'S GLISTENING WET BREASTS THEN CUTS TO GRINNING FACES OF AUDIENCE MEMBERS AND THEN CUTS TO A MEDIUM SHOT OF AMANDA

She hovered over the table with agony visible on her face. The audience were screaming, and the drumming had started again.

"Go on," shouted Dan. "You've got to go for it. Just pick one up. Pick it up and put it in your mouth."

Her hand hesitated over one of the creatures, then, with obvious fear and distaste, she picked it up between thumb and forefinger, and, making a sound of groaning horror, brought it to her lips.

The audience continued to roar at her, hungry to see her complete the deed.

"Go on. Don't think about it," said Dan. "Just do it. It's all in your mind. Just think about the money. Think about the money."

As if in slow motion, Amanda opened her mouth and pushed the spider, its legs working furiously, between her lips, and bit down on it. The creature was half in and half out of her mouth, so that it could still be seen struggling. The screaming of the audience rose a pitch in intensity.

"That's it!" said Dan. "You can do it. Chew! Chew! Chew!"

As he watched her, a strange thing happened. He had known it before, but this time the experience was especially potent and vivid. Amanda appeared to his eyes and to his innermost being to undergo a sickening transformation. She shrank in on herself, as at the touch of some foetid disease, into a leprous shape of purple-black jelly. It was a kind of necrosis. Although it seemed she was eating, and therefore killing, the spider, Dan knew what was really happening was that she was allowing the evil of the spider to conquer her utterly, and as a result was being taken over by all the qualities of the spider. She continued to chomp stupidly. A bolt of lust shot through Dan when he realised she had lost her humanity. The roar of the audience, a triumphant jeering, reverberated in his chest. Arousal was kindled in his loins. However, before his cock could harden, it was as if its tip touched some aura of the thing that was the source of its arousal, and immediately was infected by an unspeakable, purple-black nausea that turned it cold as with sickness, so that it shrivelled away. And yet, in the core of that cold disgust that had made his cock a shrivelled spider-cock, there was the white heat of the ultimate lust, so evil, twisted and intense that it needed neither erection nor orgasm, permeating him body and soul like a filthy venom.

It was only at times like this, with extremes of spider-degradation, that Dan was able to find women attractive.

Thursday, 4ᵗʰ October, 5.38 p.m.

After several minutes had passed, Zak forced himself to look back into the living room. At first glance there was nothing to suggest what had happened: the room was still in order, with Sooki sitting on the couch as he'd left her, wearing a black silk skirt, a playful smile on her face-plate. But Zak's heart was still racing from the voice he'd heard, the unearthly voice that had made him run from the room.

He listened for a while longer but heard nothing. Perhaps he'd imagined it all—the stress he'd been under recently must have been taking its toll, and he'd seen and heard strange things before when hit by extremes of tiredness and worry. Tentatively he crept towards the couch, keeping his eyes fixed on Sooki, as if she might leap towards him at any moment.

"... Sooki? Is that you?"

At first there was no response, and Zak felt certain he had been dreaming. But then a softer voice than before crept from Sooki's closed lips, and he felt the hairs standing up on his arms.

"I didn't mean to upset you, Zak. I'm sorry. But you were right— something did happen, and I might be in danger."

Her voice was low and soothing. Zak took a step towards her and gazed into her eyes, clear and cold as glass.

"Sooki ... how can this be real?"

"You brought me to life, Zak. With your love."

He reached down and stroked her cheek. When she didn't move, he sat down next to her and took her hand. He felt a kind of depressive joy, as if he had just gained something precious but given up a part of himself in return. This was what he had always wanted, and what he had never wanted.

"Of course. And I'll always protect you. But what should we do now?"

"I don't know, Zak. But maybe it is better for you to bury me for now, at least until this whole thing blows over. You can take me to St. Mary's and hide me there."

"Shouldn't I call Thad's friend Ralph first?"

"No, don't worry about calling him. Us dolls know more than people think, and I know there's already an open grave waiting for me. We just need to look and we'll find it."

"I knew you'd understand," Zak said as he leaned into her. "Sooki . . . let's never fight again, okay? We'll be stronger from now on, I know we will. This is going to make us stronger. We can think of it as an adventure. You'll go away for a little while, and when you come back we'll be better than ever. We can go on a trip somewhere. I've been saving up, and maybe, I don't know, we could go down south, to Florida, or even overseas, to Paris. Anywhere you want."

"That sounds great. I'll go anywhere with you, Zak."

Zak got up, went to the window, lifted the shades a little and peered outside. He couldn't see anyone, but lingered a while, feeling a vague sense of paranoia. Even the inside of the apartment didn't feel safe; he felt that someone could see or hear him somehow. Sooki was right: it was best to leave as soon as possible. Going back to her, he found that he was crying.

"We can't trust anyone now. Everyone is jealous of our

happiness. They want to take you from me, but I won't let them . . ."

He kissed her violently, feeling the slick coolness of her lips, the sterile flesh-plastic taste he knew so well. But he couldn't erase the sense of something wrong, a faint undertaste, the taste of someone else's mouth. Putting it from his mind, he rested his head against her breasts and listened to the silence of her heart. Then, after smoothing down her skirt, he lifted Sooki up and carried her out of the apartment. Less than two minutes later the closet door opened and a man stepped out. He went to the window and watched Zak's car pulling away from the kerb, then walked back through the centre of the apartment to the bathroom. Presteign Sainte-Croix, the mercenary ventriloquist—also known as Fred Bergen, Danny Hideki and Kurt Marlin— examined his reflection in the mirror. His hair, immaculately combed at the start of the day, was now thoroughly mussed, and his freshly-pressed suit looked wrinkled: he'd been in the closet for more than five hours. He felt like taking a shower, but knew that he didn't have time. And he didn't feel like staying in this apartment any longer than he had to. There was nothing in it: no photos, no paintings on the walls except an anodyne oil painting of an elk verging on Thomas Kinkade tastelessness; nothing but this and trunks of women's clothing. Everything smelled faintly of bleach.

As he walked to the door he briefly regretted taking this assignment. There had been that offer up in Newark to interrupt a mob funeral by projecting his voice out of the coffin, which he was certain would have involved less closet time. But then, he hadn't known it would turn out like this. Still, there was nothing to do but follow it to the end; Sainte-Croix was not one to give up on anything halfway.

The two greatest influences on his life were Friedrich Nietzsche and Edgar Bergen. As a young man he had read, or at least skimmed through, *Beyond Good and Evil* and *Thus Spake Zarathustra,* and had been impressed enough to alter his life accordingly. His interpretation of Nietzsche's philosophy of morals was that it was better to be an asshole than a moron, and since most people were morons, only the elite could truly be assholes. At around the same time he had taken to watching television in the small hours of the morning and had come across the films of Edgar Bergen. This man, now all but forgotten, had appealed to him immediately. The handsome ventriloquist had strolled godlike through his films, involving himself and his dummies in the affairs of ordinary people only as a diversion. Bergen was never truly caught up in events, but only coasted on the surface of them, his true motivation obscured. Although clearly driven by self-interest, he never let it crack his genial smile. Instead, the more brutal, animal parts of his mind took the form of his dummies: the lascivious, childlike Charlie McCarthy and the moronic, reptile-brained Mortimer Snerd. From mere pieces of wood, Bergen had crafted physical manifestations of his *id* and paraded them through a series of films and radio shows, and the public had loved him for it. But to Sainte-Croix, Bergen hadn't taken the idea far enough. A true ventriloquist superman would live underground, surviving off his wits and never exposing himself to public scrutiny. He would not even carry a dummy, but would use whatever he found at hand. And he would never accept failure, from himself or anyone else.

Outside, he walked two blocks to where he'd parked his white Mustang GT 500. Leaning against the door, he lit a cigarette and watched the setting sun cast plumes of fire over the rows of buildings. He waited a while and smoked another cigarette, then got in the car and took off. He'd given Zak enough of a head start, he decided.

On the drive to the cemetery, he put the window down and let the coolness of the evening air wash over him. St. Mary's stood atop a small hill, next to lower ground. The steeple had guided him from before the suburbs gave way, its oxidised copper siding a dark green tint like rusted jade. Sainte-Croix parked some distance from the cemetery, then, as the shades of evening gathered, walked along the path until he came within range of the graves. The hard part of the job was over; now all he needed to do was dig up the doll.

But when he came to the grave he'd prepared, he saw that it was empty. The earth piled around it looked untouched; had he beaten Zak here? He thought he'd given him more than enough time, but perhaps Zak had been caught up in traffic. Sainte-Croix turned and scanned the rows of graves for a place to hide; he needed to be out of sight when Zak did arrive. But he stopped as he noticed movement just beyond a tall headstone. A man was walking up the path, but he could tell it wasn't Zak. He looked to be in his early 50's, and was wearing sunglasses (which looked less and less appropriate as the light dwindled) and a heavy woollen coat. He did not appear especially impressive; if anything he resembled an accountant. But Sainte-Croix knew better than to judge by appearance. As if to confirm this thought, as soon as the man came within range he drew a silver snub-nosed revolver from his coat and levelled it at him. It was a fitting gun, Sainte-Croix thought; the man would have looked ridiculous aiming something sleek and modern. He walked towards him slowly, with his hands in the air.

"You shouldn't point antiques at people . . ." he said.

"I'll have you know it's fully functional. I trust you won't need a demonstration."

"No," Sainte-Croix said. "I could do with your name, though."

"Call me Mr Brooks," the man said.

"I figured you might show up some time. You or someone else."

"Where's Zak?"

"I don't know. I was hoping you could tell me. You didn't get to him?"

"No."

"Well, then he must just be late."

They looked at each other. Sainte-Croix gave a tentative smile, but the man's expression remained neutral. A few minutes passed in silence.

"He should be here by now," the man said.

"He should have been here half an hour ago."

The man removed his superfluous sunglasses to reveal a pair of care-lined grey eyes.

"Someone else must have got to him."

"How'd you find out he was coming?" Sainte-Croix asked.

"How else? By listening to the transmitter. The same one whose transmissions I'm assuming you intercepted."

"Right. I was hoping you'd miss my performance. But I guess you don't have much else to do besides eavesdrop 24/7?"

The man ignored this and kept the revolver trained on Sainte-Croix.

"Who are you working for?" he asked.

Sainte-Croix said, "What makes you think I'm not on my own?"

"I don't know. Intuition? You don't seem like the type."

Sainte-Croix laughed.

"You're right there. This whole life-size Barbie thing . . . it's never made much sense to me. I've seen weirder, though."

"So. Who's your employer?"

"Not anyone you'd know, I'm sure."

"How much is he paying you?"

"I don't like talking business at gunpoint."

"Then we'll put this away for now."

The man returned the revolver to the inside of his coat, held up his empty hands and took a step towards Sainte-Croix.

"Whatever he's paying you, I'll double it."

"Be careful. That's a lot of money."

"Money isn't the issue, Mr . . . ?"

"Karl Sullivan."

"Is that your real name?"

"It is now, legally. I was born Orson Lipschitz. Can you blame me?"

"Is that true?"

"Of course not. You don't need to know my name."

"Maybe not. But, Mr Sullivan, the issue now is whether you're willing to accept a better offer."

"That depends."

The man gestured to the rows of graves in the thickening gloom.

"My wife is buried around here, Mr Sullivan. Have you ever lost someone?"

"No. I don't do relationships, if it's any of your business. Which it isn't."

"I'm getting old," the man said. "I'm not up to rushing around waving guns at people. I'm only here because things have gotten out of hand, and I'd like for this to be concluded as soon as possible. In fact, I'd prefer if we didn't discuss things here; I feel as if my wife can hear us. She died of cancer, you know."

"And so now you need to come inside a doll? Come on, you're not going to get me with a sob story. Let's get back to money."

The man's tone adjusted instantly, snapped back to its brisk manner. Still, Sainte-Croix could see the weariness lining his eyes, and there was nothing contrived about that.

"Double what you're getting now. You'll do it?"

"Sure. If you pay me fifty per cent now, in cash. But I'm sure you've got someone on this already, don't you?"

"Of course. But my other operative is, how to put this, slightly unreliable? A fuckup, you might say. Personally I think he's stringing me out for more money."

"What makes you think I won't do the same?"

"Nothing. But I'm going to be keeping a closer eye on things from now on."

Sainte-Croix looked at the man carefully. Then he started to laugh. The *Idollatry* job had come from a private introduction, which was the only way Sainte-Croix worked. Clearly this Brooks was not familiar with the rules of the game. Sainte-Croix would take his money, then take the doll. There was no reason why he shouldn't collect a bonus now and then. And since it looked like Thad was becoming unreliable, he might save himself a bigger cut of the *Idollatry* money, too.

"You remind me of my grandfather—he was a crazy bastard too. Didn't have any Barbie dolls stashed away, but . . ."

The man smiled faintly.

Thursday, 4ᵗʰ October, 5.55 p.m.

Zak stopped at the red light and pulled down the sunblind. The rays of the sinking sun were getting in his eyes. He glanced at Sooki. Reclining in the passenger seat, her features had a look of abstraction which complemented her sudden silence—since he'd gotten her into the car she hadn't said a word. Perhaps she was sleeping, tired out from the stress, but then, she wasn't wearing her sleeping face. He reached over and gently rubbed her shoulder.

"Sooki?"

There was no response.

"Sooki . . . can you hear me? Are you sleeping?"

When she didn't answer after a few moments he decided to let her rest. She was either sleeping or thinking deeply, but either way she obviously required silence. Zak thought to turn on the radio but eventually decided against it. Sooki had always been quiet, and he'd grown used to silences such as this; knew that there was no need to fill them with empty noise. Soon the light changed to green and he turned left into the road that led on to St. Mary's. But just then the 'Bobcaygeon' by The Tragically Hip ringtone of his phone sounded.

"Zak?"

"Thad? Is that you?"

"Zak, yeah, listen—I've been doing some research about the, you know, dollnappers."

"Yeah?"

"Yeah, I think they might be getting ready to move soon. Has anything strange happened recently?"

Zak glanced at Sooki again. He suddenly felt awkward—if she was only pretending to sleep and could hear him, he didn't want her to think that he didn't trust her.

"Well . . . Sooki has been a bit more direct than usual . . ."

"What do you mean?"

Zak hesitated. "She decided . . . well, we decided that we were going to go ahead with the burial. Sooki told me to do it. She told me to go to St. Mary's. It makes sense, I think. You were right all along."

Thad sounded genuinely surprised.

"What the hell? She just started talking? Wait, like she usually does? Or out loud, you mean?"

"Yeah, out loud." Zak tried to muffle his voice. "But she didn't sound like her usual self."

"Man, this is worse than I thought. Where are you now?"

"In my car, close to St. Mary's. I'm going to bury her, just like you said."

"Man, fuck that! That's probably what they want you to do. They must have figured out our plan. This shit is hell bad, man! They're into black magic. Whatever Sooki hears, they can hear too. They've possessed her! I mean, fuck, dude! Remember *The Exorcist*? She's gonna start walking down stairs backwards if we don't do something."

Zak fumbled with the phone, trying to shift it to his other ear while simultaneously steering the car.

"Thad, what are you talking about?"

"You heard me. Put some kind of covering over her, or better yet throw her in the trunk. Don't let her hear anything!"

"In the trunk? Are you crazy? She's not some *object* . . ."

"Dude, just listen to me! You have to get over here right now."

"I thought you said your place wasn't safe?"

"Yeah, well, it's safer than the graveyard now. We'll find some place else soon."

As he shifted the phone Zak looked up and saw a red Honda Civic slowing down in front of him. He jammed the brakes but it was too late; his car jerked to a crawl and bumped into the back of the Civic, knocking it forward. Zak waited for his airbag to deploy, but nothing happened.

"Zak? Zak, are you there?"

He closed his phone and returned it to his pocket, reached into the glove compartment for his insurance information and got out of the car. A man around his own age was walking towards him from the Civic. He was short, well built, with thick black hair and smooth features.

"Well," the man said, "can't say I was expecting that." There was no anger in his tone, only a kind of bemusement.

"I'm really, really sorry," Zak stammered. "It was all my fault. I wasn't looking at the road . . . I don't know what happened. I was just on my phone, and then I looked up and . . ."

"But you shouldn't talk on your phone and drive."

"I know."

"Well, it happens."

Looking at the bumper of the Civic, they saw that it had a slight dent on it.

They exchanged their information; the man took a pen from his pocket and, squinting in the dark gold of the westering sun, wrote down Zak's details on the back of a green flyer which looked to Zak like some kind of church advertisement. It depicted a large cross radiating beams of light, beneath which a shepherd was leading a flock of lambs.

"That's Zak without a 'c'? Okay. My name's Jed."

Zak listened to his voice, which was thin, almost reedy. His way of speaking was direct, but at the same time he seemed to be looking vaguely beyond him, or through him, as if rehearsing a conversation to himself in his head.

"Guess I'm going to be a bit late getting home now," Jed said. As before, his tone conveyed more surprise than annoyance. "Then again, I don't suppose it matters, really. After a few months away another half hour won't hurt."

"You've been away a long time?"

"I was just coming back from the airport, actually. I was in Russia preaching the Gospel."

Zak entered Jed's number and insurance details into his phone. When he looked up he found Jed peering through his car window at Sooki.

"Is that a real person?"

"That's Sooki. My girlfriend."

Jed seemed hardly to have heard him.

"Is it some kind of . . . love doll?"

For the first time his tone seemed to focus, to inhabit the present. There was still the characteristic bemusement, but also a faint tremor of disgust. Zak recognised it at once. He'd heard it before, too many times to count, from strangers and former friends alike. He felt a flare of hopeless rage.

"You're going to tell me I'm a pervert, right? Well, I don't give a FUCK what you think!"

Jed's face retained its mild calm.

"Now hold on. I didn't say anything like that. You're getting defensive."

"Yeah, well you don't understand . . . you don't understand what's happening . . ."

Ashamed at losing his temper, Zak sat down on the side of the road, leaned against the car and covered his face with his hands. He didn't want to cry again today, especially not here, but the words he had just spoken recurred again and again in his mind as symbols of his own insecurity. Misdirected and meaningless, more pathetic than truly offensive, they formed the kind of desperate outburst that had characterised the worst periods of his life. He had never been good at getting angry.

Jed sat down beside him and said, "You seem pretty upset."

"I'm sorry. Things have been hard for us recently."

"God understands. You know, I think it was His will that we met like this. You're obviously going through a very dark time."

Zak looked over. Jed was staring at him with what he took to be a sympathetic expression. Not wanting to dwell on what had just happened, Zak said:

"Hey . . . do you know anything about exorcisms?"

"Well, that's more of a Catholic thing. I was raised Catholic, but I'm nondenominational now."

"The thing is . . . I think my girlfriend might be possessed."

"Could be. Possession is very serious and very real. There are evil spirits all around us. I've had trouble with them myself."

Jed placed a hand on Zak's shoulder.

"I'll give you some advice, but I want you to know I'm not judging you. I don't have the right to tell you or anyone else how to live. Only God can do that. But for what it's worth—" he took his hand away and pointed to the window "—get rid of her. You'll be better off without her. There's a real woman waiting for you somewhere, your soulmate. I want you to ask Jesus to help you get ready to meet her."

He ripped off a piece of the green flyer and wrote a number on it, then handed it to Zak.

"Pastor Phil Boughton. Good friend of mine. If you want more advice, give him a call."

He got to his feet.

"Now I think it's about time I got home. Mandy will be wondering where I am." He smiled. "She's *my* soulmate. Let me tell you, before I met her, I was a real mess. She helped me a lot. Her and Jesus."

He walked back to the Civic. Zak watched him drive off, then got back into his car and sat for a while, feeling Sooki's presence beside him. He turned to her and took her hand.

"But you are my soulmate, aren't you? Who else could it be? I'm not going to give you up, no matter what anyone says."

The resolution made him feel better. He took out his phone and dialled Thad's number.

"Hello?"

"Zak? What happened? Where in the fuck are you?"

"I'll be there soon. Just wait."

Putting the phone aside, he pulled back onto the road.

Thursday, 4ᵗʰ October, 5.51 p.m.

When there was no sound after ten minutes, Clive decided it was safe to emerge. Feeling a cramp in his leg from sitting curled up for so long, he got up, made his way to the door, and listened. Satisfied that there was no one in the corridor, he stepped outside and sneaked back downstairs to his room.

He had been lucky. At first he had been sure his father would discover him crouching behind the desk, less than a few feet in front of him, but then he supposed he never thought to investigate rooms for hidden intruders either. Of course, if his father had walked around the desk, say, to the window, he would have discovered him immediately; but after entering the room he had sat down and begun adjusting the speaker with a look of total single-mindedness. He had not even looked in the drawer, and so had not noticed the magazine Clive had taken. And so Clive had listened as his father brought the speaker to life again and tuned into the strange, continuing dialogue. As before, its literal meaning was lost on him, but the clear desperation and talk of burial filled him with dread. It was as if his father were accessing some terrible other world through the speaker, listening, perhaps, to the voices of the damned.

"You can take me to—" here the female voice had said something like "St. Mary's." At this his father switched off the speaker and left the room in haste.

That St. Mary's should prove decisive was as mysterious as anything else Clive had heard today. He knew the church well; it was where his family went at Easter and Christmas—well, before his mother had died, at least. But he had no idea what could be happening there now, although a number of grotesque possibilities presented themselves. Before he had closed the door of his room behind him, he had already conjured up images of graverobbing and Black Masses, necromancy and live burials. Whatever it was, though, he did not feel up to following his father to find out. Instead he took out the copy of *Idollatry* and began to page through it, looking for anything that would clarify what was happening.

After a cursory reading he was troubled to find that he still couldn't understand any of it. What little text the magazine contained was a blizzard of names and references which meant nothing to him. He wasn't even sure if it was meant to be pornographic in the conventional sense, although it filled him with the same convulsive feeling of depravity. He got the impression that *Idollatry* was to conventional pornography what pornography was to normal photography: an eruption of latent possibility, a rotation into another dimension. The contours of pornography were still present, but in an exploded form like a Cubist painting that, at least on the surface, left them scarcely recognizable. What was he to make, for example, of the two-page spread depicting a transparent glass mannequin resting on a plinth, its featureless skull crowned with laurels, its hollow interior writhing with snakes? Or the dwarf-sized women of pink plastic, carried on the backs of nude young men? It was only when he looked closer that he saw, or rather felt, how every angle and setting had been selected and fashioned by an obsessive lust which, as the title suggested, aspired to the level of religious ecstasy. Rather than reassure him, this under-standing only filled him with a greater revulsion. He flipped through the pages more quickly now, not stopping to linger too long on any of them. The abstract nature of many of the images heightened his unease, since it was not entirely clear what fulfilments they suggested. He was about to put the magazine aside when he felt his phone vibrating in his pocket, and then his ringtone—'Vampira (Maila Nurmi)' by Kodagain—sounded. He answered it without looking at the screen and heard a girl's voice speaking in his ear.

"Um . . . Clive?"

"Yeah? Who is this?"

"It's Marybeth."

At the sound of that name, spoken in her own voice, a kitten began to play in Clive's stomach, with its claws out. This was the first time that Marybeth had paid any attention to him, beyond the level of asking to borrow an eraser. The mystery of Marybeth's mind—perhaps the greatest mystery in the world—twitched in her voice like the whiskers of a mouse, and that twitching had turned ticklishly on his existence. For a while he could not speak.

"Hello? Clive? Are you still there?"

"Yeah. I'm here. Hi. How are you?"

He had never before asked her how she was, but it seemed a safe thing to say on the phone.

"I'm good, I guess."

"That's good. I'm good, too. Not that you asked. I mean . . . I didn't give you a chance to ask. Not that it matters."

"Right. I . . . Was there something you wanted to tell me?"

Knowing she would not see him, Clive got on his knees, as if in prayer. He could not complete this attitude by putting his hands together, because he needed one hand for the phone, but in his chest and throat he pleaded that the ecstasy that now had him in its nets would not suddenly drag him down to disaster. Words formed at the back of this throat.

"You are the most beautiful thing I have ever seen in the world."

His lips even moved. But what came out of his mouth, to his relief, was only quiet and wordless air.

"Clive? Are you okay? You spoke to my sister, Angela, and she said you'd called. Is there something you wanted to say to me?"

Clive noticed the strange emphasis in the last question.

"Yeah, I called because . . . You know, I called because . . . We see each other in class, you know, and hardly ever talk to each other, and I just thought . . . I just thought, hey . . . this is dumb . . . we should talk to each other . . . because . . ."

"Yeah?"

"Do you ever, you know, just wonder about why we're here, and time, and . . . why . . ."

Clive felt the whole direction of the conversation disintegrating.

"Marybeth." He had said her name, almost without thinking. His heart gave a delicious leap, and he seemed to draw courage from it.

"Marybeth, it's true. I do have something to tell you, but it's kind of hard on the phone. Things are a bit weird now, actually. I'm sorry, I'm probably not making much sense. You must think I'm some kind of . . . Do you know the park, just this side of the track?"

"Sure."

"Do you know the gazebo there, like, near the edge?"

"Sure. I know it."

"Do you wanna, maybe, meet there, and we can talk . . . and stuff? I don't know, or . . ."

Clive had thought that this might be a good meeting place, because it was neither too public nor too secluded, but even as he made the suggestion, it felt to him that he was asking something absurd.

"Sure."

"Sure? Okay." Clive hardly dared to ask the next question. "When would be good?"

"I'm free today. Are you doing anything?"

"No, actually, I don't have anything planned. So, say . . . an hour? Would that be good?"

"Sure."

"And we'll meet there, in the gazebo, in an hour from now."

"Yep. In an hour. Great. I'll see you there."

Marybeth hung up. Clive was left staring at his phone, before slipping it back in his pocket. He thought of his last conversation with Christie. Could it be that life was about to turn a corner onto a view of things he had never known before, in which his fondest wish stood realised as one fact amongst others? Certainly, all manner of things had been weird lately, but they had only been weird-bad, and this could perhaps turn out to be—so he prayed—weird-good. Or maybe it was just weird-weird. In any case, if he thought of it as part of life's general recent weirdness, he had a sense of things unfolding, and becoming larger in the unfolding. Weirdness now seemed to contain all kinds of possibilities. From such thoughts he looked down to the magazine he had been perusing. Could Marybeth possibly be part of the same weirdness as this? The thought came out of nowhere with unexpected potency, and he was disturbed. But there was no actual reason that she would have anything to do with any of this. Of course she didn't. It was just that, the world was full of disparities and incongruities. That's what unsettled him. Also, although it wasn't his fault at all, he now felt as if he had a secret—something he could not tell Marybeth, and from which he had to protect her—and this secret would be an obstacle in the way of his wish. Even just thinking about it, that wish seemed such an unbearable happiness that it scared him—that their two hearts should know each other; it scared him like the thought of going through the rest of his life entirely naked.

He came back to himself. He had said an hour rather than half an hour, or twenty minutes, as he would have liked to, because he did not want to sound in too much of a hurry, but he realised that, even so, he had not actually left himself that much time. He would have to go out more or less as he was if he did not want to be late. He took the magazine to his room and stuffed it hurriedly under the mattress of his bed. Then he looked at himself in the mirror. It was hardly an impressive sight, he thought, and he did not for the life of him know what to do to improve it in the time available to him. His hair, for a start, was gaying up in little spiky tufts here and there, and there were his glasses, too. He hadn't had any disposable contact lenses for a while, and he couldn't see without lenses of some kind. His shirt and pants, too, were the worst kind of casual—light brown, modest, he realised now acutely that they were clothes that seemed to declare he had given up on ever having any luck with girls. Maybe he could change his shirt. He should at least do that. The choice was between the kind of smart white shirt that you'd wear to a prom night and a slightly retro purple shirt with a large collar. Neither of them was right, of course. In the end, exasperated, Clive dragged off his brown shirt and put on the white one. Then he put on a New Jersey Devils reversible wool jacket he had bought about a year back on a strange whim, and hardly worn. It had been slightly big for him then, but seemed to fit okay now.

He looked at himself in the mirror and gave a strangled cry of frustration. But he could not bear now to put on his usual L.L. Bean corduroy jacket. He felt ridiculous, as if he were being forced to wear the clothes of a younger brother, but almost out of spite, and in a kind of rage, he determined that he would go like this.

"Why are all my clothes so stupid?" he bellowed.

Then he doused his face and hair in water at the basin, combed back his fringe with his fingers, and fairly sprinted out of his house. Slamming the door behind him, he felt somehow empty-handed, as if he were going off on some adventure for which no rehearsing would ever suffice, and whose difficulties could only be faced in the moment, as if in fact he were going potholing in some particularly deep and perilous cave system without the necessary equipment.

He had hurried out of the house, after all, and at this rate would arrive early, even if he walked and didn't take the bike. (He had not dared to stop and eat, even though he'd only snacked since lunch.) He came to a halt on the pavement. If he arrived early he'd have to endure the agony of waiting, and would probably look too keen, as well. It might be a better idea if he took a walk through the woods. That way, he could watch the gazebo from the hill through the trees for some time before he actually arrived. More importantly, the woods had always sheltered him and offered consolation when he was lonely. They would support and nourish him now, also, when he so needed understanding and acceptance. There was something very apt and calming about the idea. Clive changed direction, jogging back towards the house, past it, and up the little trail between buildings that lost itself in the old hills.

Once in the melancholy shade of leaves and branches, away from the open space of the avenue, Clive felt a little better. He was reminded of certain constants in life. His anticipation of the meeting ahead of him took on a slightly more removed aspect, allowing him to see it in a way that brought him a purring excitement rather than the hiss of panic. Even so, he was far from relaxed. The only thing he had brought with him, apart from a few dollars, that could be thought of as useful equipment on this adventure, was his phone, and he checked the time on it constantly, like a lost traveller consulting a compass.

His mind had been so much on other things that it was not until he saw a very familiar tree that he realised the particular significance of the route he was taking. He must have known, though, unconsciously. His footsteps slowed as he approached the spot where it grew, where it had grown for as long as he remembered, and probably longer than he had been alive to remember. He knelt down in the dirt at its roots as at an altar in church, and there, before him, was the heart, with the initials 'MC' inside. He had not been able to give himself to prayer fully when he had been on the phone to her, but coming on the tree like this without thinking, suddenly he was in a rare mood that was precisely right. He prayed to the tree and the dirt and the leaves, until tears rolled down his face, and then, forcing himself to be abrupt, he got to his feet again before he was quite satisfied that he had been heard. Sun was setting and the yellow light homogenised with the clustering of yellow leaves, mellow and dazzling at once. He wiped his cheeks with his hands and walked on, not troubling to brush the dirt from his pants where he had knelt. He felt different now. He did not check the time again until the gazebo was visible below, through the trunks of the trees.

He still had just over ten minutes. There was no sign of Marybeth, and inevitably his heart leapt like a flying fish when he saw this, but only for a moment. At least there was no one else around, either. A little farther along the way, there was a turning that led down towards the park, and he took it silently, without haste.

In the white cool of the gazebo, simply knowing that this was the meeting place, Clive sat on the delicate bench around its thin wall as if riveted there, unable to move his arm to check his phone, involved in a timeless, thoughtless trance. In fact, it was not long before he saw a coloured shape appear at the edge of the park's green and move towards him like a ship moving into port. He knew who it was. The red of her jacket and the blue of her jeans seemed exceptionally vivid against the green of the grass, even as the light of day weakened and flavesced. When she was close enough for him to make out her face, he realised that he had entered into a world for which he had no instincts, and for which he would have to improvise in a vacuum.

She walked up the steps into the gazebo, smiling at him faintly. There had never been anything so fresh in human history as the apparition before him. To look at her now was to know that all this solid world was a mirage, and she its only justification, though few seemed to realise this. The gazebo they inhabited could have been on the surface of the Moon. The fact that no one saw Marybeth quite as he saw her meant they were alone in a way almost eerie. He saw green grass out there instead of craters only because of Marybeth.

Clive wondered if she would take charge of the situation in some way, or whether that were up to him. Looking up at her, he made to rise, but quickly sat down again as he saw her backing to the bench behind her on the opposite side of the gazebo steps to him, so that it was as if they sat beside the two opposite jambs of a door. She seemed to check something in the bag that hung from her shoulder, then closed it and turned back to him. There were only gentle breezes, but when they shifted, one of them stirred Marybeth's hair, which was only pinned back on one side today, and brought her scent to him. The perfume was not strong. It was something mild and natural. There was also the scent, however, of her make-up, of powder, lipstick and so on. It had been applied with art and restraint, but even as the light turned chill in its shrinking away, Clive saw that these blue and silver touches served to give Marybeth's pink face a kind of electric immediacy and aliveness. It did not make her look fake, but somehow like an intensification of all that was pure and natural—the air, sun, grass, leaves and sky made female flesh.

"Sorry I'm late," said Marybeth. "Christie called right when I was going to leave, and she wouldn't get off the phone."

And Clive, even with his lack of experience in such things, knew that the ionised frisson currently surrounding Marybeth, though perhaps due partly to his own feelings, also most probably signified she had just spent some time in front of a mirror. Part of her freshness was that scent and make-up were freshly applied. And yet, even though this fact was readily apparent, Marybeth's bearing was not that of someone who noticed she was taking part in some sort of occasion.

In some way that Clive could never explain, Mary-beth's appearance there, a few feet away from him, hurt him viciously. Maybe it was because he realised now with clarity that the hardest part was not over. Air still separated the two of them. Her agreeing to meet—as she had well known—was not the same thing at all as agreeing to be his girlfriend. He had thought, vaguely, somehow or other, that that obstacle had been overcome on the phone. It had not. But beyond even this, there was something else, something shocking and wounding and tormentingly intoxicating, like a kind of madness. In his actual thoughts, Clive was only half-conscious of it, though in his heart and body he was sickened with despair. Marybeth existed in some place of madness like the starry night sky. He could never have her, he realised, simply because she was a girl. Sex ensured that for all eternity violence and lust would separate their hearts. The very fact that she was a girl—that's what hurt him so deeply and incurably. There was about her some fundamental division—and he could not now help imagining that division, despite himself—like a betrayal, and, one way or another, that division would also split him in two. He would not have dared think about it, if it were not for the fact that suddenly he could not help it, but whether he ever had sex with her or not, sex would drive a lightning bolt between them.

"Oh, you're not late," said Clive, his voice somehow feeling thin and dry to himself, like the voice of someone utterly disillusioned.

"Okay," she said, the word rising to suspension rather than conclusion.

"So," he said.

"Yeah."

Neither of them seemed to know what to do next. As they sat there, Clive's prayer before the altar of the tree trunk came back to him as if it had now been heard, though the answer was not necessarily an expected one. It brought to him, however, the shady strength of the wood, with its lonely constants, and also a certain weariness, a certain cynicism he had never known before in relation to Marybeth, but which also seemed to save him. He gave up, and, in his heart, he let Marybeth go, and watched her float away from him forever and in her place another form came, plastic, frozen and Clive was much older, the age of his father and the house was silent because she wouldn't reply. He talked to her and cried and became emotional, but she wouldn't reply.

And then, with sudden ferocity, another part of him rose up. Now that he had given up, he would do whatever was necessary—*whatever was necessary*—to have Marybeth. He would play the game in whatever way he needed to play it. He would pay the necessary price. Whether he had Marybeth or not, his dreams would be destroyed or compromised. If he had her, at least he would have the chance of knowing a compromised dream. He would worry about the compromises he had made after she was his. For now, he simply had to have her—*at any cost*. Such, he knew with unprecedented conviction, was the answer to his prayer. Some spirit had granted him a ruthless daring that would never otherwise be his—and granted it to him, no doubt, because it was his only chance.

He made himself look at Marybeth now, because if he could dare to look at her in an obvious way, as if he deserved to, it seemed like that would be half the battle won. The air was filling with shadow now. The lights around the edges of the park had been on for a while, but their glow was just beginning to be noticeable—unless this was imagination—in the quality of illumination cast on Marybeth's features. This electric-tinged twilight, cold in hue as a pebble in the bed of a shallow winter brook, was the very element in which heartbreak lived, he thought. And now her arm was resting along the edge of the gazebo's wooden fencing and she was looking out into the air and twilight, the breeze flicking her hair a little. With her other hand, she held her bag close to her. She was not looking at Clive and did not look as if she were thinking of something to say. Clive noticed the dragonfly clip in her hair that held it back a little on the left side. The silence between them now was immoderately long. It was something definite—a silence that would not have existed if neither of them had been here, or if only one. Marybeth remained as nonchalant as a dog who watched with head between paws. One thing was certain, if nothing else was—she was as aware of the silence as Clive.

"I like it here," she said at last, still not looking at him.

He was surprised that, in the end, it had not been he who had needed to break the silence.

"Yeah. I come here a lot," said Clive.

The silence resumed, but with less tension. Somehow Marybeth's words had changed the pace and tone of everything, and it seemed there was no need for a sudden dramatic release, after all. Clive looked at Marybeth now and laughed so softly to himself that it was only a quick breath of air through his nose. She was utterly perfect.

"So," said Clive, after some time, "what were you talking with Christie about?"

"Different things. School. Some party my sister's going to. Me coming here."

"Really? I spoke to Christie the other day."

"Yeah. I know."

Clive laughed, this time audibly.

"I was going to ask if maybe you wanted to go somewhere, but we could just sit here and hang out and do nothing."

"Sounds cool," said Marybeth. "Sounds really cool. But I've only got two hours, so, if you wanna say anything or do anything you should, like, do it before two hours are up. Or we can just sit here. I don't mind."

Marybeth still sat with her arm on the top of the fencework, looking out over the empty park, and her bag clutched to her, as if she anticipated the two hours being over very soon and would not have removed her jacket even if this had been a house. Then she looked towards Clive and smiled, raising her eyebrows slightly in a way that made Clive's heart do a backflip, as if those raised eyebrows were presenting the words she had just spoken in a new way.

"I guess I did say that I had something to tell you."

"Yup."

She looked at him steadily.

"It's okay," she said at last. "You don't have to say any-thing."

"Marybeth . . ." He had said her name. He wanted to let it hang there for a while. "I really want to ask you out on a date."

He was surprised at the intense rush of blood to his loins—and head—at his own words and was suddenly acutely aware of a connection between romantic concepts and his own body. He was even afraid this would be appar-ent to Marybeth. He certainly would not be able to get to his feet for some time.

"Okay," said Marybeth, as if she were simply acknowl-edging the fact he wanted to ask her out.

"Well . . ."

"Hey," she suddenly interjected, "is it true that you think I'm the cutest girl in class? *Definitely* the cutest girl in class?"

Clive looked at her open-mouthed.

"'Cause Christie said when she asked you about it, you were like, 'No, I would never say anything like that.' I just wanted to know, you know, before you asked me out or something."

"It's true . . . that I *did* say that to Christie. But it's not really true that I'd never say anything like that."

"Hmmm," said Marybeth, as if dissatisfied.

"Marybeth, you are the cutest girl in . . . In the whole school. You don't need me to say that. Pretty much everyone knows it by now. But . . . it's more than that. I don't have any idea what you're going to think about all this, but . . . I *do* wanna ask you out on a date, I really do, but I feel like even that's not what I really want to say to you."

"So, what do you really want to say to me?"

Clive opened his mouth to speak, but could not. At last he gave a roar, clutching at the air, and looking up to heaven.

"God! Here I am in these stupid clothes, and . . . Marybeth, I don't even know if there's any way that the world can understand what I'm about to say, or like, do anything with it, but there's a freckle on your neck———"

"A freckle?"

"Yeah. A freckle. And you've had it since you first came to school here, longer, I guess. I noticed that freckle when you first came, and it's moved a little, you know, changed a little, but it's still there . . . what am I saying? . . . Anyway, I'm the only person in the whole world who cares about that freckle. I mean, no one else in the whole world can possibly see what I see when I look at you . . . It's no good. I shouldn't have said anything."

"It's okay. I'm just not sure what this thing is about my freckle."

"It's not okay. I just . . . there's no way the world will ever understand, that's all. Even if we go out together, it's like the universe won't even let me say it in some way that you can understand. Or if it did, then, like, the entire universe would collapse into a black hole or something."

"Wow!"

Clive shrugged.

"That's what you wanted to tell me?"

"I guess. Except that it's not, because I can't even put it into words."

Clive realised that he had, in blindly reaching out to Marybeth, already sabotaged his resolve simply to have her by any means possible. He felt as if he had just rashly committed an act of public indecency.

"Clive?"

"Yes?"

"I like you."

"Okay."

He could feel the prickly, tingling stir of his blood again.

"I think you're making things too complicated. I feel like I've let you say too much, in a way, so I guess I should apologise."

"No, it's my fault. I should have known."

"You don't understand."

"Yes, I do."

"Hey, let me finish. The truth is, there was something I wanted to ask you, but I knew you wanted to say something, too, so I wanted to hear what it was first. I guess you'll think I'm a tease now, but I didn't mean to be."

"Wait. Stop. What do you mean? What did you want to ask me?"

Marybeth sighed.

"Do you want to come to the party with me?"

"Party?"

"Yeah. The one my sister's going to. It's tomorrow. This guy called Thad that she went on a date with invited us both and my sister said I should bring someone along. I was going to go with Christie, you know, because she's my best friend 'n' all, but we talked about it and she said that I should go with you. I mean, if you want to come."

"Wait. Christie told you to ask me? It wasn't your idea?"

Marybeth put her hands to her face in frustration.

"I'm not explaining this well. I'm such an idiot."

"What do you mean?"

"Clive! It was my idea to ask you, okay? But I didn't want Christie not to come, but she insisted that she wouldn't come, and that I should just ask you."

The explanation seemed to have destroyed the atmosphere the invitation should have created.

"Do you want to come or not?" she asked.

Clive nodded slowly.

"You don't have to say yes."

"I want to come."

"All right," said Marybeth quietly.

They were both silent for a while.

"Marybeth?"

"Yeah?"

"Will you go out with me, please?"

"Sure."

Now the tingling blood washed in wave upon rose-like wave up and down his body.

"Only . . ."

Marybeth hesitated before what she was about to say, and Clive was not sure he wanted to hear it. He forced himself, however, to prompt her.

"Yes?"

"I'm not special, you know. I'm just a regular, silly girl."

Clive made a pained expression. Marybeth looked at him questioningly.

"If I thought you weren't special, I wouldn't ask you out. It's even more than that, though."

"Yeah, I know. I understand what you said."

"I don't think you did. I'm sorry. I don't mean to be an asshole or anything. I'm sorry. It's just that . . . there's so much I want to say to you and share with you . . . God, that sounds awful . . . and . . . I don't know how."

Marybeth's eyes were lowered.

"Clive, can I say something kinda strange?"

"Why not? I guess it would make us even."

"I've had this idea, and I think maybe I want to try it out. I'm going to tell you something secret, but you've got to promise not to tell anyone."

"I promise. I won't tell."

"Well, it was Christie that told me about you. One of your friends was goofing around and said how you thought I was the cutest girl in class. The truth is, I never really thought about you much before, but when Christie told me that, I got this strange feeling. I can't explain it. I don't know what it was. I think it was those actual words—'the cutest girl in class'. But it wasn't just that, either. I guess I began to notice you and imagine you saying that, and it seemed like I would like the way you said it. Does that sound really crazy? If it had been one of the other guys, I'd have been like, forget it."

She looked up at Clive, then continued.

"But it also kinda scared me. I don't know why. Anyway, I understand the stuff you were saying. I think I under-stand. It's like I understood it even before we met today. But I don't know if we should talk about it."

She looked up at Clive again.

"So, here's my crazy idea. Whenever we're in this gazebo here, we can say whatever we like, but when we're not in the gazebo, we just talk about regular stuff, and not about the universe collapsing into a black hole and stuff. And, like, if you want to say any of that stuff while we're outside the gazebo, you can say, 'Marybeth, you're the cutest girl in class', and only that, and I'll understand, and that'll be fine."

Marybeth's eyes now were large and tender. By the liquid vulnerability of those eyes alone, Clive seemed suddenly to comprehend the meaning behind some of the words she had spoken. He understood her fear, and seemed to understand that, like it or not, she was quite right in everything she said. Marybeth looked so fragile at this moment, he was afraid that if she shivered at a stray breeze, she would break. He was afraid, too, after all. His mind searched the situation desperately for some way in which she could be wrong and he could put forward an alternative to her suggestion.

The only thing about which she might be mistaken was the idea that she was a regular girl. After all, her plan only to talk about certain secret things in the gazebo hardly seemed a regular kind of idea. With this idea of Marybeth's, Clive had seemed to glimpse the small, rocky foothills of an entire mountain range of strangeness that was normally cloaked by some spell of eternal darkness, like a fairy tale witch's curse. It was not so much that Marybeth suddenly seemed like a different person. All she had said was quite consistent in atmosphere with his image of her. It was just that he realised there was much more to her than he had suspected. Could she really be a regular girl? Clive did not know enough about girls to say. He would not have been surprised if all girls, once you got close to them, had this same alarming quality of hiding mountain ranges in a void of shadow, only to reveal the little toe of the foothills now and then—a little toe that was itself stupendous—hinting thereby that almost anything could come out of that void at any time, and you would never guess the overall shape and pattern of the contents. If so, did all girls, as Marybeth now seemed to, remain regular only because of some witch's curse that obliged them to keep the extent of their true strangeness hidden forever?

"How do I know," asked Clive, "what's regular stuff and what isn't?"

"If it's about me, or how you feel, and you feel like you can't explain it, then it's not regular stuff."

"Right. Okay. Why can't we just talk about what we want?"

Marybeth looked at him with a kind of sympathy that froze his heart.

"We can. That's what the gazebo's for. We have to both be in it, though."

"Okay. So we're both in the gazebo now, so I can ask you why you want to make this rule."

"But it doesn't mean I have to answer. That's not in the rules."

"But if you're going to make that rule about the gazebo, why can't I make a rule about always answering questions when you're in the gazebo, too?"

Marybeth laughed.

"Actually, this is kinda fun," she said. "Think about it. In this gazebo, you can say anything. If we didn't have rules about outside the gazebo, maybe it wouldn't work."

"Maybe."

"Clive, I'm just being careful. Will you trust me?"

They looked across at each other.

"Sure. I trust you."

"So, promise only to talk about regular stuff outside the gazebo."

"I promise."

"Also, please don't tell anyone we're going on a date. Not yet."

"Okay. I won't tell anyone. I promise."

"Great. I'll text you, and we can meet up before the party."

"Great."

Silence ensued.

He had been told that he could say anything here, but the immediate effect for Clive was that he said nothing. The vacuum of anything was difficult to fill. This vacuum also took the form of the physical distance that still existed between the two of them. When would this distance ever disappear? Clive looked at Marybeth's legs, encased in the blue of her jeans, the sides of which had been stitched with flower patterns at the bottom (in daylight, like butterflies, but in the deepening blue gloom now like moths). Something as abstract as the outline of Marybeth's legs was a source of pain to him.

"So, I guess we're just gonna sit here, then?" she asked.

Clive never realised that having a girlfriend would be so difficult, like trying to move with hooks in your skin.

"I've already promised," said Clive, "and I'll keep my promise, but one reason I'm worried about having to talk about regular stuff is that I don't think I'm very good at it. You know, I don't know what to say most of the time, and if I have to try and think about regular stuff . . ."

Clive paused. Something about that painful outline, which had lodged inside him, came to fruition.

"Marybeth?"

"Yes?"

"Do you mind if I sit next to you?"

"Sure. Go ahead."

She adjusted herself on the bench, shifting her bag as if it were a pet on her lap that would have to make room for the presence of Clive. He sat next to her, afraid that if their legs actually touched each other it would be too much, so leaving an inch or two of space, and then feeling ridiculous that he had done so. He laughed nervously. They looked at each other in a shy, smirking, sidelong way, and then, as if their hands had been two magnets, they suddenly sprang together. The movement was skittish, almost angry, and the two hands nearly missed each other at first. Clive felt his fingernail scratch the back of Marybeth's hand and muttered, "Sorry", but she said nothing, and soon their two hands were very tightly entwined.

Clive looked straight ahead and felt a smile being formed on his face, like an iron bar being bent by a blacksmith. It happened slowly and without his will, and he could not undo it. Then he threw back his head, into the air behind them, outside the gazebo, and laughed. This accomplished, he let out a breath.

"I'm really glad that I'm sitting here now, and not over there."

Marybeth smiled and said nothing. Their faces inclined towards each other. Before his fear could prevent him, Clive was kissing Marybeth. There was a sweet squirming of lips. Clive shuddered with a cold thrill as a long-nailed hand touched his ribcage through his sweater. He turned himself to face with greater concentration into the kiss, and with his free hand reached out to stroke the vibrant shape of Marybeth's torso. Although this was something he had hardly even dared to dream of, he knew it was actually happening—he believed it. He was well beyond the dream now and in some free-floating reality, as if he had leapt a great wall. He had something now. This was his. The movement of hands, Marybeth's and his own, made his hair stand on end with electricity. He could smell and taste the sweet milky breath from her perfect nostrils. What Marybeth had been to him for years as a distant, unbearably precious idea, he could now feel and taste perfectly, in his mouth, beneath his fingers, and penetrating to the shivering centre of his being. Thoughts that he had forbidden himself so strictly that he did not even know he had done so leapt into his mind like sparks that took flame and held strong, a powerful, repetitive affirmation behind them like a bellows beating back the former taboo by fanning those flames.

At present, however, his roaming hand was far behind his thoughts. Some unknown force field seemed to paralyse his will whenever his hand came to the edge of certain zones. Any barrier now rankled like a swallowed blade. It seemed the intensity of his experience of Marybeth was brought suddenly to half-strength by the mere existence of such barriers, but even this, after all, was a phenomenal intensity, a reality the thirst for which could never be slaked.

Clive was aware of his glasses getting in the way, a fact that brought home to him the seeming unlikelihood of all this. For girls to kiss boys with glasses had always been against the rules of the universe. Clive paused to remove his glasses and set them down about a foot away on the bench before returning to that unlikely thing that seemed to prove all that happened in life was merely self-existent, without rule or reason, part of which was the taste buds of Marybeth's tongue rasping against his own.

Clive thought that, since this did not actually lead anywhere, at some point it would simply stop. There was something exhausting about the pure pleasure and excitement that almost made him want it to stop, but he was surprised and happy also to find that it went on and on and on. There were breaks for conversation, and each time he thought the kissing was over, but, irresistibly, it would return. His phone now was there to tell him how much kissing time they had left. Within the space of an hour, kissing and talking, Clive felt deeply that they had got to know each other quite well. In between kissing they talked about their lives.

"So, I guess, maybe because I've seen how things are for my sister, I don't care about growing up so much," said Marybeth. "I just feel like, I'm not in a hurry. I'm lucky, I guess, that Angela is there and so Mom and Dad expect her to be grown up and not me. I figure that I'll have to grow up someday, so I might as well make the most of just being a silly kid now. That's what my sister always calls me, you know—her silly little sister, or her dumbass sister, when she's being mean."

Clive nodded slowly.

"I envy you, you know, having an older sister. I'm an only child. You know what they say about only children."

"No."

"Maybe I shouldn't go into all that. But it's all true, anyway. And now, with Mom gone, there's only me and Dad, and, the truth is, it's really like he's not there."

"Your dad's a businessman, isn't he? I guess he's spending all his time at high-powered meetings and stuff like that, sitting around giant tables."

"It's not really like that. He's spent his whole life working hard to build this thing up, like, this way of life or something, but do you know what it is?"

"No."

". . . Washroom services. In hotels and stuff. God, that

doesn't really matter anyway. There's something else. I don't know if I should tell you. I'm not even sure I know what it is myself. I only know it's something strange."

"You don't have to tell me," said Marybeth.

Clive could tell that this meant she wanted to hear. He looked out at the dark shapes of trees and buildings through the arch of the gazebo. He had thought before coming here that the strangeness of Marybeth and the strangeness of what was happening to his dad were somehow incompatible, but maybe he was wrong. A feeling came over him that, as he tried to put it into words in his head, seemed like nonsense—but it was alluring nonsense. Maybe one kind of strangeness could heal another. Maybe Marybeth was here in his life now partly to turn the weirdness he was going through into some kind of adventure. Everything suddenly seemed to be framed by the elegant white arch of the gazebo.

"I'll tell you next time we're in the gazebo," he said.

Sunset had long since invested its glory in the massive, commonplace melancholy of blackness. Each blade of grass in the park was hidden in the cloak of its own shadow, ready for some slow, mournful migration. Marybeth checked the time on her phone and took up her bag once more, producing a compact and trying to make sure in the gloom that there were no compromising marks or signs on her face. Replacing the compact briskly in her bag, she turned to Clive.

"I've got to split now."

"Split?"

"Yeah. I'll call you about the party. You will be able to come, won't you?"

"My dad won't even notice I'm gone."

Marybeth got to her feet and they descended from the

gazebo together, Clive a pace or two behind. He caught up with her on the grass and took her hand. There was half a question in her eyes when she looked at him.

"I'm going this way," she said, "and left on Bethlehem. Aren't you the other way?"

"I'll walk you to the edge of the park," said Clive, pleased that he had made a statement rather than a request.

"Sure."

They began walking together in silence. The evening winds were stirring with an electric chill, turning Marybeth's silky hair now and then into blue-brown streamers.

"I guess this was our first date," said Marybeth.

"Yeah. I guess it was," said Clive.

He was about to add that he felt they had been going out for years, but, remembering his promise, he checked himself. He was not sure, but such a sentiment might not constitute "regular stuff". Now that they were striding hand in hand like this across the grass, however, the pact that Marybeth had persuaded him into made complete sense. Not being able to say those forbidden things made him feel as if he did not need to say them. All that needed to be said was in the pressure of palm on palm and the interlinking of fingers. And there was Marybeth's face, too, otherworldly in the electric moth's-wing-dust of the park's illumination. It was a sheen that brought tears to the eyes the way that wind sometimes did. In that light, Marybeth's face was the pure, beautiful face of a child.

"Marybeth," said Clive as they walked, feeling himself become a child correspondingly, "you are the cutest girl in class."

It was the simple truth.

Whatever spell that Marybeth had begun to weave in the gazebo, Clive had put the seal upon it with these words.

They both stopped, turned to face each other, and kissed again. Clive was not sure he even felt anything physically this time, except a few ticklish outlines of invisible slippings and slidings, and yet the result was a pulsating orb of joy in his chest, twinned with another in his groin.

They parted once they reached the street, and Clive was exhausted enough not to be alarmed at the sight of Marybeth's back as she disappeared with quickening steps. Rather, he felt a sad kind of satisfaction. He even smiled. In no hurry himself, he put his hands in his pockets, mooching generally in the direction of home, kicking here and there a stone or tin can. He had not got very far in this way when a sudden thought occurred to him, which took hold of his chest with lightning urgency. A little way ahead, between the houses, was another trail leading up into the hills. He would take it. He felt the call of the woods now more than ever.

He ran all the way, delighting in the expansive cool of the night air, with its smells of dry soil, and in the beating of his heart and the sweat of his forehead. At the foot of the tree he knelt abruptly in the dust. The darkness was a hulking raincloud thrashing to shed a charge of sad and violent excitement. He gave thanks spontaneously and passionately for the answering of his prayer, and felt his thanks heard with the same certainty as his original prayer had been answered. That certainty spurred him on to do something he had never dreamed of doing before—something that was both an offering and a petition. He undid his pants and dragged them down to expose his groin and the tops of his legs. Then he began a frenzied, repetitive movement, with something about it of cruelty. Like a bestial cupid, he aimed for the centre of the heart in the bark of the tree, and at last the initials 'MC' were dripping with a libation more obscene with living potential and more infamous in the by-ways of destiny where lurk thieves and cut-throats of the human heart, than its crimson cousin, blood.

By the time he got home, Clive was shaking and shivering oddly. His father seemed to be out still, but he did not want to check, and went immediately to his room. He lay down on his bed, still shivering intermittently. Thinking about what he had done in the woods, he could only regret it fiercely. It was too late now, of course, he had done it, but he wished that, in going to the woods, he had been patient enough to celebrate his triumph in a different way. Marybeth had always been, to him, one of the quiet, perfect things of life. Wasn't there some way of appropriately enjoying the fact that such a quiet, perfect thing might now be his? He felt as if he had desecrated something. The thing he had done would be something—he knew—that he would *take to the grave.*

Friday, 5th October, 7.11 p.m.

The preparations had gone as Zak had expected, which was to say that no significant preparations had taken place. Sooki sat on the couch, which stood where it always had, with the table resting in front of it, and the plastic chairs had been arranged in a rough circle in front of the television, a formation that reminded Zak of some distant childhood game, fruit basket or musical chairs. One of the overhead lights had blown, stranding the further side of the room in darkness. Zak glimpsed a furtive verminous movement in the shadows, the suggestive scurrying of a mouse or roach.

"No real glasses? And you don't have any plates?"

"Paper plates, dude," Thad said. "They're all you need, ever."

He gestured to the shopping bag on the table which, in addition to the plates and a jar of olives, contained a comprehensive inventory of Styrofoam cups and plastic utensils. Thad had also abducted a large quantity of wooden chopsticks from the sushi counter at Cousin's Supermarket and placed them in a pile on the table, although as far as Zak knew no Asian food was expected. But the most conspicuous items in the bag were various sachets filled with glutinous fluid, some transparent, others red or brown with floating green motes.

"The way I figure, as long as you have sauce, you're set," Thad said. "Everything tastes better with sauce. So what I do is, I save up. Order Chinese? I ask for extra Szechuan sauce. Going for Mexican? Get doubles on the taco sauce. Arby's? You can swipe as much of the shit as you want from that place, no one cares."

"I just think we should actually order something," Zak said.

Thad made a dismissive sound somewhere between a grunt and a whine.

"People will bring it, you'll see. Anyway, yeah, when you were in the bathroom I got a call from Ralph and Lucas. They're in the neighbourhood and they'll be by soon. And Ryan, would you believe this, it turns out that he has parties at the store anyway! He says he'll let us move there later as long as we tell everyone they should help him out and buy something. Man, fuck, this is awesome! We're going to have a party at a fucking adult boutique! This has gotta be BIG—I mean, we should be out there inviting more girls now."

"I'm just wondering if Sooki will be safe with all these people here. . . ."

Zak looked over at his dear one and felt her now half separated from him by briars of love and fear that threatened to prick him if he drew too close—prick and draw blood from the sweet-harrowed heart—so the story went on.

"She'll be fine." Thad went to the kitchen. "You want a beer?" he called out. "I got Corona and Heineken."

"I'll have an, um, Corona I guess."

Thad returned with two Coronas and handed one to Zak, then went to the record player and put on Linda Ronstadt's gold-certified LP *Don't Cry Now*.

Previously at Thad's parties, music had mainly come from someone's iPhone hooked up to speakers. However, Ed Chiang, who lived on what he could pick up at thrift stores, through freecycling and so on, had donated to Thad a dilapidated Garrard Lab 80 turntable with the suspension removed, and Thad had got into the habit of only listening to vinyl at home—just whatever random, scratchy vinyl he found on thrift hauls with Ed.

As the music began to fill the room Thad made his way back to the couch. He and Zak sat with Sooki between them, listening to the songs—to 'I Can Always See It', to 'Love Has No Pride', to 'Silver Threads and Golden Needles'— and, just as 'Desperado' was beginning to play, the doorbell rang. When Thad answered it he found Ralph and Lucas standing outside. Ralph, the gravedigger, seemed made for the work, with his dense muscles and cramped posture. He was extremely short-sighted but took no action to correct it, which meant that he took in the world through a distrustful squint. Lucas was tall and tow-headed, a second-generation Norwegian import. Though the same age as his friends, his face looked ten years older, the features not so much chis-elled as inexpertly gouged—an aborted series of angular lines that collapsed on his neck in tedium. The two men held a heavy-looking brown cardboard box between them.

"What's that?" Thad asked.

"You said you wanted a fondue set, remember?"

"Oh, shit, yeah, I forgot about that . . . well hey, thanks for going to the trouble."

"Where do you want us to put it?"

"Anywhere's fine."

They eased the box to the ground and opened it. Inside were a 1 ½ quart enamelled fondue pot, a black cast-iron base, a round wooden protective tray, a nickel burner and six colour tipped fondue forks.

"We didn't bring any cheese or anything . . ." Ralph said.

"That's okay, I got some in the fridge."

Thad was about to return to the kitchen when the door-bell interrupted him again. This time it was Angela. She wore a simple white top from American Apparel and a floral skirt, along with a crystal necklace, silver bracelet and black Chinese Laundry New Capture knee-high boots.

"Hey, what's up?" Thad said. "You're alone . . . great. We got all kinds of drinks here. . . ."

"Huh? No, my sister should be along soon." She stepped forward and scanned the room. The bare walls / wall-to-wall carpeting stained with beer and semen and marked with cannabis ash. "Oh, wow, you guys really didn't go to much trouble or anything, did you?"

"Yeah, well, we're still setting shit up, right?"

Angela turned her gaze back to the four men around her and seemed to really take them in for the first time. She wondered if any of them were related to Thad. Ralph was squinting at her.

"There are going to be other girls, right?" she asked.

"Fuck, yeah," Lucas said. "Jenna and Mariah should be here soon, and my Debbie's coming out too."

"Your Debbie," Angela repeated. She smiled. "That's okay, I like to observe guys in their . . . you know . . . natural state."

Angela had intended this last line to provoke an indulgent groan, but no one acknowledged the double entendre or even seemed to understand the statement on a literal level.

Ralph twitched his shoulders.

"Yeah, well . . ." he said, staring intently at her chest. His gaze, protracted long beyond the length of a discreet appraisal, was not entirely uncritical, and Angela imagined him mentally comparing her figure with some media-derived ideal. "Let's fire up the burner," he said at last.

Zak, who had not acknowledged Angela's presence or said anything since she had come in, seemed in that state of agitation that is the edge of forgetting to care about social apperances. He was fidgeting in his seat next to Sooki like a dog making its bed, pawing her slowly and searchingly, as if to find the centre of the security he derived from her. Angela had withheld comment on the doll, thinking Sooki to be something brought in for the party, some absurdist decoration or prop for a practical joke. She decided to wait for the eventual explanation rather than ask and risk seeming ignorant. As she looked at Zak he met her eyes and then immediately looked down. He was not bad looking, but the strange pigmentation of his skin made her wonder what his story was.

Thad, Ralph and Lucas busied themselves with the fondue set. Thad was placing eight triangles of Brie cheese in the pot when Ralph said, "You need to add liquor."

"Liquor?"

"Yeah," Angela added, "I had fondue when we were in Paris. You put bread and onions in it."

"That's onion soup," Thad said.

"No. It's fondue."

"She's right," Lucas said, "you put onions and bread and wine in it."

Thad looked crestfallen. "I didn't buy onions," he said.

"But you have bread."

"Yeah, Oroweat 12 Grain."

"Is this wine?"

"Yeah."

"It says it's peach flavoured."

Angela looked at Thad. "Hey, you said no grown-up stuff, remember?"

"Haha, very funny. It's for the fondue, Miss Policewoman."

Angela smiled. "It'd better be."

Ralph unscrewed the top of the bottle and poured some in the pot, then took a swig himself.

"Not bad, not bad at all . . ."

"Peach fuzz."

Lucas took the bottle, poured some in a plastic cup.

"Madame," he said, handing it to Angela.

She hesitated for a moment and then took the cup. "I guess it really is a party," she said.

There was a tentative knock at the door, followed after a pause by the bell. Lucas went to answer it. No one paid much attention until he shouted out to Thad a few moments later.

"It's some kids. Like, kid-kids. They say they were invited."

"It's my sister!" Angela said, looking up from the pot.

Clive and Marybeth walked in. At first they held hands, until Marybeth—noticing Angela and feeling also the scrutiny of so many pairs of eyes—instinctively jerked her hand down to her side. If Clive noticed he gave no outward sign, as his entrance into the room seemed to have paralyzed him. His gaze wandered from the area of darkness at the back to the circle of chairs in front of the television, where it paused for a moment before coming to rest on Sooki. It was not the doll that froze him in place, but the way it was entwined with Zak, the human and inhuman bodies locked in symbiosis. He thought suddenly of an octopus curling its limbs around a rock, or perhaps a skull. A moment later his hand clasped Marybeth's again in a gesture of mutual protection. Angela sensed their uncertainty and tried not to feel guilty. She had invited her sister as an excuse to leave early if things got out of control, keeping Thad's reassurances in mind. But now, with a glass of peach-flavoured wine in her hand, she knew she had lied to herself. It was the same lie from college—that nothing would happen, that it would only be a fun night out. Placing her cup on the table and grinning with as much sincerity as she could muster, she called out for Marybeth to join her.

While everyone was distracted by the new arrivals, Thad slipped a bottle of Germany Sex Drops out of his pocket and poured the contents into the fondue.

"Voilà," he said.

Ten minutes later Tommy and Ed Chiang showed up. They had come straight from work and were still in their Red Kap mechanic's clothes. Cousins, they resembled each other physically: stout frames with beach-bronzed faces and thick black hair that threatened to mullet. They had brought a six pack of Climax Cream Ale but nothing else.

"Where're all the babes?" Ed asked. "Everyone here looks like they're twelve years old."

"I'm thirteen," Marybeth said.

Ed, who was clearly stoned, reacted to her assertion as if it were something a professional comedian might have uttered, the punchline to a diabolically rich and ribald joke. He fell into a fit of explosive laughter until Tommy punched him on the shoulder, hard. Then he returned to his hazy half-awareness, fixing his gaze on Marybeth.

"Wanna beer?"

"No, I'm fine . . ."

"We don't drink," Clive said. He immediately regretted not only this statement but its implication that he could speak for Marybeth—which was what he was supposed to do, he guessed, as a means of protecting her, though it still felt absurd and impossible. He glanced at her, but her expression showed no sign of disapproval. Ed had stopped paying attention to him, as he had noticed Sooki.

"Who's that?" he asked.

"Zak's sex doll," Thad said.

"Shut. The. Fuck. Up." Zak said, not so much thinking but believing *love is beyond their understanding throne of light above the high cliffs lap and beyond the wide oceans you Sooki of my tender thoughts my heated mind a matrimony made our own private bathing place.*

While everyone was talking, distracted, Ralph pulled out a quarter ounce of Washington state shrooms and, looking around cautiously, dumped the contents into the fondue.

"Fuck it," he murmured.

By the time Debbie Lawson and Mariah Mendez arrived, almost everyone had dipped into the fondue, most using chopsticks to skewer their torn-up shreds of Oroweat 12 Grain bread. Thad looked up as Mariah filled the doorway. Rubicund, Rubenesque, she wore ruby-coloured sweatpants, and as she moved, her thighs rubbed together, wiggling like rubber. Lucas went to embrace her and she ejected him, like a bouncer. Debbie, frizzy-haired and slender in slacks, dwarfed beside her friend, held a half-drained bottle of Margaritaville Tequila Silver.

"Ta-killya," Ed Chang said.

Beside him, Tommy moved his hand to the fondue and, under the pretext of stirring it, slipped in four MDMA capsules he had scored from a roving biker earlier that day.

Thad surveyed the room and felt a dim satisfaction. Several spirited conversations and non-tentative dance moves had broken out amidst the general levity. The party, which had come to life like some jump-started vehicle in fits and false-beginnings and sputters, had now shot out of the gate and was wheeling around, seeking identity and direction. Thad roved from person to person, making sure everyone had enough drink. Sooki still dominated the room, but the party had shaped itself to accommodate her silent presence, the lodestone on the couch acknowledged only in surreptitious glances.

Clive alone felt completely out of place. He had secured a fork and now he stabbed a chunk of bread, dipped it in the fondue and lifted it onto Marybeth's plate, loading it with what he thought the choicest chunks for her. When he passed the plate to her, she took it as if this intimacy were becoming natural. Half-abstracted, Clive watched her tender lips wrapping themselves around that saturated bread like two clouds around a mountain peak.

Soon after their introduction, Angela and Mariah had begun talking excitedly.

"Anyhow, I started taking these diet pills—ECA Stack they're called. The granddaddy of all fat-burners. So we'll see. I'm sick of being hit on by guys just 'cause they think I put out," Mariah said.

"Wow . . ."

"I gotta use the restroom, honey. I'll be right back."

Ed Chiang noticed with sleuth-like attention that whenever anyone walked by him they left trails. He put his beer bottle to his lips and tipped his head back, his eyes still moving side to side observantly. Debbie, already on her fifth tequila shot, was pushing herself against him.

"I looooooove your um," she said.

"I love yours too," Ed replied, believing he was beginning to get a handle on this case.

𝔇𝔦𝔫𝔤-𝔇𝔬𝔫𝔤!

"Ah, Thad! Thad-O! Is this a Thad I see before me? Thadonicus! In the glory of your organism you are Adam, the first man! What a piece of work is Thad! How noble in reason, how infinite in faculty! Come over here, you paragon of animals, and see what sweets I bare!"

Ryan had arrived in a flourish of shirt-cuffs and held a giant cheesecake in one hand. He had a stud earing in his left ear. His tight jeans lent exquisite definition to a male enhancement that made telephone poles, tall trees and water towers bow their heads in reverence. Ryan was a man of two halves. Put him anywhere in the vicinity of a camera and he seemed forged of an earthy frankness that provoked an uneasy trust-distrust. Place him in a natural environment and he took it on himself to play with affectation as if fingering the keys of an accordion so that the question of trust or distrust was in creepy abeyance. His face now was a garden of innocence and understanding and, after a platinum-edged display of bonhomie, he ushered Thad confidentially towards the kitchen area on the pretext of depositing the cheesecake there.

"Hey, Thad, I notice the Matsushima Series Real Doll over there. One that looks familiar. Very familiar. Destiny? Destiny. Is this your plan? Dolls are where it's happening, believe me. I'm going to hurt my own self here, but I do it out of a kind of fraternal love and also disinterested scientific and artistic admiration. I'm going to give you some important information because I think that the world of the young Thadonicus and the world of love dolls can do beautiful things together."

"Right," said Thad, who was now attempting to keep Ryan's facial features in their accustomed outline by blinking and squinting. "Did you just say something about dollnapping?"

Ryan fixed Thad with an intense, and, it seemed, compassionate stare. He appeared frozen in time, and yet his smile became gradually warmer and more generous like the rising of yeast. Then, in violation of time's apparent paralysis, he raised his right forefinger to his lips and winked.

"I said, dolls are happening." He leaned in towards Thad until they achieved conspiratorial intimacy.

Thad nodded.

"Yeah. You're right on that, Ryan. They're happening all over."

Ryan reached into an inside pocket and drew out two colourful-looking pamphlets that had been neatly folded in two.

"Start with these," he said. "Doll factories. They're always looking for a competitive edge. A couple of hundred years back there was money in taking corpses to doctors—'cause what good's a doctor without death? He needs his corpses, right? Times have moved on just a teensy bit, bro. The entrepreneur has more options today. You know, medicine has branched out into cosmetics, and here in our sparkling 21st century . . ." Ryan paused and took a number of deep, satisfied breaths, as if to relish the bracing pine freshness of the air, ". . . your resurrectionist is just as likely to use rohypnol as a pick and shovel, you dig?—Babe-burking, Thad, that's what I'm talking about—sleeping beauties. Parties is where the babe-burker harvests. Parties like this one, maybe. Save the numbers on your SIM, ditch the pamphlets, and call them when you've got an A-grade baby doll for a mask model. Depending on who's asking, they sometimes go for body models, too."

Thad took the pamphlets and nodded again. He wasn't quite sure what Ryan was talking about, but it sounded important.

"Hey," he asked, "about those Germany Sex Drops I got from you."

"About?"

"Um, like, how long do they take to work? None of the chicks seem horny yet."

"Worry not my exiguous amigo, for a-horny they shall be. First they will start peeing with great frenzy and then they will be on your cock like juice on fruit."

"Yeah?" Thad grinned.

"Yes. We'll talk more later. I'm going to mingle and groom. And I hope you're coming to the shop for your second leg—or should I say third? I have to be back myself, soon. Juan's bringing the roulette table. We're going to r-r-r-r-r-release the spiders tonight!"

Thad had been grinning for some time when he realised that Ryan had already gone.

Then, for another considerable duration, he tried to remember something he'd forgotten. In his mind he moved through the slalom of dolls, corpses and spiders that were the psychic remains of Ryan's conversation increase tonicity of vagina shark extract chewing gum she's wrapped in a matrimony vine activate the sexual glands to generate sperm if erection appears time after time or last too long time drink a cup of water please.

"Party . . . drugs . . . fondue . . ."

The checklist led him back to the present. He fished out a small Ziploc bag from his shirt pocket and swallowed the two white pills it contained. That would do for now. Everything else was in place. He just had to change the music and stake out Angela.

She was in conversation with Ralph and Lucas now. They were sitting cross-legged near the sofa. Lucas was smoking a Camel cigarette and Ralph was talking, hunched to one side as if carrying an invisible sack of body parts on his back.

"I know what I like. That's what I'm saying. I agree with Angela. I'm liberated. I'll go down on a girl. I don't care."

I always knew you were a fag how is that a fag I'm talking about pussy fag pussy what's the difference you're a gravedigger you should know what a clit is what I don't get it a clit is a dick that means you are a dick-licker what are you talking about, asshole how can a clit be a pussy fag pussy dick well let's say how can a nipple be a tit see man you're full of shit no it's a scientific fact men pussy fag pussy have nipples because pussy fag pussy they're not women it's the X and Y factor you switch down one track your nipples grow into tits down the other your clit grows into a dick that means Ralph pussy fag pussy you are officially a dick-licker wait pussy fag pussy wait hold on man there's got to be a mistake is this true this isn't true right you don't have a dick well pussy fag pussy I kind of I mean do you have boobs pussy fag pussy no right I don't so that means she's just trying to pussy fag pussy confuse you because she knows I'm right wait wait said Angela patting the ground with the palm of her hand I know right Lucas if a pussy fag pussy girl sucked your nipples would that make her a lesbian of course but I would never let any woman pussy fag pussy have lesbian sex with me.

Angela opened her mouth but appeared to be unable to find her next words and, from the corner of her eye, noticed with first disapproval, then resignation, and finally relief, that Ed Chiang, Tommy and Debbie were smoking a giant joint in the corner.

Someone had been playing Lynyrd Skynyrd's *Street Survivors*, the 1977 album whose title was to take on an ironic and sinister significance when, three days after the album's release, the band's chartered plane crashed, killing some of the crew and three band members. Thad stopped to orientate himself by the music:

Ooooh that smell
Can't you smell that smell
Ooooh that smell

He lifted the needle from its groove with a reckless flick and replaced the Lynyrd Skynyrd with Volume I of the *Hell Comes to Your House* compilation, released in 1984 on the Music for Nations label, a UK import from the precise year that was the eve of thrash metal's breaking into wider public consciousness, the inchoate and exciting period when it was still associated with some pre-thrash bands, such as Venom, Manowar, Hellhammer and some bands in the New Wave of British Heavy Metal. Indeed, it was an offering from Manowar with which the record began.

As the first chords of 'Blood of My Enemies' rang through the speakers, Thad turned to face a room of which he felt himself newly in possession. He advanced in the direction of Angela, watched by Zak, who remained with his arm around Sooki's shoulders, paralysed by fear on the one hand, and drawn-out expectancy on the other. Since his arrival at Thad's yesterday, he had been sleeping in Craig's room with Sooki, two concerns continuously sharpening themselves on the whetstone of his attention. One was the imminent threat of Sooki's abduction—imminent since the dollnappers were apparently watching their every move—and the other was the question of Sooki's possession. The second was even more troubling than the first because its causes, boundaries and implications were so nebulous. The voice had come, yesterday—Sooki's, he had thought. And yet it was not Sooki's. And now that intrusive, different voice was silent again, and this silence was not like any si-lence that had obtained between him and Sooki before. It seethed like a cloud hiding thunderbolts.

Before, her voicelessness had been for him as crystal-transparent as her body was opaque. She was subtle, factual; honest, mysterious. She yielded, or she did not yield, with precision and completeness, and was without evasion. Since the possession she was murky, hard to read, and he waited again for an actual voice, not knowing whether it would truly belong to her.

Naggingly anxious to penetrate the now-stubborn mists of the crystal ball that was Sooki, and conscious each moment of the danger that threatened her, Zak had barely left her side for a minute all the time he had been at Thad's (he had swooped on the fondue as nervously as a raiding pigeon, and swooped back). As he watched Thad take his position on the floor near Angela, however, Zak became aware of something happening in his brain. Was it the movement of the party, stirring up currents in him? For some reason his attention was freeing up. The clutching sensation in his chest was relaxing, allowing him to breathe more easily, and he found his gaze was not now magnetised by Sooki. The thought struck him—he did not have to stay here on the sofa. He could move, too, if he wanted.

Something was definitely happening. Brilliant shadows were rippling across the entire room, as if cast by shoals of unseen fish in some eucalyptus-fresh ocean that cleared not only the sinuses, but the synapses of the brain. He felt opened up as the air in the room itself expanded. All of a sudden he was holding his head high, aware he had been hunched for a long time, but now unable to return to such a cramped posture.

Now that he felt ventilated and lubricated, he chose to look at Sooki again, and there was a feeling of sweetness and apprehension in the choice. Recent events, as well as the long routine of daily life, had dulled him. He did not know why, but the veil of that dullness had just been lifted, and he saw something that made the air thrill in his lungs—Sooki. Her eyes under the shiny lace of that dark fringe, the suggestive delicacy of her inorganic contours. With or without religion, sometimes a person is granted a spring-like knowledge of the tender precariousness of things in his life, how more-than-I-could-ever-wish-for they are. Even in the abysses of his fear for Sooki, he had been taking her for granted. Now was the time, knowing the preciousness of things—to stand up and make a decision.

Literally—he would literally stand up. That was how to live the dream. And so he stood, and then crouched over Sooki, and stood again, carrying her in his arms like a film actor carrying his leading lady.

Exciter's 'Violence and Force' was now playing. It did not seem so much to be coming from the speakers as to be the sonic crystal within which the hologram of the room was embedded. The shadows of shoaling fish had transformed to a rotor-blade chop and whir. Zak thought he could feel the wind from that blade; it sent waves through the carpet as if through long grass.

He strode towards the stairs, feeling more visible than he could remember feeling in his life. They could watch—they were watching—but they couldn't stop him doing what he had to do. As he approached the stairs to the upper floor, he could hear Thad say, "Gone to get a room."

There were three rooms upstairs—Thad's bedroom, a bathroom, and Craig's bedroom—where he and Sooki had been camped out since the night before. He took Sooki into Craig's room. Craig played drums for a local band called Jinx Proof, and the room was cramped by his five-piece drum set. The only pieces of furniture in the room were a chair and a bed and the walls were decorated by countless classic Van Halen posters that Craig had purchased on eBay.

Zak seated Sooki on the chair in such a way that she could look out of the window at the now starry blueness of the evening. Taking the stool from the drum kit, he sat opposite her. The night itself seemed to have become almost unbearably sensitive, and it was sharing that sensitivity with all who breathed its air. He could hear the music coming from downstairs, but, intertwined with it, thought he could make out voices from back yards and from inside houses farther down the street and then from downstairs the hoppy smell of beer and the queasy wafting musk of marijuana seemed to drift up and insects were singing as if it were only their constant trill that kept the sweet dark in place. The pavements and the genetically enhanced, hormonally boosted, space-age lawns, exhaled the tragic warmth of unsustainable prosperity, but, laced with the moon's silver, there was a scent in the air that was the nervous chill of tomorrow morning's dew. In the breeze-blown, lacy half-light, Sooki appeared to be covered with a taffeta swarm of butterflies. Moonlight and streetlight unmasked a skewed rectangle across her eyes and the bridge of her nose.

"I think we really need to talk," said Zak.

He paused.

That morning, when he had come out of the shower, he had found Thad coming out of Craig's room. When he went in, it seemed to him that Sooki was in a different position than when he had left her and her dress seemed to have been adjusted.

"I guess we both know that things are changing between us. I don't know what's happening for you, Sooki, but before you say anything I just want to say a few things of my own."

Zak was scared to bring Sooki back to his apartment, but also was not sure he trusted Thad. Yes, after the party he would have to bring her home. Life, after all, was for living.

"First of all, whatever happens, I will always consider you as a blessing in my life—maybe one that no one else will ever understand—and I will cherish the memory of the times we've shared forever.

"Secondly, I want whatever is best for you—wherever life is taking you that can most fulfil what you are and what you can be, I . . . I don't want to stand in life's way.

"Third, I want you to know . . . I'm not giving up on you, Sooki. I'm right here, and I'm ready to listen to whatever you have to say right now.

"And . . . that's it," Zak concluded, as if himself surprised to have spoken so soon all that was of importance.

For a moment Zak wished he had managed some kind of oratorical flourish that provided an irresistible cue (for instance, for applause), but after a few moments of silence he decided he had truly said what was needed and he could dispense with all the prestidigitation of prompting and coercion.

Looking across the window's spilt light to Sooki, Zak found he trusted her again. It was not that the clouds had departed—no. But the Sooki he had always known was present in their midst. In fact, his trust was an act of consciousness and courage; he trusted her because he recognised the reality—its exact nature not yet revealed—that meant he might lose her.

"I'm listening," he said, and bowed his head.

After a while, he raised his head again, cocked to one side in attention.

"Yes. I do believe you. Yes . . . You're right, it isn't easy."

He wanted to kiss her now—was pierced by the desire—now that he knew it was not the time to do so. He was not sure such a time would come again.

Yes, anything. Just tell me what you want . . . The kids? Which kids—? Oh . . . yeah . . . Okay. Sure. I'll introduce you. I don't know them myself, but . . . You want to talk to them? Sure. Okay. I understand. Let's do that.

Angela had told Marybeth not to wander far, but a short while after they'd started eating the fondue, both Marybeth and Clive had felt an urge to go outside, as irrepressible as the need for a bubble to rise to the surface of a body of water. At the back of the condo there were some steps leading to a watered patch out back, fences, lawns of neighbours, thin strings falling from a sky that seemed to trump mundane reality with a full house of stars, took on the ragged charm of a dandelion in seed.

Immediately they had the door closed behind them they were kissing in a way that usually occurs, in any one life, seldom enough that it may be counted—kissing as if they were in a song. Clive was aware that they had no heads, or that their heads had become transparent, the way a finger does when you hold it very close to your eye, and in place of their heads were planets and stars, and this kissing.

They broke off the kiss. Clive thought that Marybeth had broken it off, but it was hard to tell. She belched softly, like a fish gasping in air. Marybeth seemed like a different person now. He took this opportunity to examine her features closely. They were the features he knew, which had become familiar and strange to him—strange and familiar—in uncountable cycles over the years. But this was a new strangeness again, and he couldn't quite make these known features blend into the face they had so long been for him. A whimsical idea flitted into his mind like a wild bird from nowhere: It was like knowing someone you have never heard talk anything but English, only to learn, after some years, that her first language was something else—something obscure and Slavic—and when you heard her speak her native language, you wondered who she was, after all, because even her body language changed with the change in her spoken tongue. That soft belching, too, he thought, was part of this new language.

"So how are you feeling?" she asked.

She took both of his hands in hers, and he was reassured. "Actually . . ." he said. "Actually . . . I think I'm butter."

"Butter?"

"Yeah."

"Does that worry you?"

"Worry? I guess . . . not."

"Cool. You know what . . . I'm butter, too."

And, strangest of all, at this point Marybeth actually took her hands away from Clive and started examining them, back and front, as if seriously bemused by some buttery melting that was taking place. Clive, wishing to be helpful, but also becoming puzzled—*concerned*—stood back a little and started inspecting her, head to foot, trying to work out exactly what was happening. There was much that he saw, as he did so, that amazed him, but after a while his eyes fixed on the region of her belly, which was becoming clear like the surface of a lake from which the ice was melting. There, in pellucid darkness, a bright shape curled—a dragon, perhaps, or a horse with a long, beribboned, fantastical mane, like a toy from some haunted and melancholy nursery. Looking closer, he saw that it was, in fact, a human being, made of plastic—a doll.

"What are you looking at?"

The lake grew dark; her stomach was opaque again.

"I . . . Did you just say you were butter?"

She began to giggle.

"It's okay. It's okay. It's okay. It's okay. Come on."

Soon they were kissing again, but now it was not quite like in a song. Clive had become sure of something—he now had a girlfriend. This was a great thing, but it came with a great shadow. He did not know who his girlfriend was, cloud, crack or clock and all was peaceful all was one they were on a fruitful isle and he remembered the gazebo. More than anything else, he wanted to say those words to her—the ones they had agreed on—but he could not. Then, as he was kissing her, he saw something. It was the freckle on the left side of her neck. The freckle was the same. He began to kiss downwards, and for the first time in his life he was kissing that freckle. He thought it tasted peppery. Then there was no thought. His mind was wrung out like a cloth.

"Wait. Wait." It was her voice. "Please don't. I don't want a hickey for school."

"Oh. Yeah. Sure. I'm sorry."

For some reason they stood still now, and looked at each other.

"Hey," said Marybeth. She reached up and wiped a tear from Clive's eye. "What's this?"

A creaking sound made them both jump at the same time. The back door was opening. They moved a little apart, watching the door. Manoeuvring awkwardly with the doll in his arms, it was the man they'd seen earlier, Zak, apparently a friend of Thad's.

"Hey, guys," he said in a soft voice. "Sorry to interrupt. Do you mind if we join you for a minute or two?"

"Sure. I mean, that's fine," said Clive.

He felt that perhaps he had rushed unnecessarily to answer, and looked to Marybeth to gauge her attitude, but was unable to read her blank-azure face and Zak was now on the top step and closing the door behind him with his buttocks. He looked from Clive to Marybeth and back and then sat down on the steps.

"This won't take long," he said. "I mean, you don't know who I am, so I should introduce myself. And Sooki. This is Sooki. My name is Zak. Zak Landers. I guess there's not much to say about me. And maybe you kids are too young to understand."

"Probably," Marybeth murmured.

"What it is is . . . You guys don't know anyone here, right? Sooki just thought you might be feeling awkward being . . . not knowing anyone. So, she just wanted to come and say hi, and make you feel more comfortable. She's like that."

Marybeth looked at Clive. Her flat lips twisted at the ends and she began to giggle. Some indeterminate period of absurdity, Zak watching her in a manner almost intense but without impatience. The giggles took on a chaotic momentum of their own, and Marybeth threw back her head, horse-like, half turned away, and even, at one point, stamped her foot three times a moon shattered on a windswept lake.

While this was taking place, Clive was looking closely at Zak. That was why—he realised—his attention had been drawn to Zak and Sooki since he'd arrived; he knew them. So, apparently, did his father. Yes, Sooki. The box. The speaker. Dolls. Dollnapping. It all made sense.

Or did it?

Some mechanism, like a fairground grab-arm, had deposited Zak and Sooki before him, in the trough of here-

and-now, but not at random. The connections that formed the joints of the grab-arm, though, were invisible to Clive. In any case, perhaps Sooki had some message for him.

Marybeth began the entirely visible process of calming herself down in a state of neither existence nor its opposite a flower that stares at the light and finally she let out a breath as if to say, "I'm ready", and then, in a conspicuously composed voice, she spoke:

"We're here with Angela. She's my sister. But we don't really know anyone else. Except Thad. I sort of know him."

Zak continued to stare at her for a while.

"So, you were saying," prompted Marybeth, "about, um, Sooki wanting to make us feel more comfortable."

"Yeah. Yeah. That's right."

Zak turned to look at Sooki and began to adjust her in his arms.

"Oh my God!" said Marybeth, "Can I just say this one thing? You look just like you're about to sing a song. I mean, like you're tuning a guitar or something and you're going to burst into song."

"Yeah," said Zak. "I guess . . ."

And he continued to mumble for a while as he adjusted Sooki. However, the mumbling did not come to a natural conclusion. It persisted as if running into an unexpected and insoluble complexity that required a kind of repetition and Clive listened **listened** *listened to once upon a star . . . steps to Heaven . . . makes no difference who shot off the locks and stormed the house of Mrs Fox am I more like my mother or father who am I and I started to see hair grow where it had never grown before*

Where'd you get those?

Eyes

I mean the hair had never grown there before **YOU HAVE A BONER**

And that   slither

*Where did you go did you go mother earth opens you in her locks and
her box and her fox and no one to cook me dinner to fix me stitch me
to love me is all I ever wanted was to be loved and does she have hair
growing there too?* **WHAT COLOUR IS YOUR PUSSY?**

*Dark reflection . . . adjust your idol eyes I guess that is what it
is to be a man but do I care but do I care?* **AT LEAST I'M NOT
GAY!!!** *A fag a female fag a fag whose fleece is white as snow.*

*I'll still be there to unlock the locks that bind the box that holds
the ball that spreads the pox and when I saw there was hair growing
there I didn't know who to tell a secret me and my secret hair.*

It's war!
Take me home
On the trail of the loathsome slime
To the place
Gotta make way for the holo-Siberia
I belong
Don't put your ferrets on the ground, Mrs Worthington,
Where any chap can kick them around
Is this the stairway to once upon a star three steps from Heaven
Eye in the sky
I
I
Pretty little angles
Angle eyes
Those twilight eyes
Idol's tears
Is this the way . . . ?
To the place
Descended from a
*Curved stairway to the hula box, unlock the locks and spread the
pox*
Where'd you get

The place
Where'd you get those
I belong
Where'd you get those eyes? ***I AM SORRY FATHER BUT WHO ARE YOU IF I GO TO PRISON FOR RAPE IT IS YOUR FAULT SO JUST REMEMBER THAT SHE IS NOT A REAL WOMAN!!!***
    Give up hope hitch your rope upon a
Every night is rape night ***SHE'S A DOLL PUT MY HAND DOWN HER PANTIES***
Organ turns to rust
If you never come in the sheets I just had to change them before father got home but where else can I come where else till the torches turn to ashes
Star

"Wait," said Clive, "what's happening?"

"It's okay," said Zak. "Sometimes she needs a bit of translating."

"Did you just sing 'Date Night in Hawaii'?"

"She's been a little hard to understand recently," said Zak.

Clive was not sure if this meant that Zak had sung 'Date Night in Hawaii' or not.

"Okay," said Zak, looking back up at Clive and Marybeth. Somehow a stage had been prepared for him, there on the steps, by their laughter and confusion. This was the moment before approaching the microphone, the silence of an expectant audience, before the engagement has begun, yet with an almost-certainty that the engagement will succeed. "She wants to tell you Three Things."

He looked from Clive to Marybeth to confirm their attention. They both nodded in turn.

"The first thing," said Zak, "is just because there's no name for something it doesn't mean it's not real. The second thing is kind of two things, really. The biggest problem in the world is that people don't trust each other—the real heroes are the ones who know how to trust. That's number two. And number three is this: Fear is the past; love is the future. Those are the Three Things."

The silence that now descended, full of stars, was the mirror image of the silence that had preceded the Three Things. Zak, Marybeth and Clive looked at each other, almost-uncertain, yet seeming to know that the silence so fully occupied the present space and time that the meaning of any words now would automatically be displaced into superfluity.

Zak bowed his head slightly. Ever so prematurely—and yet at exactly the right time—he rose awkwardly to his feet and said:

"I have to go. I have to take this little lady home. It is past her bedtime."

Somehow he manoeuvred back through the door, and Clive and Marybeth were left on their own.

Facing Marybeth, Clive saw her eyes had become cartoonishly liquid and wide, though they were dark and glistening as any real, organic eyes on a moonlit night.

"I want to write them down," she said. "Do you have a pen and paper?"

Clive began checking his pockets, uselessly, as he knew he had neither.

"Hey," he said, "did Zak just play us songs?"

"No. I mean, he looked like he was going to, but he didn't."

"I was sure that he started playing Sooki like a guitar, only it was like the guitar was playing him in a way, like she was a ventriloquist guitar making her dummy player sing. And then he became John Denver. And he played a couple

John Denver songs. And then . . . he turned into someone else."

"I must have missed that, I guess. Who's John Denver?"

"Someone my dad likes. That's so weird. Er . . . Also, I guess I don't have pen and paper."

"That's okay. I just remembered, my sister always carries pen and paper. I'll go ask her. Be right back."

She disappeared back into the condo, the sound of music growing louder and then muted again as the door opened and closed. Since she had said she'd be back, Clive felt he had been instructed to wait. He stood, not moving from the spot. Something was troubling him severely.

He was sure Zak had sung 'Date Night in Hawaii', except, he also thought that the chorus had actually been sung as—or maybe he had changed it in his own head to—'Every night is rape night in Hawaii'. This little earworm had begun to drill into his brain. One thing was overwhelmingly sure—it was in very bad taste, and he was ashamed because of it. That song, or that one line of it, had grown with great fecundity into a verdant and blossoming Hawaii in his mind. It was a Hawaii permeated by the jaunty melody of the song, but there was incongruity here, for every night—what detail he envisaged it all in—the sandy beaches and the warm purlieus of the towns were the scene of something gratuitous and cruel. He heard the moans, the screams, saw the atrocities. The song continued all the while, jaunty, melancholy, mocking. It appalled him, and yet he seemed gleefully to lose himself in it, as if to punish himself for ever having imagined it. It was as unspeakable as it was inane, a bad joke insisting on itself for the very sake of its badness. He had carefully—as if avoiding treading in something—given the proper title of the song when he named it aloud. But Marybeth hadn't heard Zak sing it, so this was surely Clive's own stupid secret. If anything could drive him to insanity, it would be this.

The song was still tormenting him when Marybeth returned.

"Hey," she said, "you haven't moved."

Surprised, he tried to loosen up his posture. He felt relieved she was back, but also guilty.

"I got the paper," said Marybeth, and she passed him a small piece of lined paper on which the Three Things were written.

Clive read them to himself in a mumble:

> *1. Just cuz something doesn't have a name, doesn't mean it's not real.*
> *2. The biggest problem in this world is that no one trusts anyone. The real heroes are those who know how to trust.*
> *3. Fear is the past. Love is the future.*

He felt as if he had just opened the mother of all fortune cookies, but he struggled to apply it to his situation. He wanted to tell Marybeth that he knew about Sooki, but that would mean talking about his dad, and about his eavesdropping, and about a whole spiral of other things. The laws of physics dictated that he could not talk. And since he couldn't talk about Sooki, he contented himself it was only natural not to mention the irrelevant absurdity of 'Rape Night in Hawaii'—that song, somehow, was the very essence of something he had to *take to the grave.*

"I'm gonna keep this," said Marybeth, and, taking the scrap of paper back, put it in her breast pocket.

"Ay, what shall we play a game?"

"A pound a game."

"Between her legs."

"What are you?"

"Nothing."

"The fuck? The walls aren't . . . connected right?"

Tommy moved his hand in front of his face as if to clear away an invisible membrane, then shifted his leg and knocked over a half-empty bottle of Climax Cream Ale. Or was it half-full, Thad wondered as he watched it spill onto the carpet. Tommy stared at it for eleven seconds and then reached out a lazy hand to grab it. Thad sympathised with the delayed reaction; several other beers had been spilled and righted over the course of the night, but none of it seemed to matter. He realised he'd been thinking about Sooki again, wondering what Zak was doing with her (taking her upstairs, then outside, then upstairs again). He had some idea, and could feel the thought lulling him into an unpleasant reverie. Shaking his head, he forced himself to concentrate on what was happening around him.

The tempo of the party had both slowed and accelerated; less seemed to be happening, but it was happening more intensely and in greater detail. Each stray movement seized Thad's attention. Jenna Pryce had shown up, along with someone he didn't recognise: a tall Hispanic girl with braided hair. Now they were staring at Mariah's digital camera as she showed them pictures of her new dachshund. Before Thad's eyes the two-dimensional dog elongated like an accordion and then contracted back into the camera screen. Pizza had materialised like manna and been launched at the walls, red blotches and vertical smears in the wake of stray slices. On the other side of the room, Debbie was sprawled on top of Ed Chiang, the two of them kissing with long, slow swallowing motions. Thad remembered Lucas making a claim on her earlier in the night, but at present Lucas was engaged in the monastically rapt contemplation of a stray wad of bread on the table. Thad reached out and tried to pitch him over. Lucas wobbled but did not fall down.

Thad was seated close enough to Angela that he could smell her jasmine perfume, which seemed to him only the outermost veil of a more intense scent inside her, a fog hiding some ultimate experience. The words 'ULTIMATE EXPERIENCE' appeared in his mind as a block of solid letters that cycled through hundreds of fonts before dissolving into disconnected scribbles. He felt the blood pounding in his head like a drum. Something clicked in his ears. He wiped a sheen of sweat from his forehead.

"WARHAMMER FORTY K!" Lucas blurted. "Has anyone played . . . I mean . . ."

Angela's crystal necklace kept glinting, an effect Thad attributed less to the overhead bulb than to his own altered chemistry. The silver band glowed as if superheated, and the individual crystals vibrated with a sound like the subtlest pressure on piano keys. Angela moved and her leg came to rest against his; he could see and feel her *cool bare thighs white swan curving take to um private bounce my inner white ingress flower pattern skirt of flower forest air all pressure blonde hair the bracelet around inner nerve forest under my dick is too hard cant stand up suddenly.*

He felt total calm. The moment, the time for action had come. He acted cleanly and without hesitation, placing his hand on top of her thigh but exerting no pressure, only mapping her skin with his palm. Angela looked at him and opened her mouth but finally said nothing, holding his gaze for a moment before looking away.

"Shit, it's getting pretty hot," he said. "Let's go take a break, I'll show you my, um, collection."

"What collection?"

"You'll see."

"I want to go outside, actually," Angela said. "Smoke break. I don't usually smoke, just . . . social occasions."

"We can do it upstairs. I mean . . . there's an ashtray."

"Okay."

He took her hand and led her up to his room, which he had tidied earlier in the day by jamming everything in the closet and fixing its doors shut with a coathanger. Angela glanced at its bulge before moving to the window and taking out an unopened pack of Marlboro Menthols. She stripped off the plastic wrapping, tapped the pack on the back of her hand, flipped the top and took out a cigarette. Watching her light up, Thad felt waves of *altered alertness heaving fullness close to illness tight lips closed clenched soft puff of smoke taut backs of cool bare thighs humming in air all dark forest pressure under blonde hair bracelet breasts and flowering skirt hurry up and touch her.*

"So what collection?"

Thad took the cigarette out of her hand, tossed it to the ashtray on the sill and embraced her. Their mouths met and he felt the wet smoky warmth of her tongue, and at last his hands were digging into her clothes, the soft cotton of her shirt and synthetic silk of her dress; and then he was pressing against her tightly, her body moulding to match his frame.

"Stop . . . stop . . ."

Words were escaping from her lips, so he kissed her more forcefully and moved his hand to her breasts.

"Stop!"

He could feel the yielding outline of her bra and the softness beneath it, *soft hot glistening flower forest tangled damp nerves humming in air—*

"STOP!"

She pushed him away, hard enough that he stumbled. He felt a sudden rage and moved to grab her before regaining control of himself and straightening up. Angela took a step away from him, towards the door.

"Why do you want to kiss me so much?"

"It's no big deal," Thad said. He moved towards her. "But you look tense. I'll give you a massage. . . ."

She pushed his hands away and held up her own, the palms open in warning.

"No, really. I want to hear what you think. Why do you want to kiss me so much?"

Thad started to answer, then stopped himself. This was not the time for talking. Arguments at times like this, he knew, were impossible to win; even consenting to argue implied losing. He had to keep things physical to prevent the deadening words from taking over.

"'Cause it's what's real when we forget about all the bullshit."

"You mean you want to fuck me."

"I didn't say that."

"So you don't."

"Well um, like, what you, it ain't like, like I don't NOT want to . . ."

"Nice grammar."

"Sorry, can't compete with you college girls."

The pounding was back in his head, and he noticed that the walls seemed to be dripping something that looked like static. But only from the corners of his eyes—when he moved his head, the effect vanished.

If that's all you're interested in why don't you become in her heart as a unique grandiose incomparable man just jerk off I jerk off every day and I still need to have sex is that a problem how do you know that you mountain snow-lotus.

"What do you mean? I just know."

"Do you feel better when you jerk off?"

"No. Yeah. No, I mean . . . maybe I need to do it more, maybe I'm just a high sex-drive kind of guy. How much is too much?"

His legs felt leaden; he needed to sit down. Angela receded in front of him, then snapped back into place; he doubted she had moved at all, but suddenly it was impossible to fix her form.

"I don't have a number for you, Thad, but if jerking off every day doesn't satisfy you, I don't think more is the answer. Maybe there's something else you want. I want to help you to be more conscious about your sexual motivations. What is it you really want?"

Thad sat down on the bed. The interrogation seemed to be happening somewhere distant, some minimised chat window in the corner of his consciousness. He could still make out Angela's words, but they were stripped of all meaning, nothing but fluttering veils sustained by the lines of force in the room.

"Shit, I don't know. . . . I like girls."

"Okay, but you feel agitated. Let's be aware of what that could be. I think that sexual energy by itself feels great. It's an important source of vitality for people, our senses are heightened . . . we feel invigorated and alive. But you aren't enjoying that, you're frustrated. Why?"

He forced himself back to attention.

"Are you going to make me say it?"

"What?"

"Well, like, um, I haven't gotten any for a while."

"But you get physical release every day," Angela said.

"I meant with a real woman."

He thought now of Sooki and the frantic minutes he had passed alone with her in Zak's apartment, and earlier today. Even at this moment, with Angela's body imprinted on his hands and the scent of jasmine in the air, the doll loomed up as a monument to impossible desire. Why did something not real seem more than real?

"What do you crave about a real woman?"

"I don't know, just touching . . . talking . . . everything."

"Okay, so you're lonely?"

Thad faced the floor and steadied himself, feeling the static from the walls buzzing faintly. Angela at last relaxed her posture and moved closer, stopping on the verge of sitting beside him.

"Yeah. That's true," Thad said. "Just haven't, like, actually admitted that to myself, I guess."

"How is that to admit to yourself?"

"Sad."

"What's sad about it?"

"I feel like a loser. Like I'm not any different from Zak."

She sat next to him. "Because you're avoiding your own feelings, your desire to connect with a woman is manifesting itself as wanting to have sexual intercourse all the time. Do you see how you're substituting one motivation for another?"

He turned on her sharply and felt the moment snap back into focus. "Well, that might be true . . . smart. So you think you got me figured out, just 'cause you went to college. Well, let's see, genius. What do YOU want?"

"Me?"

"Yeah."

Angela smiled. "I want to live without lying to myself and I want to make a difference in the world. I'm trying to get into journalism . . ."

"Journalism about what?"

"Everything. This kind of thing. The social situation, where we're at now."

It sounds like a bunch of bullshit there is no social situation things just happen so what about your future are you men are born with great sexual energy and strong persistence as their rights going to work and get married like everyone else or just keep working and increasing sperms pretend it's important I haven't it's too soon to know but I believe that people should have relationships based on equal standing the orgasm time no one should have to feel desperate or coerce anyone else.

"Yeah, except that's not the way it works, is it? Someone has to make a move or nothing happens. I'm not, like, claiming to be the greatest guy there is, but at least I'm honest."

"I don't think you're honest," she said. "Not to yourself. You don't really know why you're doing anything."

"And you do?" Thad asked.

"I try to have principles."

"Principles, that's more bullshit . . . you just think what all your friends think."

"And you don't? What makes you different from those other guys down there? Because none of them seem very appealing to me. So where's this leading?"

Thad shook his head of sandy-coloured hair and threw up his hands in mock protest. "Too many questions . . ."

Angela walked to the window, took the ashtray from the sill and carried it back to the bed. She lit a cigarette and smoked it in brief, shallow inhalations.

"I'm a journalist. Asking questions is what I do. Why do you think I came here?"

"I don't know . . . because you were into me?"

"You really think I was into you? After you tried to bribe my little sister and called me a bitch in public?"

"Yeah, I think you were. You were probably around a bunch of pussies up in that . . . where was it, Vassar? And you got bored with them. I'm not some uncontrollable maniac, but I do what I want, when I want, right? So yeah, I was into you, and I gave Maryann a little tip and told her to go enjoy herself. 'Cause I felt bad, yeah? Same way I felt bad when she walked in the door tonight. You know this isn't a party for kids?"

"You said there wouldn't be anything bad."

"Yeah, and you really believed that? Come on, girl genius. You knew what it was and you still brought her. Do you even know where she is now?"

Angela hesitated. "She's . . ."

Don't worry she's got her little boyfriend down there with her you know I don't think you're really trying to protect her I think it's the other way around you're trying to use her to protect yourself but she doesn't promoted clitoral stimulation give a shit she's chilled out she's more like me than latent lesbianism you Angela laughed in the midst of inhaling and fell into a coughing fit Marybeth like you yeah she's a total dude Thad said a deadhead she'll be into reggae next year just wait without waiting for her to answer Thad took off his shirt his muscles well-defined by genetic disposition clitoral but softened through idleness glistened with a layer of sweat his face was flushed promoted clitoral stimulation his eyes sparkling Angela broke into another coughing fit of laughter and you're stripping down why fuck I want to fucking fuck you now that's your problem not mine fuck you let's go on a real date what to Burger King the movies again no one clitoral goes on dates.

"I'm old-fashioned. I want to go on a real date with you. With waiters and wine and everything. I'm not as poor as I look, you know? I just don't give a shit about looking like some rich asshole. What you see is what you get. But I can do classy."

She laughed once more and looked at him. Feeling the cigarette's heat edging to the filter, she pushed it into the ashtray.

"Hey," she said in a serious voice, "I need to go pee."

"Just outside the door, to the left."

After she had gone out of the room Thad looked down and noticed that he had a huge erection.

It then occurred to him that *of course oh motherfucking Christ yes the reason yes that Angela had to yes Ryan's a genius go to the toilet!!!—the motherfucking Germany Sex Drops, fool!* He had a sudden vision of a dam breaking and water flooding the land.

He took off his jeans and underwear and climbed under the covers of the bed.

"When she comes back, the talking's over," he thought to himself.

He fished under the mattress until he found a Trojan Brand Fire & Ice lubricated condom which he shoved under his buttocks and then positioned himself, one arm behind his head, chest showing, so that he would look as enticing as possible.

And he waited.

He waited.

Waited.

The night was deep and right for stimulus, but without stimulus soft, and after about fifteen minutes he realised that he was bored and that Angela probably wasn't coming back. He got up, got dressed and went downstairs.

The only people there were Clive and Marybeth. They were holding hands. A Rick Springfield record was spinning on the turntable.

"Like, um, where is everyone?" Thad asked.

"Some people just left. My sister and a bunch of

other people said they were going to some sort of adult emporium."

"They said you knew about it," Clive put in.

"Fuck," Thad said.

He took out his cell phone and texted Angela:

U MISSED OUT

About a minute later a reply came:

SORRY FORGOT MY SIS CAN U TAKER HER HOME ADDRESS 679 LANDRELL DRIVE THX

Thad stood staring at the message for a few moments.

"Angela wants me to take you home," he said, presently.

"Me?" Marybeth asked.

"Yeah."

"Can you take me too?" Clive asked.

"I got a motorcycle. Just room enough for her, dude. Sorry."

"I'll let Clive walk me home," Marybeth said.

"Sorry," Thad said, "no dice. Your sister wants me to take you. She doesn't want you to get into trouble."

"It's okay," Clive said. His face looked sad. "It's okay," he said.

Saturday, 6th October, 1.03 a.m.

Ryan g(   )ngela, Maria(   )d Jenna a ride to the se(   )op in his imp(   )nge Lotus. It had(   )en diffic(   )m to convi(   )m to come, although An(   )iced some concerns. Ralph and Lucas follo(   )m in Ralph's old Chevy sedan, Ra( )h's hand(   )he wheel and Lucas's v(   )n his ear. A( )er a w(   )lt themsel(   )used into one mind, som(   )tative new orga( )sm crammed inside (   )ke a mollusk in its sh(   ). Lucas (   )f other analogies of var(   )acy as he (   ) Ralph to swerve arou(   )he few night tim(   )estrians who crossed the(   )th: two peas in a tin, sardines (   )*od of conjoined dol(   ) sonar streaking hands across ( )vement intergalactic ic(   )mers scooping oyster sex gut(   )tuned fucking monolith time beam of (   ) June purple holocaust ringing in the (   )ed night mom(   )een each breath.*

     They sti( )d: tequ(   )onas, joi(   )ol Ranch Dor(   )izza slice(   )ills, two pack(   )arettes. They stopped (   ) fed each other until a D(   )uck pulled up behind them and honked. Somehow they (   ) yan's Lotus and fol(   )strip containing the sex shop, which (   )ontained *strip gea(   )ldos leath(   )icate fish scale n(   )f lace encasing plastic limbs and (   )atures linked in tourni(   )ments tied together under raw pink light at the back.* They pulled in(   ) the conjoined organism staggered onto the pavement, vomited, then righted itself.

Ryan go(   )f the Lotus an(   )he door for the girls.
H(   )is eye on Jenna, whose blandly dyn(   )re suited
his tastes, b(   )ela came in a close second. Mar(   )e,
beneath con(   )e looked up an(   )aced as Ralph's
Che(   )lled into the lot. The car, old and po(   )d-for,
offended his sensibilities.

"Wel(   )oks like tha(   )ne," he said. "Ni(   )uan
should be inside already. I told them to get started early. It
c(   )tty wild in there."

"Wild is good," Jen(   )id.

Rya(   )red at her raptly. Like a raptor.

"We nee(   )quila!" Mariah said.

"Got a(   )rinks you n(   )ide."

A SCULPTURAL SUGGESTION

The shop enc(   )ilities through its light(   )ec-
ture: not that the two c(   )rated. The decor an(   )
ested within the architecture like (   )itants,
w(   )ests. Now, under the auspices of its organ-
iser, the (   )ome to an agreement with the s(   )ral
elements, and certain corners beckoned to Angela, Mariah,
Jenna and Ralph, Lucas and Nic(   )urn, suggesting
obscure (   )ests, moving through space at the
whims of their own internal (   )es, fell into complicated
rhythms. Without (   )us (   )ness they (   )ed to each
other, (   )n by the walls and the floor beneath them, a
warm complicity presen(   )cts thronging the room.

THE BACK ROOM CONTAINED

Obj(   )rts in storage. (   )os, masks, lea(   )
mes, bod(   )s, hot ( )x, rings, cl(   )chers, cha(   )gs

and restr(   )ks, posters, magazines, kni(   )aine,
anal b(   )gs, contrace(   )ible underw(   )ible
underwear: pant(   )dies, briefs, thongs, str(   )o press-
on na(   )etics and role-play scenario sourceb(   )
nted candles and nurse uni(   )lice uniforms and airline
stewardess uniforms and cat(   )bra suits and tigersuits
with tig(   )ini briefs and soft claws. And metal, plastic
and rubber (   )s. Enem(   )s. And a bag of unopened
diapers.

"RELEASE THE SPIDERS"

   Juan g(   )e ( )l table and all the girls (   )nd all
the boy(   )aled when Juan r(   )iders and Ryan
laug(   )nd ope(   )eer and all the spiders came skitter-
ing tittering twittering in on hot l(   )s all eyes and
hot se(   )uths but really ( )ed of the blood-warmed
drugged human flesh filli(   )om. An(   )he spiders
skitt(   )nd tittered and wa(   )ed across th(   )elt of
the ta(   )nd Angela wandered up and down the aisles w( )
Rioko Tomita from Tokyo a( ) Benjamin f( )m the te( )
i( )ze in a da(   )wirled he( )ms and felt high hot whit(
)aven melt(   )he air whi(   )railed past her visi(   )d
she felt t(   )rs flowing in a rive(   )ind dragging he(
)motional muck bu(   )et like a sundae and Azealia Banks
ca(   )ers from somewhere an(   )uld see Jenna and
Ry( )re kis(   )d boys she d(   )ow were dancing
to the m(   )rinking and taki(   )ff their clo(   )
he laughed at how rid(   )ll see(   )t a lit(   )en
though it intere(   )s Jenn( )d Ryan su( )d e(   )er's
fac(   )hen he w(   )ing her up a(   )ing her aro(   )e
room while she laugh(   )ariah moved by he(   )ike some
anc(   )ility god(   )midst the flowing (   )ot *magic ruby*

r(   )ance curv(   )ht exposu(   )sh (   )ving arms this emo(
)ght in webbed lig(   )nd outside all bo(   )ling free in the ai(
)ms waving servant of the ru(   )dess of night while the lights
changed overhead and Ra(   )as were (   )ing and ( )
king and she almost forgot about the spiders.

PARZY VS JUAN

Parzy was from New (   )and and had a (   )
ner, or it could (   )ect of the room and whatever
he had taken. Juan had already released the spiders and w(
)rk. They g(   )wn to i(   )ps and limbs locking in the
aisles, amidst the m(   )e racks, the r(   )ncient magazine
plastic limelight fi(   )ts and ancient hair all tented in pu(   )nts
and waxed lips and plastic-bagged periodicals whose mod-
els were now mostly dead or married or both, reduced to
revenant ang(   )ographic after(   )aller than
Juan, overshadowed him; and on his knees (   ) his pale
th(   )is in his mouth and massage(   )skin and
gl(   )ing th(   )er with his hands. The se(   )
ts and pooled in a puddle, a little lake Juan cupped in his
hands and r(   )th. He wa(   )is ( )e and Parzy
knelt and licked it clean.

NICHOLAS COAKLEY FUCKED HER UNDER RAW PINK LIGHT

Nicholas Coakley, a (   )de ( )th from ( )land, had
been ( )ed by ( )an; they were (   )f Justin Isis.
Nick had h(   )veral bee(   )oint and was feeling utterly
bl( )d. He felt li(   )ed into an ac(   )y he had long susp(   )
ut which had taken the cur(   )nces to reve(   )
ll. He notic(   )riah dancing and w(   )er to join her. His

consciousness s(   )at and th(   )re enmeshed in
each other and her b(   )ed endless; he could m(   )ide
it and they would ext(   )ever as one sub(   )nce. Nicholas Coakley fucked her savagely under raw pink light,
Mariah's h(   )t in his h( )r, Nick's h(   )n her br(   )
s, her mouth f( ) of t(   )a. They enveloped the room and
it c(   )side them l(   )test pink mote, a ti(   )all of
sound and fire.

THE BLACK MASK

The black mask came out. N(   )eneat( )ight bene(   )
ight be( )ath night be(   )th night beneath n(   )scended.
Angela in the ais(   )onger list(   )o the s(   )*ties and the*
crawl(   )ngs com(   )gh the seco(   )cing chop(   )nd
strobe li(   )dless exten(   )ed with fles(   )
ask and the craw(   )ke a tin(   )ll of f(   )
d cra(   )ack cat with a human face.

OUR FLUIDS FOR THE ANTI-WOMB, CONCAVITY
OF THE PORCELAIN CERVIX

Hunched over the bowl the white warm mother wel-
coming him back.

THEY MADE IT HOME SOMEHOW

They did.

Saturday, 6ᵗʰ October, 1.32 a.m.

Thad wondered why he had agreed to take Marybeth home. He'd much rather have explored the sex shop with everyone else. Maybe in the end he would have got somewhere with Angela. He hated to think that one of the other guys, like Lucas or Ralph, would be harvesting the fruits of his German Sex Drops.

He saw that his gas was low so slid in front of the pumps at Buzzy's Mini Mart, got off his bike and let Marybeth sag forward onto the handle bars. Whatever she'd consumed at the party, her comedown was a sleepy one—almost comatose.

Two shapeless characters were standing by the ice cooler in front of the store.

"Hey bro, can we borrow a quarter?" one of them said as Thad approached.

"Naw man."

"How 'bout a dollar?"

Thad didn't reply. Just as he was opening the door to go in, one of the men said:

"What about the doll on your bike, she got any dough?"

The door closed behind him. A lightning bolt went off in Thad's head. The motherfucking pamphlets Ryan had given him! He fished in his pocket and pulled them out. There were two, to two different places.

He took out his cell phone and looked at the time. 1.36. He doubted if he called anyone would be around, but it could be worth a try.

He dialled the number of the first and a somewhat chipper female voice with a heavy Indian accent came through.

"Bhansali Discount Love Dolls and Trading, can I help you?"

"Yeah, um, you guys open?"

"Yes, our business hours are from 9 P.M. to 9 A.M. seven days a week. And how may I direct your call?"

"I have a girl that I thought you might want to mould."

"Is she sexually attractive?"

"Very."

"Yes, we might well be interested."

"How much do you, um, pay?"

"We offer a hundred dollar coupon to either the Dosa Hut, which has a fine array of idly feasts, or Mr Song's Korean Palace, which is very much popular with the young and hip crowd."

"You offer dining coupons?"

"Yes, sir."

Thad pressed the End Call button.

The second number he dialled was to a place called Sundown Dolls.

A deep male voice came from the other end.

"Yeah?"

"Is this Sundown Dolls?" Thad asked.

"Yeah."

Thad explained what he wanted.

"If she's cute you can bring her by," the man said. "But don't get your hopes up."

"Um, like, how much do you pay?"

"We don't talk about money over the horn. Just bring her by."

Twenty minutes later Thad pulled up in front of a large brick building on Euclid Avenue.

Thad rang the bell with his left hand, Marybeth propped up in his right arm, her head sagging against his shoulder.

An overweight man in white sneakers and huge baggy jeans came to the door. His eyes took in Marybeth from toe to head and then splashed over to meet Thad's half-grinning face.

"You the guy that called?" he asked.

"Yeah. I'm, uh, Brian."

The man stuck out his hand—a hot, unctuous paw that gripped Thad's in a lingering moment of companionship.

"I'm Fernie Gonzales. Product manager. Come in."

Thad dragged Marybeth into the front room—a small, pink-carpeted area furnished with four Lesro Savoy Series Bariatric Guest Chairs with black urethane arm caps. A large framed photo of goldfish hung on one wall and on another a framed *Grandeur Nature* poster. New Age keyboard music was being piped in through a sound system. The smell of Seven Archangels Darshan incense lingered in the air.

Thad flopped the girl down on one of the chairs.

Gonzales looked at Marybeth and whistled. "She's a cute one."

"Yeah."

"How old is she?"

"Don't worry about that."

"Do I look worried?"

"So you're interested?"

"Well, she has hell of nice features. Hell of nice. So, yeah, I guess maybe I am interested." He shifted his weight from one foot to the next. "The truth is that a lot of people come here with gals they want us to mould—and I'm always willing to take a look, but I turn almost everyone away. They never seem to got the umph. Most of them couldn't be used to mould an anime frog pillow doll. So in general we just use professional models, but even a lot of times they don't have the umph. But this girl . . . she's interesting."

"She's got the, er, umph?"

"Her nose, cheekbones. I guess she does. Reminds me a little of one of those Candy Girl Petite Series Fs. Wait here and I'll get Mariya. She owns the place, so it's her show."

"Right on."

Thad sat down. There were a few doll catalogues and various magazines on a glass-topped table next to him. He picked up the October issue of *Idollatry* and started to leaf through the pages, checking out the various photos, briefly scanning over an article on how to modify a Plush Double Heart Beetle bear Sleepy Doll for the most pleasure and was just starting to read another on bamboo wives when the door opened and Gonzales walked in accompanied by a woman.

"Brian, this is Mariya Oksana, CEO of Sundown Dolls. You can talk business with her."

"Okay, cool."

Gonzales left and Thad sat staring at the woman.

At first he thought that it was some sort of joke, and that Gonzales had dragged in a doll instead of a living person. In fact, most of the dolls Thad had been checking out in the magazine looked more like real women than she did. Her skin had a decidedly plasticky appearance. She had a Swarovski crystal bindi on her forehead. Her long blonde hair was parted in the middle, the part being marked with pink kumkum powder, and the hair was brushed forward so it spilled in dual waves over massive silicone breasts which were imprisoned in a skin-tight vomit-green blouse with black polka dots. Her feet, strangely large objects that seemed to have been made under the influence of Alberto Giacometti, were balanced in high heel platform shoes.

She stood fiddling with her iPhone, her eyes flicking from the phone to Marybeth and back to the phone. Then her eyes suddenly darted up and, like two intense blue rays, met Thad's.

"Your name is Brian?"

"Yeah, um, right."

"You are good-looking boy."

She spoke almost correct English with a heavy Ukrainian accent.

"Thanks."

"I recognise you."

"Recognise me?"

"Indeed. We held hands on Teutonia. You were called Valiant Odr but then received your mission to help the Adamic race and disappeared."

"Um, yeah."

"Your girlfriend. She has a handsome face. It has a very high frequency. Her face on woman's body would make a nice model."

"So, you'll, like, take her?"

"Indeed. If you let us mould her face, you can have full doll afterwards. I will give you some Ancient Shrine Oil to rub on her. You can then play with her whenever you want and instead of wasting your life chasing girls around city, you can have more time to surf internet. I will give you lessons on lucid dreaming."

"Yeah, like, um, that sounds real interesting. But I was thinking more in the line of cashola."

"Well, indeed, money is 'nother matter. Our custom-made dolls sell for five thousand U.S. dollars and up."

"Yeah, okay, so like, if you give me five grand cash that would be groovy."

She frowned. "I will give you two thousand dollars."

"Cash?"

"You Americans!" She frowned. "So materialistic! Yes—you will have your CASH! Now, you wait here or go into the mould room. Indeed I cannot stay and chat with you, I must do meditation, astral travel and internet search."

She turned and wagged her meagre bottom out of the room and a moment later Gonzales returned.

"Sounds like you got it all worked out," he said.

"Yeah."

"You gonna wait here or go into the mould room and watch?"

"I guess I'll watch."

"I'll carry her bro," Gonzales said.

Thad followed him through the door, and found himself in a giant room. Doll parts were everywhere—arms, legs, torsos. Hairless heads were ranged about, their faces blank—eyeless, lips and skin unpainted. Moulds were stacked on giant shelves. Jars full of eyelashes, bottles of wig shampoo and other things were scattered about. On one wall was a sort of rack on which were placed numerous faces. Partially finished dolls hung from hooks.

Four women, between the ages of forty and seventy, were sitting at tables assembling dolls, but they hardly looked up when the two men passed through.

Gonzales carried Marybeth into another room towards the back, large, but much smaller than the first.

There were various work tables and projects in progress and, in an open space in the room, a man in his mid-thirties wearing a t-shirt and bandana, was doing Pa-Kua.

"Hey," he said, stopping and turning towards them.

"Hey Trevor, we got a face for you to mould." Gonzales set Marybeth down on one of the work tables. "In and out job."

"And who's this guy?" Trevor asked, jabbing his thumb towards Thad.

"This's Brian," Gonzales said as he walked out of the room. "It's his whatchamacallit."

"Hi Brian, my name's Trevor."

"Hey."

Trevor looked closely at Marybeth.

"Okay, I guess I better get to work."

First he took a number of photos with a Vivitar Vivi-Cam X029 and then slipped a plastic hair net over her hair, put a straw in her mouth and inserted one up each nostril. He then sprayed her face with a coating of Brownells T.F.E. Dry Lube & Mould Release. He put on a pair of yellow plastic gloves, opened a bucket of moulding rubber and began to paint her face with the thick purple liquid.

"She's really enchanting," he said as he applied the latex. "I can see how her face could have sex gong magic fu."

"What?"

"Oh, sorry, it is something my teacher was telling me about."

"You mean Mariya?"

Trevor laughed. "No, she's my boss, not my teacher. My teacher is a guy named Joey Si. He does videography and web design in the Yon Yat lineage. The goal of the whole thing is knowledge and wisdom. I'm a certified believer. I already did the Little Dipper Program . . ."

"Hey," Thad asked, "how long will this take? It's just the face, right?"

"Yeah. Not long. Couple of hours. Why, afraid she'll wake up?"

"Kinda."

"What's she on?"

"Just some beer and fondue I guess."

"We better give her a little prick then," Trevor said.

He went over to a desk, opened a drawer and pulled out a hypodermic needle.

"A little Zolpidem'll do ya," he said as he jabbed it into her arm.

"Hey, you mind if I like, um, look around while you're working?"

"You feel anxious?"

"Um."

"You should really be taking wild mountain root. If you take the four gentlemen decoction it'll help calm the hot palms."

"Yeah, um, right. I'm going to take a look around."

He wandered back into the large room. The women were now taking a break. Three of them were eating out of Tupperware containers (noodles, bean salad, cold turkey dog) while the fourth, the eldest of the party, was partaking of an eel roll that she had got at Cousin's Supermarket and drinking a diet root beer. She glanced up with an annoyed look at Thad and then turned her face back to her bad sushi.

Going further on, he found a corridor that led to the left, which he turned down. Through an open door he saw Gonzales at a desk engaged in paperwork, but the latter didn't notice him, so he continued and came to a pair of partially open BM-1-2 Avanti solid bamboo flush panel doors.

He slipped his head through the opening.

There were no chairs in the room, only HANZHIYUAN velour, heart-shaped meditation cushions. Various large crystals were positioned about the place. To one side of the room was stationed, away from the wall, a Korg Krome 73-Key Keyboard Workstation. Hanging from the wall behind the keyboard was a framed 24 x 36 inch poster titled 'The Key to Eternity'—a garish slab of spiritual mediocrity, featuring an owl, a purple rose, a blindfolded woman and the sun setting behind Stonehenge. On one of the other walls was a painting Mariya had done herself—a multi-coloured pyramid against an amaranth purple background.

Mariya was sitting cross-legged on one of the cushions staring at her iPhone.

She looked up and noticed Thad.

"Indeed, enter," she said. "Close doors behind you."

He did as he was told and swallowed hard.

"Sit," she said.

Thad went over to one of the cushions and sat down. He felt nervous. He looked over at Mariya and wondered if she would invite him to have sex with her. If she did, he was determined to really put on a show. Angela hadn't put out, but Mariya was on a totally different level. She took out a Zippo 24472 Yin and Yang Black Matte Lighter and lit a stick of incense.

"Now we meditate," she said.

"What do I do?"

"Concentrate on point."

Thad closed his eyes and tried to concentrate, but he wasn't sure where the point was *this chick is cold but hot would um love to get down her like um pants it was all okay in the sex had no problem sex lasts no more than like five minutes before saving the um like long-lasting condoms any sensations the same problems even if I can't um like do it with a doll again even with the excitement not felt like um what's in a doll's rosebud um all okay in the sex had no problems even with the um astral donger excitement not felt but like the plastic cockpit right now like let her feel the drumstick even the normally excited I cannot possibly by the fact that a previous partner was more articulate and stimulating sex had not previously steamed himself infuriates the fact that like stroking the bratwurst the state me on the strength do not even know how to live have not had sex in the day Zak's a pussy of our acquaintance pink taco now go and all the you care about Sooki right men begin to argue say women are giving me on the first date I'll ding dong McDork tell me what to do because no normal sex would not be normal relations I cannot possibly give a like inorganic girl the meat sword um by the fact that a previous partner was more articulate and stimulating sex they call me Longfellow ha ha had not previously steamed himself infuriates the fact that the state of the wang dang doodle me on the strength of my lap rocket do not even know how to live.*

Suddenly he felt something warm touching him. He opened his eyes. It was Mariya, but she was diaphanous, see-through—and behind her was another Mariya—the Mariya of plastic-like flesh, sitting cross-legged.

"What's going on?" he asked

"Now we engage in astral body travel," she replied.

She took his hand and pulled his astral body out of his physical body.

"Yeah," he said.

His eyes wandered to her breasts, but, large as they were, they lacked definition and he felt somewhat disappointed.

Holding him by the hand, she led him to one of the paintings, that of the pyramid, and together they floated into it. The triangular object was at some distance, placed in the midst of space and they glided towards it. When they came close, Mariya pointed to an opening and led Thad through it into a high hallway painted with giant grimacing emoticons.

The way was strewn with tiny green and yellow plastic elephants.

"In the temple," Mariya said, "adorable elephant is playing as sign of Aquarian energies. When it moves, its head shakes up and down, indeed its ears shake front and back, its tail shakes right and left and downloaded is purest essence. It is the best guide in the temple in playing for harmonic resonances."

Moving on, they came to a vast chamber done in purple tonal hearts pre-pasted wallpaper. In the centre of the place was a Max West 3pc Red Bonded Leather Living Room Sofa Set.

A figure rose up from the 58 x 32 inch loveseat. He was extraordinarily tall and his muscular physique was apparent beneath his burgundy Alexander Del Rossa Men's Water Absorbent Fleece Bathrobe. His hair was done up in numerous long braids. A bright-white goose was sitting on top of his head.

"Like, um, who the hell are you?" Thad asked

"I am the Queen of Heaven, dear one," the other replied in a somewhat fey voice.

"I have brought Valiant Odr," Mariya said. "Long ago we did vibration activity in Azure."

"Did you give him any glow enhancement sessions?"

Mariya shook her head in the negative.

"Well," the Queen of Heaven said, turning towards Thad, "it seems to me that you don't got the electric polarity to really attract women. I'd really just LOVE to give you what you're looking for, dear one, but, y'know—what is it?"

"Um, I dunno."

The Queen of Heaven laughed. "That's the point. Maybe you're just here to feel my oneness! It's perfectly deliciously satisfying."

"I'd like to, um, know my future."

"Indeed," Mariya said, "tell this Valiant Odr his future."

The Queen of Heaven lifted up Thad's hand and gazed at his palm.

"I see a paradigm shift," he said in a serious voice.

"Huh?"

"You gotta recalibrate your frequency, otherwise your earthly manifestation is gonna be overcome by dark energy. Yes, dear friend, bliss and joy can permeate the minds and hearts of any soul who becomes opened to the higher realms and the brimming energies and communications we of the higher realms have to offer, and you are feeling the after-effect of certain aha moments you foolishly ignored."

Thad was about to say something when the goose flew from the Queen of Heaven's head and started flapping its wings in front of his face.

Suddenly he was back in his own body, his eyes open. Gonzales was in the room talking.

"Hey Mariya, some guys are here to see you."

"Guys?"

"Yeah, they say they're from *Idollatry*. Got an interview with you or some jazz."

"Indeed this is impossible. My iPhone alert told me nothing."

"Well, they're here all hopped up to see you."

"Ah, well send them in."

Two men came in. They introduced themselves as Sid Modimolle and Billy Glandzk. Sid was wearing a grey Apollo King Men's 2 Piece Executive Discount Suit in luxurious wool feel fabric that he had bought at the Clothing Connection Online for $64.78. Billy was wearing jeans, sandals and a bright orange vintage Hawaiian shirt.

"Welcome," Mariya said.

"Hey," said Billy, "we met before. Last year's doll expo."

"We on schedule for the interview?" Sid Modimolle asked.

"Indeed I had no iPhone alert," Mariya said in an agitated voice. "Interview impossible."

Modimolle frowned. "What the hell? We talked on the phone yesterday!"

"Just wanna snap some photos," Billy added.

"Very well," Mariya said, holding up one hand in a gesture of universal peace, "we will engage in interview."

"Far out," Sid said. "The first thing I want to ask is———"

"Indeed the problem," Mariya interrupted in a high-pitched, loud voice. "Indeed the problem with our time is that people have forgot the secret of the Egyptian sexual orgasm. With proper orgasm function, power is brought to the Mer-Ka-Ba lightbody. Sundown Dolls are specifically manufactured to enhance sexual orgasm of the Mer-Ka-Ba. Our plastic пихву are the only in universe designed on the Ankh system and we rub with DNA molecule. Sex with Sundown Dolls produces deepest physical levels of rejuvenated life force."

"So," Sid asked, "you believe that sex with Sundance Dolls is superior to sex with other doll brands?"

"Indeed, I do not wish to despise other brand dolls, but our doll is the only one on the market designed to aspect of both Tao te Ching and revelations of divine Atlanteans. Indigenous people spirituality has been practiced in Baltic before recorded history. The fundamental premise of all indigenous spirituality is to honour and respect пихву."

Sid grinned. "Care to give us a demonstration?"

"Indeed I will now engage in beautiful song."

She went to the keyboard and, after lighting further incense, set her fingers to the keys. A choir of sound spilled forth and she began to sing in a high-pitched enchanting voice:

Приходьте купити цю
пластикові піхви
зроблений
У сонячних НД

Приходьте купити
це піхву
Венери пелюсток
Ця пластикова дівчина
Зроблено з використанням сонячної енергії

Two hours and forty-six minutes later, Thad was dragging a still unconscious Marybeth out of the moulding room. Gonzales walked up to him and handed him an envelope.

"The boss told me to give you this."

Inside were twenty crisp new hundred dollar bills as well as an invitation to attend one of Mariya Oksana's out-of-body-travel classes.

"She's a real smart cookie," Gonzales said.

"Yeah."

Outside, the cool night air partially revived Marybeth. Thad managed to get her on the motorbike and she clung to him weakly as he sped through the streets.

It was 5.22 in the morning when Thad dragged Marybeth from the back of his motorcycle to her doorstep, leaned her there, rang the bell and took off.

Monday, 8ᵗʰ October, 10.19 a.m.

Thad had long since lost track of who had said what to whom and who was supposed to have said what. It had come down to a simple equation: steal Sooki first; ask ransom money later. Outside the door of Zak's apartment, Thad looked back at Ralph and Lucas, who held a quantity of paint-stained decorator's canvas between them, and put a finger taut with the latex of a surgical glove to his lips.

"We've got to do this professional," he said. "Not a sound till we're out."

Then, with a motion as if to say, 'watch this', he extracted a key from the back pocket of his jeans and slid it smoothly into the lock.

The door swung open on the tilting fizz of silence, the rooms of the apartment seeming drunk with their own waiting emptiness. Thad stepped forward onto the spotless, studio floorboards with an exaggerated caution learned from the big screen. He almost forgot his own injunction, and was about to say, "Let's go!", but remembered in time, and, holding up his hand instead, gave a flicking beckon with his fingers.

They went straight for the bedroom, bundling the supine figure into the canvas with such ruthlessness it seemed that they expected resistance. They lay their catch upon the floor while Thad knelt with one knee beneath each armpit and, his manner that of someone cracking a safe, removed the sleeping face from the front of the head. Getting to his feet, he took the face to the back of the room, placed it on a shelf, and, from a stand on the same shelf took a different face whose open eyes seemed to look on helplessly at all that took place. He put the sleeping face on the stand where the other had been, and, from a rack, he picked out the pink blur of a tongue more or less at random. Returning to the figure on the canvas sheet, he affixed the seeing face and the tongue in the place where there had temporarily been nothing. Something troubled him. He snatched the choker from Sooki's neck and held it out as if it were a grenade sans pin. Standing and looking about himself, he left the room, searching with an increasingly frantic manner, and finally deposited the unwanted item in the ice-box of the refrigerator before returning to the bedroom where Ralph and Lucas were wrapping up the inanimately startled Sooki like Cleopatra in a carpet.

Soon they were outside and wrestling the canvas bundle into Lucas's '98 Plymouth Breeze Sedan. Thad got into the back seat with the bundle propped next to him. There was a jolt as they sped away from the kerb. With the car moving, the three of them began to relax a little. Thad and Ralph lit up cigarettes, and Lucas, who was driving, turned on the radio. By the time they had got out of town, their tension had almost entirely evaporated. They sped between wooded hills with the windows down. For no obvious reason Thad suddenly let out something between a howl and a yahoo. He flicked the butt of a cigarette out the window.

"Well, no one seems to be following," he said. "Jesus, this shit's making me paranoid. Lucas—you sure this place we're headed is empty?"

"Yeah, I'm sure."

"We got the camera, right?"

"Yeah, we got it."

"I gotta admit, this is a first, even for me."

Thad was silent for some time, serene, letting the wind blow through his hair. To the left, the variegated colours of the trees cried out autumn's splendour. Some of the land around here was state forest and they passed a blueberry farm. Thad saw part of a derelict old iron bridge, penetrating the canopy of trees, flash by, no doubt a marker of local history.

"I'm gonna see if we got her the right way up," said Thad.

He began to unravel the paint-stained canvas, and to pull down its edges, until Sooki's head was revealed, her hair badly ruffled and her lipstick smeared. She stared straight ahead. Thad, in turn, stared straight at her.

"Your old man's not here now to stop me having a good look at you, is he?" said Thad. "Hmmm. You're not saying anything, but I notice you didn't put up much of a fight."

"Hey dude," called Ralph from the front, "what're you talking about?"

"Nothing. This is between me and this bitch."

"He's nuts," Lucas said.

"Yeah," Ralph agreed.

Thad let them talk.

Without taking his eyes off her, he extracted another cigarette from the packet and lit it. He inhaled and then blew smoke into her face. What was it that he found so provoking? Inhaling sharply again, he could not deny that in the presence of this non-organic bitch, he felt nervous and excited in a way he could not remember happening since he was a kid.

Yeah, in the end Angela had nothing on this chick.

It was stupid, of course. He couldn't recall now all the materials Mr Magister had so lovingly recited and described, with all his half-cracked reasons as to why they were superior to flesh, but he knew this doll was basically plastic and rubber.

He could hear Mr Magister's voice now, or was it his own from a preternaturally articulate dream?

"But why do you imagine that plastic is not alive?

"Contour and line—these things are the spirit. They tell a story we understand. But so far the only thing in human knowledge to have contours with which we could communicate, with which we could experience union, has been flesh. When other kinds of matter begin to speak our language, too, they can take us into such new worlds . . . the equivalent of exploring other planets."

Thad had sometimes wondered why Mr Magister had been so ready to talk about his obsession in such an intimate way. It suddenly occurred to him that he might be the only person that Mr Magister had really confided to. Was that why he had kept on paying money? In any case, Mr Magister had a story to tell, and Sooki had a starring role in it.

So, what was the story of this silicone slut, exactly? There was an expression on her face, it was true, but it was like that Mona Lisa painting that he had seen some nun talking about on TV saying that no matter where you were in the room the painting seemed like it was looking at you. The look on Sooki's face, in her eyes, could mean anything. Maybe no matter what man you were, Sooki put on an act of liking you.

"I'm beginning to think you had this all planned out from the start," said Thad. "I'd like to know what kind of fucking game you're playing."

Sooki, as usual, was demure.

"As if you're not Zak's fuck-puppet."

Then it came to him with the clarity of Sooki's perfectly moulded, story-telling contours—the reason that she turned him on so much (so much that he was ashamed to admit it and afraid he might lose control) was because she looked simultaneously as if she would do nothing and as if she would do anything.

Fired up, Thad grabbed her cheeks roughly from beneath the chin with one hand and jerked her head around so that she was facing him. He looked into her eyes, his mouth as tight and sneering as that of someone spoiling for a fight. Nothing was going to make him look away. He would see how demure this bitch was now.

Looking into her eyes, without thinking, he identified that they were blue. Then it seemed to him the colour was changing, like a butterfly's wing, from blue to kind of unearthly grey. And then he thought that the pupils were dilating. No, it was not just the pupils, the irises, too, were dilating. Hadn't this happened before? He seemed to half-recall something from his previous intrusions into Sooki's personal space. It was spooky, but he remembered his determination not to look away, no matter what she threw at him. He kept his eyes fixed on hers. There was a whoosh, and he realised that the irises were not dilating—he was falling into them. For an instant he felt a strange panic as he wondered if he would be swallowed up by the black holes at their centres, and then the black holes vanished, and he seemed to vanish, too, and all that was left was the blue-grey of a lunar landscape. The landscape became more distinct, and resolved into a hillside, a forest, trees. There could be seen, among the monochrome trees, some small stirring of movement. Behind the trunk of one of the trees was a boy, a look of solemn determination on his face as his arms worked with slow, repetitive force. There was a blade, gouging into the tree's bark. It was carving the shape of a heart. Inside the heart there seemed to appear some unspeakable secret, but this, for some reason, was hard to grasp.

Then there was a sense of falling away and with a jolt Thad found himself on the back seat of the car again, looking into the glassy blue eyes of the doll. He glanced over at Ralph and Lucas, but they did not seem to have noticed anything. The radio was playing and they were talking, but not about him. He let out a deep breath. Clearly there was something deep going on here, but he was not going to let it faze him. He had been through wild times before, and especially lately.

"So, Lucas, how much further to this house?" he asked, raising his voice over the combined roar of the engine and radio.

"Still a little way. I mean, you wanted an out-of-the-way place, right?"

"That's right. And you're sure the owners are away?"

"Yeah, it's one I've been scouting for a bit of a rumpus. It's some rich fucker's vacation place. They probably use it, like, two weeks in the year."

Monday, 8th October, 11.52 a.m.

The house was large, with a raised porch and whitewashed walls, and set, in peculiar isolation, some distance back from the road. Lucas, skilled in such things, swiftly dealt with the front door, and let them inside with a flourish, as if he were the master of the house. Once inside, the three of them rampaged with an urgency that suggested they were being timed to break a speed record.

Ralph tore through the liquor cabinet, sampling some bottles and handing others to his friends. After throwing furniture, ornaments, paintings and so on about in a frenzy of such focused energy that it seemed there must have been a purpose to it, even if none were apparent, they calmed down a little and paused in their activity, their chests heaving.

"Okay," said Thad, "let's get the stuff."

From the car they brought an assortment of objects and equipment, including Sooki, a camera, a length of chain and a hook on a screw.

"Ralph, see what you can find upstairs. Maybe some chick's clothes or anything interesting. Lucas, you get the chain fixed to the ceiling. Let's go wild."

While Ralph and Lucas busied themselves with the tasks assigned to them, Thad cleared a space in the middle of the room, placed a wooden chair there, and carefully seated

Sooki upon it. When he had arranged her in such a way that she would not fall off, he stood back and considered.

"No," he said, shaking his head. "Definitely not. We can't have the house as a background, even if it's fucked up. It's too fucking amateur. Lucas, you gotta hitch up the canvas for a background, like it's a studio . . . or some fucking sex dungeon or something. Have you got your spray paints?"

"Course I have."

"Great. We need some, like, real snuff-movie kind of graffiti on the canvas. Think you can do that?"

"Not a problem."

For some time the three of them were industriously absorbed in their respective tasks, punctuated by the sound of a power drill, hammering, the hiss of aerosols and so on. After twenty minutes or so the preparatory industry came to an end. They donned black balaclavas that they had tossed into an armchair. There were holes in the balaclavas for eyes and mouth only. Sooki now had her hands raised above her head, handcuffed to a chain suspended from the ceiling. Behind her was the canvas backdrop on which Lucas had sprayed evil faces, crude pornography and obscene slogans, such as, "Here's to the fuckpig!"

Now Lucas had his camera in his hands and was clicking away from different angles.

"Well, well, well," said Thad. "She really didn't put up much of a fight, after all. This is getting interesting. Okay, Lucas, keep shooting. I'm gonna take this bitch first."

Lucas and Ralph looked at each other and then back to Thad.

"Er . . . What are you talking about, Thad?" asked Ralph.

"What the hell do you think I'm talking about?"

"Are you . . . ?"

"I am."

Ralph squinted.

"Yeah. Okay. Thad, this is getting a bit weird. I mean, this is Zak's chick, right?"

"Yeah! This is his chick, and look at her! And what the fuck d'you mean 'getting weird'?"

"I think Ralph has a point," put in Lucas. "I mean, some things are sacred, right? I mean, this is just to scare him a bit. Just for the money, right?"

"Fuck that, man! Look, we've already broken the law. And, guess what, last time I checked, raping a doll was not a crime in this country. I don't know. D'you want to phone a lawyer and check now? Anyhow, who says it's even rape?"

"Well, I don't know . . ." said Ralph. "Did you actually check that?"

"Chickenshits! I'm doing it, and you guys can do what you like. Report me, if you like. Watch. Don't watch. Take photos. I couldn't give a shit now."

Thad's face had taken on an almost neon strawberry tint. He kept clenching his hands into fists and then opening them.

Lucas shrugged.

"Okay. It's your choice. Er . . . actually, I think I will take photos, if you're sure about that."

"Damn sure. Glad I remembered to put the tongue in this bitch," said Thad as he took a hank of hair at the back of her head in his fist and yanked her face up to look at him.

She still felt as if she had jumped from the door of a moving car, and it was already a week later. There was a kind of twitchiness in her body, and just how you knew when a cloud was gathering itself to rain, Angela felt sure that soon she was going to have a bad attack, and perhaps be sick in bed for a couple of weeks. She was determined to get something of substance written before then, while it was still fresh as hot puke in her soiled memory.

But everything was against her. Maybe she'd been a cruel elephant driver or something in a previous incarnation, because it was hard to work out the meaning of this cruddy karma from what she'd done in *this* life. The ring finger of her right hand was swathed in white gauze—not only useless for typing, but an actual impediment. Her middle finger kept dragging it down, so that she tapped keys she hadn't meant to, and she had to use her other fingers very deliberately to compensate for the keys the bandaged finger would ordinarily be tapping. Too bad she wasn't a two-fingered typist, she thought, or she'd be used to it. One thing she couldn't remember was exactly how she'd injured this digit. Why this one? It was disturbingly specific.

To make matters worse, her computer had been infected with something virulently wrong since she'd rashly clicked on a link in an e-mail sent to her from an unknown address. The screen kept freezing, or the computer wouldn't respond correctly to the keyboard. The link had been to a deeply weird video that still left her feeling rattled when she thought about it. The whole thing had been presented as a hostage video—the kind sent by kidnappers to anxious parents. But in this case, the hostage had been a doll—a sex doll. Was it a joke? Somehow it just didn't say funny to her. At least, though, the doll was no one she knew—well, not personally, as in, being a *person*. Presumably she'd been sent this by mistake. Was it spam, then? But she'd never heard of any spam like this. Also, looking closer at the doll, she had a pretty good idea she did recognise it. The kidnappers wore balaclavas, avoided looking in the camera, and so on, but she began to get a weird feeling that this hadn't ended up in her inbox completely at random.

What she *didn't* know—that was the maddening thing. Like how she'd injured her finger, and why Marybeth had come back from the party so late and with little bits of some purplish gunk in her eyelashes and hair and one or two other odd places. How big was this blank? What did it contain? She'd been so stupid to take Marybeth at all. Somehow, she'd trusted Thad. Not trusted him to *not be* a douche (to use the kind of grammar Thad and *Delilah* both favoured), but, without knowing it even, trusted him to be something *like* a decent human being. If only she knew exactly what had happened.

When she thought about it, something threatened to collapse inside. She had to be honest to write a good article, but, recalling the advice of Julia Westbrook, she just didn't know what was required of her: "We're all about that guys shouldn't be creeps not that women should be nuns." Well, it was true that Angela hadn't been much of a nun at the party, so that should count in her favour, but she wasn't sure that this was so commendable, after all. Besides, her not being a nun somehow overlapped with Thad's creepiness. The more she thought about it, the less likely it seemed she could be selective in a way that would highlight a message of which *Delilah* would approve. And, if she was *completely* honest—that she had gone to the party with some half-baked hope of scouting out a story—in view of all that happened after, and of that big, ugly gap of who-knew-what, it wouldn't sound like gritty journalism so much as the hysterical confession of a hmmm-okay-next-caller-please lunatic.

She sighed. She'd never had an assignment as tough as this at college. *Delilah* would reject the story. That was for sure. There wasn't going to be any shortcut to dreams for her. Really, she should start thinking about a day job.

As if it were of the utmost urgency, she broke off from writing her account of the party, clicked open a few browser windows, and began scrolling helter-skelter through Craigslist and the sites of agencies she'd used to get part-time and summer work.

She clicked on a side-bar ad and a looped video began. A short, firmly built brunette in tight navy blue pants and a hardware store-looking shirt took an electric screwdriver from her tool-belt and leant over a household work surface in order to inspect some kind of problem area.

"You could be an electrician," came the subtitles. "You could be a <u>sexy</u> electrician."

She closed the window with a huff and returned to the others. Nothing was inspiring.

Flicking away a stray lock of hair, she paused for reflection. Justine, at college, who was studying Arabic, had said she was going to be an electrician. Maybe it wasn't such a bad choice: good pay, independent, no need to work in an office, plus having an excuse to walk around all tooled up.

She couldn't find the ad again now, which was typical. Taking a tiny notebook with a pencil in the spine from her breast pocket, she opened it and wrote the single word "electrician", underlining it three times.

That decided, she felt less panicky returning to the article. The words from Julia Westbrook's e-mail returned to her: "Uh . . . duh . . . No?" Funny how the world of the magazine seemed so casual and accessible until you actually started chatting back to it. Then, up goes the casual drawbridge and down comes the casual portcullis.

She would write the article anyway, and send it anyway. She was a woman of wiles and means and grit—an electrician! Possibly.

She began to type at speed now. Her bandaged finger bobbed . . . and batted some random key.

"What the fuck! Where's it gone?"

Somehow the document had closed without saving.

She would have to go back to the last saved version and start again.

Just as she was opening the folder she'd been saving the document to, the cursor stopped moving, the whole screen seemed to give an electronic wince, and then went blank. The computer had crashed.

Wednesday, 10th October, 3.18 a.m.

Everything pushes—as a panicking crowd to the exit of a blazing building—towards the simple idea that it's okay, that 'it might never happen'. For Zak, it *had* happened. At least, while there was still some hope for an outcome that would restore détente between his soul and the universe, the truth had to be faced that the universe had not, on this occasion, hesitated in making a violent incursion into the territory of his soul. His defences had been almost non-existent, and he was quickly overcome. Without Sooki, sleep patterns, appetite and concentration were all fatally destabilised. His integrity, his autonomy, were revealed as fragile systems, and, as such, illusory. Yet he could not live except through those systematic illusions. When they were damaged, it was something like a moral duty to be distressed. Futile as it was, he had to torture himself, rehearsing acute vigilance for what had already taken place. Perhaps this was a form of prayer—bargaining with one's suffering. Zak had entered a desert of unforgetfulness—forgetting was the merciful shadow absent here. His every thought and feeling now was gritty with the sands of this desert. Fear was a constant thirst, and his skin burned with empty strangeness. He reclined in the shocking chill of his perfectly clean bed, and even in the folds of cotton abrasion he fell into a shallow sleep. This sleep was a two-tone landscape like the patterns of sand dunes and dry rock formations—curves and points of sun and shade—only this. Wandering through this landscape he began to have an idea that the two tones were sleeping and waking, but he did not know which was which. Then he found himself wandering into the polished bareness of his front room and sitting in the armchair. The bed had become somehow uncomfortable for him again—it seemed like an object of concentrated superfluity. It would be better for him to sit here for a while with the light on. Was the light on, in fact? He was not quite sure. The lighting effects were anomalous. The strangeness of the shadows in the room suggested a light source such as external street light or moonlight, but there was too much contrast between light and dark for either. Zak was no more than mildly puzzled by this. He rubbed his chin. He only felt vestigially sleepy. He was calm and awake. Realising this, he also realised that for the first time since Sooki's disappearance, there was no band of crippling pain contracting around his chest. Like a bubble breaking the surface of the sea, his indifference, becoming conscious, swelled in a moment of wonderfulness. Sometimes, sometimes, not to care—not to mind—phrase it any way you like—sometimes it was a beautiful cool wind. Because there was nothing he could do. That was it. He nodded to himself, having grasped this. There were still jagged days ahead, and the outcome might be terrible, but he would sit here for a while, calmly, sleeplessly, emptily. After some time, Zak understood that he was staring at one particular spot in the room. It was a corner of the ceiling, on the room's far side, to his left. The strange shadows were particularly thick there, like dark drapery. Also, he thought he could hear a slow, repetitive, creaking sound from that direction. The more aware he became of the sound, the more he looked for something in particular. Then, suddenly enough that it startled him, something emerged from the shadows. And disappeared. Creak. Sigh. Creak. And there it was again. And again it disappeared. This second time, Zak knew what it was. The curves and lines that had whitely emerged from darkness like an archipelago from the sea, were Sooki. His eyes adjusted, or the shadows in that corner became fractionally less dense. Now he caught a suggestion of movement, of web-like stirring. Sigh. Creak. Sigh. The darkness was like a great aperture. It couldn't really be there. Sooki, obviously, could not be swinging through empty space, as she appeared to be, where the walls met the ceiling in his front room. But still he felt only vestigially sleepy—a sensation, he felt sure, he had never known in dreams. He was soon convinced, also, that Sooki could see him, just as he could see her—perhaps better. She appeared again, and disappeared again—a mournful pendulum swinging between shadow and light. Zak . . . Her voice was clear. It was different to that voice he had heard, too, the time he had planned to bury her. This time he did not feel the same confusion. It was simply Sooki's voice. Zak . . . She appeared again, glass eyes staring, lips unmoving, and disappeared. Yes? His throat seemed parched, and his voice barely escaped his lips. Zak . . . There is an object, round, the size of an acorn . . . Light. Darkness . . . it hears all things, but it can also speak . . . Creak. Sigh. Darkness. Light. Again, without opening of lips, the voice: Wit it now well that it is no raving that thou seest to-night, but take it and believe it, and keep thee therein, and comfort thee therewith, and trust thou thereto, and thou shalt not be overcome. Light. Darkness. Sooki . . . ? Where are you . . . ? Creak. Sigh. Darkness. Light. Dark lines were crawling down the white surface of her forehead from her crown of black hair, the space between them becoming webbed—a descending curtain of crimson. Sooki . . . ? Are you coming back? Zak's voice was returning to him. Sooki . . . ! What should I do? Tell me. We were lovers . . . Zak. What do you mean? Do you still love me? Sooki! Be . . . reasonable . . . Zak. You are not . . . my . . . uncle . . . We were lovers . . . lovers . . . Light. Darkness. Creak. Sigh. Darkness. Darkness. Silence. Eventually, Zak assembled within himself the courage to approach that corner of the room. He reached out and patted the walls. There was nothing there. Or rather, there was something—the something that should have been there. Of course, he could not go to bed. He returned to the armchair and sank into its cushioned support again. Though he had been—at some point—certain that he had remained sleepless, suddenly he awoke, still in the armchair. How peculiar it was; as if, for once, he had just woken up from wakefulness itself. The lighting of the room was suddenly different—natural. It was daylight, and the impressions from the night just passed were beside him like an extinguished candle whose final flickering he had not witnessed or could not remember. He closed his eyes, and after a time opened them again—he repeated this a number of times before, at last, getting to his feet and going to the bathroom to splash water on his face. It was still very early, he discovered; his phone told him it was just past seven in the morning. After some coffee and a leftover croissant, Zak flipped open his laptop and typed some phrases into the search engine. He started with "thou shalt not be overcome". It wasn't long before he found the source of most of what Sooki had said to him during the night. He remembered having watched a documentary about reincarnation or telepathy or something, in which a scientific expert on something else had said that "in cases like this", knowledge that might seem to have been transmitted through reincarnation (or telepathy, or whatever) had actually been picked up by the subject incidentally somewhere, and then forgotten, only to resurface when triggered by the right circumstances. The question was, had Zak ever before heard of Julian of Norwich? It was possible, since she seemed like the kind of person one might hear about somehow without paying attention. And yet his memory remained stubbornly vague on this point, giving no indication either way. The result was a kind of flatness; if he chose, there was a perfectly good rational explanation. This robbed his experience of its vitality, but, at the same time, did not give complete sceptical 'closure', since it was not, in itself, a very compelling explanation. But what about the meaning of the words? Thinking of these, and reading more of the writings of Julian of Norwich, Zak did something he had not done for a while; he took an old cardboard container of incense sticks from his closet and lit one. Then he began to arrange some of the text he'd been reading on a parchment-effect background he'd found in his e-mail stationery. This done, he began to read. Slightly dissatisfied, he searched out some choral music on YouTube and played this, too. After three or four minutes reading in this way, with the incense and the choral music, he began to feel irritation in his throat and sinuses. Then the coughing started. He took the incense to the bathroom and ran the tip under the faucet. It hissed out immediately. He remembered now—that was why he didn't burn incense. Too cloying. He would be late for work if he wasn't careful. Did he care? He decided he should probably go.

Wednesday, 10th October, 12.14 p.m.

Ralph and Lucas each sat on a plastic chair. Thad had given Lucas the key to the place and said they could hang out there while he "took care of business". A record was spinning in the background titled *El Fabuloso Vicente Fernandez* (LP-12-38537 of the Orfeon label—ORFEON VIDEO-VOX, S.A., Calle 8 Esq. Alce Blanco Fracc. Alce Blanco 2a Sección, Naucalpan de Juárez, Edo de México)—a music full of pathos and energy that served well to paint the mundane surroundings with an orgy of dahlias and prickly pear cactus, hissing snakes and quebrantahuesos.

The place had not been cleaned since the party. The remaining fondue sat hardened in the pot. Empty bottles were scattered about, cigarette butts and saliva fermenting within.

Lucas had a Trippel ale brewed with coriander between his legs. Ralph was taking a hit of ghost train haze out of a metal pure pipe[1]. He held in the smoke as long as he could and then started coughing, his face the colour of a freshly killed sea star.

"25.49% THC," Lucas said sagely.

---

1. This pip is the best I've ever seen in my life we pack wont beast boul and when its done won of us pass out or strip like crazy and it takes they best hits iv ever seen.

"Where—COUGHCOUGH—did—COUGH—you get that—COUGHCOUGHCOUGH—shit!?!?!"

"A homeboy of mine gets it down in Atlantic City. But it ain't cheap. It's meant for high rollers. This is the weed Archie Karas smokes after a big win."

Ralph nodded his head. Tears were rolling down his cheeks.

Lucas took a drink of his beer. "Fuckin' Thad," he said.

"Yeah."

"Fuckin' fuckin' Thad."

"Yeah."

"He's all horned out over that doll. I dunno if his buddy offers to pay the reward if he'd even return her."

Ralph took another hit from the pipe by way of reply.

Lucas took another drink of his beer and continued his soliloquy.

"Yeah, I admit, she's pretty hot an' all. But she's, like, a fuckin' doll. Hell, I'd rather go balls deep with Mariah than a doll. I mean, at least she can groan."

"Yeah."

"Hey, don't bogart the weed bro!"

Lucas grabbed the pipe from Ralph and thrust the stem between his lips and was just sucking a huge toke of the powerful marijuana into the pits of his respiratory organs when he heard Ralph say:

"*Cocksucker!*"

Lucas looked up.

"Huh?" he said, a fog of thiol-smelling smoke issuing from his thin lips.

"Huh what?" Ralph asked.

"You, um, calling me a cocksucker."

"You're fried. I didn't say anything."

"Yeah, um, whatever."

Ralph shook his head and squinted and took the pipe from Lucas and took another hit. He flicked the lighter and petted the bowl of the pipe with the dancing flame as he sucked.

Lucas was gazing at the hair on his left wrist and wondering why his best friend had called him a cocksucker when he heard:

"You got sialorrhea or just love dining at the Y playin' the skin flute pussy. May the magpie drink from your brains you bearded clam panty hamster bitch and I'll cum in your lungs."

"Hey, fuck you!" Lucas said leaping up from the plastic chair, which fell backward.

The song 'Corazon de Niño' lurched up from the stereo.

Ralph was staring up at him in surprise, his face resting in a mist of blueberry-coloured smoke. His mouth was almost closed, but insults kept coming out of it:

"You're a hair pie eating muff diving take it up the ass peach licking chili cheese dog sucking handy bracejob auto-fellatio loving fuck start. Your dick is too short. Eat vomit while every Chinaman fucks your mother's broken meat flap."

"Shut the fuck up!"

"Your mother blows as good as your sister like walrus pork by the pound you licking los cocos let me fuck your ass through the gravel road or maybe you better just loan me your cunt. Go pick your ass with your nose after I shave it with green glass and fuck you in the forehead."

Lucas' brain was suddenly embroidered with rage. He lifted up his right foot which was sheathed in a red, white and black Adidas Crazy 8 basketball shoe[1] and planted it solidly in Ralph's face. The latter fell back in his chair, banged his ear against the wall and then found himself on

____

1. the white things on the shoe are so 3D makes the shoe look huge it's really hard to put insoles in them but other than that they are pretty good maybe get a size bigger it's a little heavy but they look really good

the floor, a lithe stream of red flowing from the crushed remains of his nose. He waved his arms about frantically, but still would not be silent.

"*May you get fucked by a blind wolf,*" he said. "*Limp pencil dick-chewing milk-swallower I'll put my cock in your ass so hard it comes out your mouth so you can give me a blow job.*"

Lucas was quivering with fury. Aborted thoughts boiled about in his head, thrust out their claws and strangled each other in grunting orgasms of vendetta. He gripped the handle of the beer bottle, brought it up and then swung it down, smashing it against Ralph's skull and the latter's neck bent as his eyes rolled around.

Ralph lay there stunned. His mouth moved, pleading for help, but the words, instead of being those of supplication, were of utter insulting filth.

"*You menstrual meat wallet result of a defective condom I slapped your mama's legs and rode the waves. Beer dick beef curtain eating muff teaser semen pig. Tit wanker. You eat the mushrooms that grow on a whore's tampon pocket so should shampoo my magic stick with your———*"

Lucas yanked the fondue pot from the table and flung it down as hard as he could on Ralph's head, cracking both open in one swift motion of violence.

The fingers of Ralph's right hand twitched and then he was still.

"Fuck," Lucas said. "Why couldn't you just shut up? Fuck."

Ralph's eyes were open, glassy. He was dead.

Lucas was wondering if he should cry or not when he heard a sound and turned his head. A man wearing a light green beltless action-stripe poplin jumpsuit came padding down the stairs.

Lucas' face assumed a panicked expression.

"Who the fuck are you?" he asked.

The man grinned. "My name is Presteign Sainte-Croix, but you can call me Bergen. I am looking for Thaddeus."

"Thad? I don't know where he is."

"You do, and you shall tell me."

"No."

"You killed your friend."

Lucas looked down at Ralph lying dead on the floor.

"Yeah, I guess I did," he murmured.

"Now, be a good boy and tell me where our Mr Thaddeus is. I, in turn, will refrain from informing the authorities about your little tracasserie."

"Yeah?"

"Yeah."

"Yeah, okay. Thad's, um, over in Ocean County."

"Address?"

"Number 7 Mt. Misery Road, Longwood."

"I take it this is correct? Things could get very nasty if I found out you were telling me an untruth."

"I'm not lying bro!"

Presteign Sainte-Croix shrugged his thin shoulders, extracted a 13-inch AKC stiletto with a green pearlex handle[1] from his pocket and snapped it open, revealing a gleaming Swedish 420 Stainless Steel blade, performing the action with such nonchalance that Lucas seemed hardly aware what was happening before the bayonet sang over his throat and a three-foot jet of purple blood shot into the air with a hissing sound as the young man swung backward onto Ralph's body, their sap being joined to the folkloric strains of 'Cuanto Te Debo' as interpreted by Roberto Cantoral.

---

1. Yeah it's HUGE 13 INCHES LONG, becha hear that a lot. YEAH

Wednesday, 10ᵗʰ October, 1.34 p.m.

The house Presteign Sainte-Croix pulled into first on his way to Longwood had hardly changed since his last visit some two years before, its lawn and small garden carefully sculpted into miniaturist perfection. Sainte-Croix noticed several new additions: marigolds and rose bushes and a small fig tree covered with a protective net. The damp grass brushed his leather shoes as he walked up the path.

He rang the buzzer and was soon greeted by a middle-aged woman in a black coat and evening dress. She looked competent but pained, somehow distant. Her lips cracked into a smile.

"Sarah," Sainte-Croix said, avoiding the term *aunt*; avoiding, as always, the atavism.

"I'm glad you could make it. Leonard . . . well, he's upstairs as usual. He's been expecting you." She paused. "And I appreciate . . . you know, this is really the only time I can have to myself. You know how he is . . ."

"You don't have to explain," Sainte-Croix said. He understood her problems, her constant sacrifices, but remained unmoved; only Leonard interested him. Presteign Sainte-Croix had reached the age when he no longer saw exceptions and inconsistencies as faults in a philosophy. The enlightened man could afford some flexibility, provided his general idea was sound. As such, he did not think

"

too hard about how his renunciation of human ties squared with these infrequent but regular visits to his cousin.

Sarah ushered him inside and led him up the carpeted steps to the second floor. They entered the first room on the right, which appeared to have materialised inside the house like a sudden cyst, its near total disorder contrasting with the elegant hallway outside. But when Sainte-Croix looked closer his eyes took in the greater order within the disorder. The piles of papers, stacks of books and endless sheets of graph paper attached to the walls all hinted at a totalising system, bewildering but not incoherent. At the centre of the room a man sat in a pile of cushions, staring intently at the pages of a notebook. He wore grey sweatpants and a stained white singlet. His hair was long and stringy, his nails yellow claws. He glared at Sainte-Croix in greeting and ignored Sarah.

"Leonard, it's been a while," Sainte-Croix said.

The filthy man did not blink.

"I know why you're here. So SHE can leave with him." He fixed his gaze on Sarah. "HIM. An interior decorator from Sears. NOT a mathematician. NOT an intellectual. She isn't acting like my mother. SHE'S ACTING LIKE A WHORE."

Sainte-Croix felt stray flecks of saliva lash past his face. A look of sudden and immortal hatred animated Leonard's features, then passed like a wave. But the muscles did not relax and the posture did not slacken.

"Leonard . . ." Sarah said. "We know you've been working hard. I think it would be good for you to take a break from your research. You know, take the night off. I need a break sometimes too."

Leonard took a ceramic plate from beside him and hurled it at Sarah's head. She dodged it with a practiced movement and took a step backwards.

"Leonard . . ."

"OUT. NOW."

Sainte-Croix met her eyes. She nodded, paused, and then went to the door without saying a word. A moment later Sainte-Croix heard her footsteps padding down the stairs.

"ACTING LIKE A WHORE," Leonard repeated.

Unlike Sainte-Croix, Leonard cared greatly about consistency. He was another superman, though he was neither a mercenary nor a ventriloquist. Leonard, who had not appeared in public for ten years, had won and then refused the Clay Mathematics Institute Prize for demonstrating the truth of the Hodge conjecture, and was widely seen as deserving the Fields Medal. And unbeknownst to all but himself and Sainte-Croix, Leonard had killed more people than any other internationally-recognised mathematician in modern history (the second-place contender was a Serb whose motivations had been quite different).

It was true that, were it not for Sainte-Croix's influence, Leonard never would have killed anyone. As a teenager Sainte-Croix had, upon determining his future career, decided that he needed practical experience in homicide before he could advertise his services with any confidence. Not wanting to join the military, he had decided to enlist Leonard's help in a series of murders, and the two had set off armed with various stolen weapons: ropes, pipes, knives, a machete and several firearms. Striking in random locations at night, preying always on the weak and alone, they had exploited each weapon's full potential on each chosen victim. The first had been an elderly pensioner whose home they broke into after midnight; Sainte-Croix had elbowed her in the face and then continued striking her skull with his fists and feet until she died, which took much longer than he had expected; he and Leonard subsequently ruled out aggravated battery as an efficient first option. They had moved onto edged weapons next, which considerably improved the time ratio when combined with their research into the locations of major arteries. A truck-stop prostitute named Reza, with a torso like a freshly-sculpted statue, seemed only mildly surprised when Sainte-Croix cut out his eyes, as if being stabbed in the head—and later dismembered and thrown into the forest—were only the latest in a long series of indignities. A small boy in a Catholic school uniform, whose student card identified him as William Flinders Ferguson, barely struggled when Sainte-Croix abducted him from Liberty Landing Marina at dusk, took him to a garbage dump and held him down while Leonard beheaded him with the machete. Neither Sainte-Croix nor Leonard remembered having identification cards in elementary school. Ballistic weapons were effective but noisy, as they discovered when shooting a vagrant at point blank range with a Smith & Wesson Model 500 as he dozed under a pile of cardboard boxes. The recoil was so great that Sainte-Croix thought the gun had exploded; later, he and Leonard bathed in the Saddle River to wash the brain and skull fragments from their clothes. Through it all Sainte-Croix had tried out his voices, projecting the accents of demons from cans, empty boxes, picture frames, television screens and whatever else was at hand.

Despite taking no especial forensic precautions, they had suffered no consequences from any of these murders. This confirmed Sainte-Croix's belief that as long as you killed the very young and very old, the ugly and the poor, those with no connections, no one cared. Killing the important and connected was therefore a profitable skill. But Leonard was not interested in money, whether it came from assassinations or intellectual achievements. After he and Sainte-Croix had killed ten vagrants, four pensioners, three prostitutes and two children, he announced that the murders were diverting him from important research on topological vector spaces. By this time Sainte-Croix felt ready to advertise his services, so they had agreed to move on.

"I thought you might like to come along on a job, for old time's sake," Sainte-Croix said. "Someone I need to take care of. It's a long story."

Leonard got up from his cushions, took a book from the shelf and then dropped it in disdain.

"Donald R. Hickey is a DISGUSTING FRAUD," he said. "The Chesapeake Bay Flotilla NEVER EXISTED."

For the past year Leonard had been dividing his time between consideration of the Moore space question and an increasingly detailed attempt to prove that the War of 1812 was a hoax.

"What else have you been up to?" Sainte-Croix asked.

"Nothing. Hobbies are a weakness."

"Well, come along. I don't want to stay in here all night."

They walked downstairs and out the door, across the lawn to Sainte-Croix's car.

"I detest leaving the house," Leonard said. "Surrounded by degenerates."

"I've met a few of those recently," Sainte-Croix said. As they pulled out of the driveway he briefly explained the assignment from *Idollatry*. When he finished, Leonard spat in disgust.

"Watch the upholstery," Sainte-Croix said.

"I ESCHEW sexual activity. A non-Pythagorean attachment to the temporary, instead of the higher Ideals."

"You're still interested in killing degenerates?"

"I'm interested in killing Paul F. Freeman from Princeton University," Leonard said. "I want to CUT HIS HEAD OFF. For making INACCURATE STATEMENTS ABOUT SET THEORY."

"What are you going to do with the head?" Sainte-Croix asked. "Dissolve it in quick lime? Bury it?"

"I wouldn't even feed it to mongrel dogs. It would poison them. It is full of UTTER NONSENSE."

The Carpenters came on the radio, 'Yesterday Once More'. They drove in silence for an hour and stopped at Carl's Jr. for dinner, where Sainte-Croix ate a Jalapeno Turkey Burger with a side of chili cheese fries and an orange cream malt. Leonard, a vegan, had a cup of water.

When they arrived at the vacation house, Sainte-Croix gestured for Leonard to open the glove compartment, where he found a Ruger SRC9c and a Springfield Armory XD-S. He handed the 9mm to Sainte-Croix and took the Springfield for himself.

"I have TERRIBLE AIM," he said.

"It won't matter."

It was a still night, and the moon was visible. They performed a cursory check of the perimeter and found only a black cat chewing on the remains of a sparrow in the grasses past the house. Sainte-Croix projected a living bird's shriek and the cat jumped away and retreated into the bushes. They concealed their weapons and headed for the front door, which was unlocked.

The house had clearly been vandalised, its chairs and tables overturned, graffiti scrawled on the walls. They found Thad asleep, snoring on a couch—or divan, Sainte-Croix supposed, given the house's estimated property value—in the living room, Sooki lying face-down beside him in clear disarray. Sainte-Croix took a glass bowl from the table and threw it against the wall, where it shattered into crystal fragments. Thad continued to sleep, so Leonard kicked him in the face. He started awake, blood streaming from his nose.

"What the fuck!?!"

Sainte-Croix and Leonard raised their guns. Taking them in, Thad scrambled backwards and held up his hands, knocking Sooki to the ground in the process.

"Mr Bergen! I can explain . . ."

"Can you? I'm not surprised, Thad, but I am disappointed. What exactly was your plan? Soil the merchandise and sell it to another client for less than you would have made by sticking to the plan?" He took a step closer, keeping the Ruger trained on Thad's head. "Or pass it off to Mr Brooks? Small time. You could get bigger ends from the change in that divan."

"Mr Magister, I mean Brooks has more than you think, listen——"

"Are you a FUCKING MORON?" Leonard interrupted.

"Well no, I . . ." Thad paused. Startled out of sleep, his mind was completely empty. He looked from Leonard to Sainte-Croix and back again, his thoughts racing for an explanation. But none emerged.

"I'm a big believer in survival of the fittest," Sainte-Croix said. "Had you successfully fucked me over, I wouldn't have held it against you. But you have unsuccessfully fucked me over, thereby successfully fucking yourself over. I find that . . . contemptible. But I am not without compassion. Leonard, do you think we should give Thad a second chance?"

"NO," Leonard said.

"Look please," Thad said. "I was playing against Brooks all along. I was going to get more money from him, more from Zak, then cut them both off and go ahead with the plan. Like a bonus, yeah? I was going to surprise you. I thought you and the client would like that. Like its ingeniousness, right?"

"Ingenuity," Sainte-Croix said. "Not ingeniousness."

"Yeah, exactly."

Sainte-Croix lowered his gun.

"Thad, Leonard is going to ask you a question. If you answer correctly, you earn your second chance and we leave now. If you answer incorrectly . . . then there's no forgiveness."

"A question," Thad said, wiping the blood from his face. "Okay . . ."

"READY," Leonard said. "Is the ring of invariants of an algebraic group acting on a polynomial ring always finitely generated?"

"What?"

"FIVE SECONDS TO ANSWER. FIVE . . ."

"Wait, repeat the question!"

"FOUR . . ."

"Mr Bergen . . . listen . . ."

"THREE . . ."

"Is the ring . . . the what . . ."

"TWO . . ."

Thad ran for the door, fast enough that Leonard's initial shot missed him and punched a hole in the wall.

"Let's go," Sainte-Croix said. "Target practice."

They chased him out the door and into the bushes behind the house. Sainte-Croix fixed him in his sights but did not fire. Leonard stopped, gripped the Springfield with both hands and took aim.

"NOW YOU DIE!!!"

A momentary explosion later and Thad dropped to the ground, falling forward as he pitched down the incline.

"Was that supposed to be a head shot?" Sainte-Croix asked.

"I told you I had TERRIBLE AIM," Leonard said.

They hurried over and found Thad lying face down on the ground. The gunshot had blown apart his kneecap, and the fall had shredded his face with gravel. He was breathing heavily, his eyes white ghosts of themselves.

"That looks painful. But I'm sure you'll survive. Fitness test, Thad. Just like in school. Do you deserve to be alive? It's up to you now. Were you ever a Boy Scout?"

"Bergen . . . fuck you . . ."

Thad's breaths came in shallows; he let out a sudden involuntary scream as Leonard kicked his wound.

Sainte-Croix reached down and removed Thad's cell phone from his pocket.

"We'll be cutting the house lines too. Doesn't look like there's anyone around for miles. Think of it as the wilderness challenge! Goodbye, Thad."

Leonard gave him a final kick, which sent him tumbling further down the incline. He landed in a pile of moss and wet leaves.

He lay on the ground taking ragged breaths. After a while he reached into his pocket and retrieved a miniature plastic Ziploc bag. There was one white pill left, which he took. He would have to make it to a rest stop and get help; surely there was one around somewhere. It was only a matter of staying focused through the pain. Clenching his teeth, he forced himself forward on his hands, stopping only when the core of agony in his knee became too great. On one of these breaks he yelled out for help but only exhausted himself. He could hear night sounds—scurryings and scrapings, the continuous chitter of insects—but no human voices answered him. He would rest, regain his strength and then continue on to the road. He stretched out and tried to forget the constant sun-sharp pain that had become the centre of his existence.

When he next looked up, under starlight, tiny Disney characters were crawling from his shattered knee, and he realised they had established a mining site in his wound. Miniature Donald Ducks were shoveling out bone dust and solid fragments, passing them along to jiving Mickey Mouses and wildly gyrating Goofies dancing on the edge of his ragged flesh.

"Bastards," Thad said. He swiped at his knee and felt a fresh explosion of pain.

Ants were crawling all over him.

He thought of Angela and suddenly the entire situation seemed only an absurd inconvenience; he would make his way to safety, have his wound treated and bang her as planned. He would think of a better method this time; confident, infallible.

He heard a buzzing close to his ear and felt a slamming instant of needle-sharp pain, as if someone had jammed a pencil into his head. His hand jerked up instinctively and came away with something hard and black and yellow. Dimly he could see other wasps circling overhead. No nest was visible, but he knew there must be one nearby. He struggled forward and bumped his knee on a rock, which set him to screaming. Another wasp landed on his arm. Fresh blood drenched his pants.

He moved without thinking, spurred on by the pain. Minutes passed, or hours, he couldn't tell.

A pinging sound caught his awareness. When he looked up, a cloud had formed in front of him. As he watched, it congealed into the shape of a man, taking on colour and definite detail. This figure wore a grey suit with an open collar, and he was tall and broad-shouldered, with a square jaw and blond hair. His expression was ineffably wise and compassionate.

"Thad, I'm glad I caught you," the man said. "We don't have much time."

"You can help me," Thad said. "You can . . .can't you?"

He broke off. The man seemed to shimmer, as if the moonlight were passing directly through him.

"I can help you in the way that counts, but not the way you might be expecting," the man replied.

"Who are you?"

"I'm post-Singularity Ryan Gosling. You may have seen some of my films. I'm still the Ryan Gosling you know, but I exist in your future. I've become a bodhisattva of sorts, travelling back to help those on the verge of death."

"I'm not going to die . . ."

The man ignored him. "The important thing now, Thad, is that you get your karma straight. Looking back over the past few years, can you identify some mistakes you've made? Attaining clear consciousness is the first step towards learning real life lessons. As I said, we don't have much time. What might you have done differently in your interactions with Angela? I assume you've read *The Laugh of the Medusa* by Cixous and the later works of Kristeva. In fact, you———"

Another pinging sound diverted Thad's dazed attention. He heard a voice from behind him.

"Drop that zero and get with the hero!"

He turned his head, feeling fresh pain with each move-ment. Another man now stood before him, dressed in a silver and green jumpsuit which appeared to be made of shining tinfoil. He had handsome but aggressively linear, regular features. His hair had been sculpted into a quiff and buzzed short on the sides, with shaved lines. He resembled a surreally camp astronaut Ken doll, but his expression was all calculated disdain.

"Yo Thad, don't listen to this tool. Post-Singularity bodhisattvas never really help anyone, word to your mother. There is nothing to be learned and no spiritual progress to be made. Inhabit your last breath like the party don't stop, word to your mother."

The first man's expression darkened.

"Post-Singularity Vanilla Ice? I might have known you'd show up. Thad, don't pay any attention to this impostor. He's not even the real Vanilla Ice, just a simulation based on old video recordings. A copy of a copy of a copy."

"Ice is Ice," the man in the jumpsuit said. "I'm beyond your outdated notions of authenticity, which no longer apply to our post-scarcity and in some sense post-material context. And if you want to talk unconvincing mimesis, I could mention your acting, dog. Shit is whack."

"Ice, I remember you from my childhood," Thad said. He started crying. A cloud of darkness settled over him.

Something heavy brushed past his face. He felt a sniffing snout, then teeth. The tiny Mickeys and Goofies were back at work on his knee, and now they had installed miniature charges of dynamite. In a few moments the charges would blow. He could already feel his leg moving away from him, separated at the joint.

The teeth bit into his face.

At once he saw Sooki, filling every aspect of his awareness. He realised that he was seeing her for the first time as she really was. Nothing about her had changed, but now everything about her was different. Stripped of her glamour, transfigured through subtraction, she had no face, no eyes, no hair—these were human things with human meanings, but Sooki was not human, and he looked on the thing that had camouflaged itself as a woman and knew it for what it was: a mineral being of lines and angles, more house than person. A house of worship.

He passed through her stained-glass eyes into the inner landscape, cool and echoing. The pleasure he had known before was nothing now that he would soon occupy the silence of her ultimate heart. Seeking it, he turned corner after corner, moving through the curved hallways in a place stripped of shadows.

The moon fell and the sun rose in turn, casting pink light over the forest.

David Whitaker had strayed from the camp site to relieve himself. His father was already up, cooking eggs and sausages on the grill. When David came across the shape sprawled in front of the stream, covered with dirt and moss and insects, he took it at first to be a fallen scarecrow; derelict, a doll.

Thursday, 11ᵗʰ October, 1.04 p.m.

Remy Mi-ti was sitting at his desk smoking a DJ Mix Apple Green cigarette and looking through eBay for doll offerings. He almost never found anything he wanted there, but continued to look obsessively in the hope that one day he would find a great deal.

He read:

> *Virtual Girl is composed of high density Iso-Foam, sheathed in a soft, durable, oxygenated latex blend. IsoFoam is an ultra-resilient foam compound. What this means is that you can pounce and bounce on Virtual Girl's body. Even when subjected to full body weight, she will always return to her original, perfect shape. This resilient, heavy-gauge foam is incredibly lightweight and durable. Because of Skinthetic technology, Virtual Girl's skin is highly elastic, and very durable; you can squeeze her and tease her as much as you like.*

"Load a crap," he murmured.

The wind passion bamboo ringtone of his cell phone began to sing. He picked up the phone and put it to his ear.

"Hello?"

"Mr Remy Mi-ti?"

"Yeah, this him."

"This is Fred Bergen."

"Great. You got business?"

"Indeed I do Mr Mi-ti."

"What plan?"

"Excuse me?"

"What plan?"

"I'm down here on the street with the doll right now. Shall I come to you or you to me?"

"We come together right now!"

"Yes?"

"Bring doll up right now. We have wing-ding."

Less than three minutes later Remy Mi-ti and Fred Bergen (that is to say Presteign Sainte-Croix) were shaking hands in the editorial room. Sainte-Croix was wearing a dark-green lightweight Highlands tweed jacket and a pair of brown linen houndstooth D-ring waist pleated front pants with besom pockets. Sooki was sitting in a chair next to them.

"She so hot," Remy said.

"And now about the little matter of pay."

"Restroom down hall to right."

"Excuse me?"

"You need go pee?"

"Pay, Mr Mi-ti, pay. As in money. Moola. Scratch. Bread and honey."

"OKAY! You **WAIT** few minute 性交."

Bert Seidman was hunched over the proofs of the interview Sid Modimolle had done with Mariya Oksana, marking up the text with a Pilot Cavalier Fountain Pen filled with red ink. A half-eaten egg salad sandwich was sitting near him and a cold cup of coffee.

Billy Glantz, who was sitting at his desk wearing a pair of Maui Jim 103 Stingray sunglasses and reading a book titled *The Decaying Aplanatic Moons of Old Europe* that he had got in the mail from a Romanian publisher just that morning though it had been ordered two years earlier (in order to get the book actually dispatched he had had to buck the slobbering donkey on web-camera three times, but he felt extremely grateful since the volume was printed on exquisite and heavy cardboard paper and had arrived in a clothed box with only a minimum number of tripe soup stains), looked over and saw Sooki. He felt a sudden interest, put down the book and rose from his seat. He hoped that some day, after Mi-ti had soiled and used the doll a great deal, he might get the cast off.

Mi-ti held up the doll, beaming.

"So happy merriment!" he said.

There was a boom box in the room. Billy stalked over to it and put in a CD titled *Greatest Hits of the 80s*. The song 'Safety Dance' by Men Without Hats began to play **March, 2012, *SOFT ISSUE cute fluffy cute cartoon characters to attract countless eye smiling eyes looking at you like to tell trickling affectionate or lively or shy sensitive show so you can not help laughing and all of them are so touching!***

Mi-ti began to dance with Sooki, a burning cigarette jutting from his grinning lips—his hips wagging from right to left and his right foot sliding smoothly over the floor the anthropoid riddle / **a vintage scene** / female principle a fragment of a poem:

Thin beautiful elegant representing girl
Smooth lithic SPERM equidissection SPERM
Enneagon grows again
Labyrinthine I pushed my hand on her neck
And then to SPERM gyronny spheres parfilage

Carmen walked into the room holding a bottle of Parrot Bay coconut-flavoured rum and some plastic cups.

"Hey, sounds like a party!" she cried, thrusting out her breasts.

Bert looked up from his work. "I'll take a little sauce," he said, picking up his cold cup of coffee and waving it in front of him.

Carmen danced over to his desk and corrected his coffee with a generous slug of rum and then poured drinks for everybody in the plastic cups **May, 2009, DOLL BROTHEL ISSUE—doll head practicing wiggling sex addict LURIDLURIDLURID comes off during intercourse**.

'Hearts on Fire' by Randy Meisner came on the boombox. Carmen's breasts began to bounce up and down. Billy's ponytail swayed back and forth. Bert took a sip of his coffee and frowned **tonic angles / dominant angles / modiant angles of HER**.

It was then that Sid Modimolle came in. He had just had a pork and clam plate and a couple of bald pussies over at the Iberia Tavern & Restaurant over on Ferry St. and was feeling a bit high.

He began strutting about like a rooster, knees high in the air, head nipping back and forth, the fingers of his right hand snapping.

"Whoo!" Carmen cried wiggling up near him, her blood running like a raging river.

The kickdrum pounded out from the speakers with a steady thump-thumpety-thump like the heartbeat of a frisky rhino depths and altitudes of prophetic buttocks.

The mood of the music suddenly changed to the witchcraft of 'One Shot Lover' by Venus **August, 2011, AUSTRIAN GOTHIC ISSUE SPIDER WEBS CHAINS TORTURE INSTRUMENTS**.

Bert Seidman slowly got up from his chair and with deliberate steps approached Sooki. From Mi-ti's hand he took her hand. *He took her hand.* **He took her hand.**

"Enchanté," he said in a barely audible voice and then she was in his arms and they began to featherstep. **Featherstep.** Hover feather block of feather finish in triangle of plastic cunt.

Carmen was sitting on Billy's desk.

"It's a shame you don't like **HOT** women," she growled.

"I'm an antinatalist," he said, nodding his head.

"You a what?"

"I don't believe in babies."

"Oh, baby!" she said in a pitying tone of **sympathetic attraction**.

Her heeled foot dangled over to his thigh / some hope of physiological rectangle.

Remy was not altogether pleased that Bert Seidman was dancing with Sooki. He grabbed her away, leaned her against the wall and then opened a double-door closet which was stuffed with doll samples *Idollatry* had been sent by various manufacturers, mostly in China, South Korea and Japan.

"Dance these dance these!" Mi-ti cried flinging them around the room.

There was a DBJ-204 Real Natural Lady[1], a TCM-021 Masturbation Cup Real Vagina Sex Doll, a Rude Girl[2], a

---

1. Real Natural Lady your virtual partner for you next sexual. Technologically advanced silicone material replicates soft, realistic human skin. Explore new worlds of sensation with dual entries. The vaginal is textured to mimic virtual penetration. Open ended vagina makes clean up quickly with soap and water. Reach intergalactic levels of ecstasy with Sex doll.

2. With a human voice jump egg, warm up wand, lubricant, air pump, mending equipment. The doll can sustain a pressure of 300 pound.

Lovehoney Magic Wand Vibrator Deluxe Mains Powered Massager Sex Toy Sex Product[1], a Shizuka wig, Real Love Doll Ange with Boing extra body hole, one HitDoll (redhead)[2], a carton of newMan Spider Airplane Masturbation Cups[3], Sex Women Doll[4], a cardboard box full of products from Nicejoy Global Limited[5], an Inflatable Tina Doll by Shenzhen Fanrefond Plastic Products Co. Ltd., two pairs of Dick Nose Novelty Glasses, a Man Adult Toy[6], a

---

1. The Lovehoney Deluxe Magic Wand is a new and very much improved UK version of the Hitachi Magic Wand Vibrator, which was withdrawn from sale in the UK. Now market North American.

2. HitDoll uses high intelligent technology on our dolls. We can feel your action's speed & frequency by using intelligent chip sensor and offer you the real girl's distortion voice accordingly. Also our doll has recorder functionality. You can use this functionality to record the voice of your loving girl. Maybe in the near future, you can hear your favorite star's voice in your bedroom.

3. Korea Jiangnan style into the onslaught of China, South Korea imported adsorption male masturbation cup masturbation in the history of the first with adsorption function spike all manual masturbation devices!

4. Shenzhen Mroow Electronic Co., Ltd., is located in shenzhen and is specialized in manufacturing silicone rubber products. With an experienced and professional team, we have exported our products to many countries and regions all over the world, especially Europe. Our products enjoy a good reputation among our customers.

5. We are pleased to introduce ourselves and inform you that we are a large manufacturer of sex furniture, and a distributor and wholesaler of many other high quality sexual products and toys. We invite you to please check out our complete product catalog including a large array of erotic products and toys, lingerie and lubricants. Also please take the time to view our premiere manufactured products, a line of sex furniture that's guaranteed to add the spice back into your customer's sex lives!

6. It's very lifelike. It's the same as real girls' ass. It have a vaginal and anus, and have public hair. It can sex with mans.

Hairy Vagina Toy[1], a Karl MarXXX Doll[2], a box of Orgasm Key Chains by Selon EB Firm.

Purity girl, men's first love

1. Purity and beatiful girl, I believe that you can love it first time

2. The period of use is very long

3. It is natural like a real person

4. Many style you can choose

FLASHBACK!!! {Billy suddenly, and for no apparent reason, recalls when he was a teenager and would hide in the bathroom, read Lovecraft and masturbate with wadded up toilet paper in his mouth} **FLASHBACK!!!** {Bert Seidman punching hole between the legs of his little sister's Palmolive Soap Advertising Promo Storybook Doll *SOFT LUST*}

FROM THE LENGTH OF THE UPPER EDGE OF THE SWORD-SHAPED CARTILAGE OF THE STERNUM.

APEX XIPHOID.

Sid put on a pair of Dick Nose Novelty Glasses.

Remy dragged Sooki into his office with Sainte-Croix following.

"See," Mi-ti said, "this doll with soft mouth nipple real unique. Made by unique vagina. Pursuit of high quality life

---

1. Ultimate pleasant sensation, reappearance, pursuisex toy adult toys pussy sex doll for man this private Erotic Doll features a soft pussy and ass with the all new expandable mouth design. Almost seamless, life-like feeling shin, head with long flowing hair, large breasts ad jointed This private Erotic Doll features a soft pussy and ass with the all new expandable mouth design. Almost seamless, life-like feeling shin, head with long flowing hair, large breasts ad jointed arms with orbital sockets.

2. When bending or moving, please treat him with the respect he deserves.

experience's successful man. Got to fuck flat to be on level. At Shenzhen Guangdong they make ten thousand piece crap doll every day. Sooki one-of-kind with Noel Toy 阴道. Man want pretty nurse got to be patient. She, Sooki, like strawberry. Sweety and hot! It has not only a beautiful looking!"

"Yes, I see your point," Sainte-Croix said. "But about that payment . . ."

"Okay, great! Now you watch me huan huan," Remy said. He set the doll down on his desk. "It don't matter how slowly you go long as you don't stop."

He pulled down his trousers to reveal a penis that, by even the most lenient standards, would have been considered modest at best.

Sainte-Croix raised his left eyebrow.

Mi-ti thrust the doll's legs apart and bent his own knees in preparation.

"Hey, like, um, what the fuck."

Mi-ti hesitated. He turned towards Sainte-Croix.

"Do not look at me," the latter said. "If there is someone tossing their voice about in the room, it is not I."

Mi-ti's eyes travelled back to Sooki's vagina which, at that moment, began to speak in an extra-ordinarily clear voice, that was not of a woman, but rather that of a young man.

"Yeah, like, um, what the fuck. His friend like, um, fuckin' shot me in the knee-cap."

Mi-ti stood staring with open mouth.

"You Sooki talk pussy?" he asked.

"I'm not, like, Sooki, dude. I'm Thad. I got shot in the knee-cap. By that cat over there in the tweed jacket and his psycho fuckin' friend. I'm, like, looking for Mariya."

"Mariya?" Mi-ti queried.

"Yeah. Mariya Oksana. Sundown Dolls. Y'know?"

Mi-ti turned, shouted, "Modimolle! Modimolle!" and his voice travelled through the open door of his office, jutted about in the form of a Lemoine hexagon, before performing a reverse one and a half somersaults with three and a half twists into the reporter's right ear, and this latter gentleman swayed his body into the office and was instructed by Mi-ti to call Mariya right away.

Sid, a graduate in journalism of the University of Dar es Salaam, hit his boss with the Five Ws.

"Sooki pussy now talking here don't know why!" Mi-ti screamed.

Sid got out his cell phone and dialled Mariya, telling her she was needed urgently. As fortune would have it, she was at that very moment buying a bottle of Zico Coconut Water at the Amazonia Brasil shop on Prospect Street and in less than ten minutes walked through the door of Mi-ti's office. She was wearing a pair of beige skin-tight Tracy Nguyen designed sequin leggings with a non-visible panty line.

Her eyes glanced disapprovingly at Mi-ti's sustained erection.

"Indeed I have come," she said, "but do not wish for material altercation."

"The doll's vagina is talking," Sid explained. "It's asking for you."

"Yes?"

"Yup."

"A strange stagecraft," Sainte-Croix added.

Mariya stared intently at the doll's vagina.

"You speak to me?" she said. "You ask for Mariya?"

"Um, yeah. I need your help."

"Indeed I know this voice. Valiant Odr, you are here?"

"Yeah, like, um, my material body got totally fucked up. By that jackass in the ugly tweed jacket."

"Valiant Odr you release negative emotional content and listen, okay?"

"Yeah, um, okay."

"Indeed you listen. This destiny of astral body was the cause of last thought at time of demise, was it not?"

"If you mean was I thinking of fucking Sooki. Um, yeah, the answer is yeah."

"Attachment to material plane піхву must be released. Must think of great піхву of Star City. Must concentrate on this. You hear me?"

"Yeah."

"Time on planet Earth reach cessation. Explore gateway of time stream. Pleasure destinations many. Access realms of energies. Now look hard you see shining cord."

"Shining cord?"

"Indeed look hard Valiant Odr."

"Oh, like yeah, I see it."

"When you hear my shout wander fast along cord. Mission with Adamic race completed. Events in the Venus-Sun-Moon move quickly. Your Solar bhukti follows whilst Rahu-Ketu continues to transit. Travel fast along shining cord to Teutonia. Indeed you understand?"

"Yeah, um, I think so."

"Now I shout."

"Um, okay."

"!!!піхву!!!"

A slight whining sound came from Sooki's vagina. And then there was silence, only the sound of Shakin' Stevens' 'You Drive Me Crazy' coming from the outer room.

"Indeed it is done," Mariya said gravely. "May you travel well Valiant Odr, may your travel be well."

Sooki lay glowing beauty chiselled out of plastic **EMBLEMATIC** *emblematic* diamond-shaped lozenge.

Mariya lowered her eyelashes, turned, and, taking out her iPhone to check her e-mail, left Mi-ti's office, going through the main room where Bert Seidman was performing symmetrical sex on the Inflatable Tina Doll / prehistoric style / Carmen stood in profile eyes octagonal and wide gyroid pond mucous membrane **FERTALIZATION** *of* plastic or you magic wand cast your SPELLS! She was steatopygous. Cleanly cut. Angular. Breasts taut triangles of heat which both interested and frightened Billy whose hemispherical eyes were locked on her as he manipulated a foreshortened newMan Spider Airplane Masturbation Cup.

Sooki lay on the desk glowing beauty of moulded gold eyes of ventriloquist meet those of merry pubian symphasis lust erection now primitive semi-comic hieroglyphic **SPERM OIL**.

"Now, about that money . . ." Sainte-Croix said in a somewhat sharp voice.

"Casual platonic friendship."

Mi-ti pulled out a honey-tan genuine crocodile-skin wallet, opened it and extracted nine crisp new thousand-dollar bills. He peeled two off, put them back in his wallet and handed the balance to Sainte-Croix.

Paper money passing from one palm to another, crisp as autumn and the turned back of the Machiavellian ventriloquist—with this descended calm; the almost-sad lotus calm before wide incandescent license.

Remy's fingers on Sooki's back as he hefted her over his shoulder—normal NORMAL *quite normal*. No backstep of amazement, but so totally your own pace—anti-fanfared, almost. No flags but unresistance.

Better this way—made patient by an astral Thad. Let the cat's paws ripple the pond.

Pausing by Bert's gluteal obeisance mantra.

"Bert, I need extend project work now. I take Sooki in Forest of Voice and search Internal Orgasm."

Bert tipped his head so far forward that his wig fell off CRANIUM.

"You're in the workshop, sure."

Bert—looking up.

"If anyone need me, this is too important work. But after forty minute knock—make sure I answer."

"Mazel tov!" Bert raising his palm for a high-five.

"Will be number one employee and customer satisfaction. Now do not disturb."

Walking to the door of the room Bert called the Workshop, Remy, with eyes contained in chest, saw, escaping those narrow walls, a landscape. The doll-trees waiting, electronic rain, zingy fresh with tantric qi slipping from their sentient subtle-leaves.

The spoor of labial concepts—the way through. To crest it this time. To crest, and there to find the placid flatlands where runs the river, the pristine crunch of a car door in a new universal normality—the Internal Orgasm *daily* **Daily** DAILY public—TRANSPORTING upskirt of God's simples, my hand read the palm of between your lakes and hills Will Be WILL BE—milk and honey portfolio

Freshly printed

Vulval fanlight

offshore for all the

first morning

AND SID IS A MONOLYTHIC HEAD.

Friday, 12ᵗʰ October, 2.19 p.m.

Where that strange room of work or play or something else was located, the Magister house had, on one side of its top floor (excluding the attic) a long corridor, somewhat bare, lined with windows, which anyone in the habit of naming rooms and other areas of a house might have called 'the Gallery'. Neither Clive nor Mr Magister called it that, or anything at all. Nameless as it was, however, Clive had spent a lot of time here, intermittently, over the years. People often think of the accumulation of time in terms of hoarded clutter, cobwebs—Miss Havisham's decaying, uneaten wedding cake. This corridor, bare as it was, and open to sunlight, gave Clive a greater sense of accumulated time than any other part of the building. Perhaps it was because it functioned as something like a watch tower—a place of vision, waiting and rest. Watch towers, lighthouses and so on—these are surely the kind of place where the heart is most purely conscious of itself and where memory can most freely play.

Clive was supposedly ill. His father, in the guise of treating him like an adult (which really meant continuing the usual neglect of the past years) had not questioned his barely-even-feigned illness. This in itself filled him with lassitude. But his real reason for ditching classes and skulking in solitude like this was Marybeth.

Time had passed again. With his elbows on the sill, gazing—almost serenely—through the glass of the window, Clive felt himself looking down upon that time, and the tiny, antic, half-engaging events it contained. Opposite these windows were the hills, crowded with those woods through which Clive liked to walk. The sun striking them now, catching the grey and reddish trunks under the grey, green and yellowing leaves, contained the dregs of summer even in the placid resignation of autumn. Clive knew where his tree was, on which were carved the initial 'MC'. He saw himself carving those initials, a thin-shouldered boy, saw himself later lingering, uncertain, later again, excited, offering those same initials a furtive, hurried libation of guilt, covetousness, regret.

Perhaps, he thought as he gazed through time's soundless telescope, perhaps his instincts had been true when, on the eve of his possessing Marybeth he had been so crushed by that sadness his tongue could not conduct into words, but which steeped and tormented him in the presentiment of also losing Marybeth—or all that was most precious in her—whatever else took place.

He was afraid he was doing a terrible thing by being here, now, at home, with these dark thoughts, when he could have been at school, watching over her, and stealing a moment here and there to speak with her, to touch those fingers, to breathe the very glances of her eyes. He should really ask her to come to the gazebo again. But he was more afraid of that. On the one hand, he was a fairy-tale fool who had planted a few magic beans to discover a gargantuan beanstalk growing from them, writhing serpent-like to the sky. It was obviously too vast for him to control or cultivate. On the other hand, he had been bequeathed a seedy little gospel from somewhere, written in dust, which told a desiccated tale: There is a girl, haunted by beauty, as by a ghost. A boy sees the girl, so beauty-haunted, and admires then desires her. Finally, he grasps her, but he cannot grasp her beauty. It haunts him, but floats away, eludes his grasp even as it haunts. She herself does not seem aware of the existence of the ghost. The ghost and the girl have become separate through his intervention. His presence somehow displaces the ghost, divides ghost from girl. He no longer knows her, nor himself. Time passes, and in this confusion he loses them both—girl and ghost. He leaves her forever, and looking back at her from a distance he sees that she is more beautiful than ever. The ghost has returned to her. It has swollen and grown brighter, since it has swallowed another ghost—his. He has lost her, lost beauty, lost his soul, forever.

Such was the dusty gospel of love that Clive read silently to himself these days. He feared it was inevitable and that his most valiant efforts would be torn feathers in the wind of this gospel; he feared that he was making it inevitable.

His mind wandered along the desolate track of these thoughts under a spell until it came out at a clearing of sad and mysterious silence.

He grew aware of noises in the house. He had forgotten that his father was also at home, apparently catching up on some administration for which he preferred domestic isolation. Then he heard the sound of tyres against the concrete of the driveway at the front of the house. A car horn sounded there. The sounds from his father's study grew more pronounced. Then the doorbell chimed.

Although he had an excuse—false, if that mattered—for being at home, he was in a mood where any kind of interaction would be bothersome to him. If his father emerged now, he might be seen. Almost involuntarily, he opened the door of the room behind him and, slipping within, felt immediately safer. This had once been a guest room, but there had been no guests in this house for a long while. In the meantime it had been used to store old paintings, photographs, stacks of papers and so on. For a moment, Clive was caught in the room's stilted atmosphere—it was an overflow for the by-products of neglect, procrastination and compromise. Then he realised that, from the far window, he could see the front drive of the house. His father's footsteps were already sounding in the corridor and—in obvious haste—down the stairs. Instinctively, he moved to the window, freshly curious about what was transpiring.

A large white van was parked in the driveway. On its side, a black sunburst radiated from the single word "Sundown". The driver, a man in his mid-thirties wearing a T-shirt and bandana, was standing near the van's open door, shielding his eyes as he surveyed the house-front. His workmate remained in the van's passenger seat. Clive had lost track of his father's footsteps, but the latter emerged now onto the driveway as if a separate, smaller entity to the man who had just left his study. Clive eased the sash window open a little and listened to the voices, which, even on the still afternoon air, only came up to him patchily.

". . . not exactly discreet . . ." Mr Magister was saying.

"Afternoon's the most discreet time of day . . ."

"Never mind . . . the one I ordered?"

"First out of the mould. She'll have that fresh rubber smell . . . something for you to sign . . ."

And further words were exchanged before the driver and his assistant began to unload a large bubble-wrapped bundle from the back of the van.

In a minute or two, the entire tide of Clive's blood seemed to have turned. He was alert now, present. Whatever was in that bubble wrap—he knew it with a keenness like the proximity of something long lost—it would tell him exactly what was wrong in this house.

He closed the window again, sat down on the stale carpet, listened, thought and waited. He wanted to be sure, by sound alone, exactly where his father went now in the house. There were some noises first on the ground floor, then, he thought, after the van had driven away, in the garage, then the ground floor again. Surprisingly soon, his father's footsteps re-ascended the stairs, slower than in their descent, almost laborious, and with a suggestion of stealth. Clive was beginning to feel something resembling his sensations when he had hidden from his father in the study a week or so back—like the sugary panic of blood loss. But, he noticed, he felt it now more on his father's behalf. There was something in that tread and in the whole situation. On the one hand, his father was on guard. On the other, he had become careless.

Mr Magister was simply returning to his private room. The footsteps stopped, the door opened, and it closed again. Clive got to his feet—he was about to engage with this half-flaunted secret.

Mirroring his father, when he closed the door of the guest room behind him, he only made a limited effort to keep his tread quiet. Or rather, some reaction against stealth forced a squeak here and there from the bare floor of the corridor. Now he gambled everything and knelt at the keyhole. If his father came to the door he would have no time to conceal himself, but he felt increasingly the need for secrecy heavier on his father's side. He seemed almost physically borne up in the scales, since his father weighed them down opposite him.

Adjusting his eye to the keyhole, the first picture he snatched of what was taking place comprised a figure seated upon his father's desk with his father standing in front of it, his back to the door. Clive's view was cut off just below the shoulders of both figures. He was, however, able to see the moist, hairless pinkness of the seated figure's right knee and calf. The only voice was his father's, clearly muttering as if he thought himself alone.

". . . see what you got here. Uh-hmmm. I think you just might be the finest doll I've landed so far. Maybe even better than that Sooki tramp. Jesus wept. Sundown know what they're doing. That Ukrainian broad is not so crazy . . . I think I'll call you . . . I think I'll call you . . . Hell, why don't we talk about names later?"

The seated, unspeaking figure was wearing a black evening dress, the hemline high, and somewhat ruched, of the kind that a sorority girl might wear to a social event. Clive observed his father's hand tugging down this dress from the right shoulder with impatient movements, and even more hastily tearing aside the cream-coloured and rose-dotted bra beneath.

His father now leant a little forward and to the right, and then drew back again. Somewhere on the back right corner of the broad desk, it seemed his father was playing an audio or video file on his laptop. From what Clive could make out it was porn. It sounded like heterosexual porn, too, but it was hard to tell, as all the voices were male. Clive caught a name: "Yeah, Sooki, you silicone bitch. Don't pretend like you don't want it." His father's voice mingled horribly with these background voices.

"Really?" his father now said with playful incredulity, as if responding to something the other figure had said. "You do, do you? Uh huh?"

Clive was beginning to feel sick. He knew it would have been actually impossible for his father to speak this way had he been aware of Clive's presence. In effect, this was no longer his father. Or, it was his father, but the filial bond was now stretching like sticky bubble-gum to breaking point. Clive thought that he should stop watching and go, but it was too late. If he went now, this heavy sickness would settle in his stomach forever. He had to see this through. He had to actually be sick, though he didn't even know what that might mean.

". . . so let's see what a tight little cutie . . ."

". . . *waiting for this, haven't you, silicone bitch?*"

His father's words, out of rhythm but in the same spirit with the digitally recorded voices, were becoming intermittent, punctuated by other sounds. His hands and mouth were busy—drunkenly busy. The sounds from the computer came to an end, but his father continued. He crouched, so that Clive could now see his face in quarter-profile or full profile at times. Was this how he had looked when he was bringing Clive into being? The thought made Clive feel as if he had never been born, like a ghost who had entered upon this life directly, without biology. His father was undoing his very conception.

". . . why you like an old guy, huh? 'Cause we got no dignity. Yeah? Well, what about you, little missy, when you're lying on your back?"

As he said this, Mr Magister swept some folders off the edge of the desk and forced the mute figure with wanton clumsiness into a horizontal position. She fell back with a jounce, her head just out of the keyhole field of Clive's vision.

Now came the motions and sounds that proceed from a crouch, a thrust and open legs—the rhythms that lose harmony with each other and turn into chugging spasms and begin again in a percussive spiral to release, the demented, asphyxiated voice that surrenders to its own grunting and bellowing gracelessness.

And then the final roar and gasp. Mr Magister appeared as if struck by an arrow. Solemnly, he sat up straight, moved back a little and pulled the supine figure towards him so that her head came into view.

Her horizontal profile was like the enunciation of a tip-of-the-tongue word, finalised into something written indelibly in the brain's neural map.

Her face . . . She did not breathe. Was she alive, or dead? For a duration, Clive did not understand what had happened and his breath also ceased. He was empty, yet heavy. Everything in him had melted through his feet into the floor.

Had she been coated in rubber? Suffocated? How had this happened? Why?

His father was unconcerned by the questions that strangled him, and was crawling between the knees he'd pushed apart.

With a strange lop-sidedness, Clive got to his feet. He fumbled with the doorknob, rattled it, threw the door open.

His father looked up.

"What are you———?"

"Get off her," hissed Clive.

"Clive, listen, I———"

"Get *off* her."

It was hard to say exactly where in the room it had its centre, but there was a sense of irreparable ruin. The deadly fear of both, around which their mutual agony of restraint had constricted, was revealed too plainly for excuses to obscure its edges. Words could no longer contain it. It was still possible for exultation also to be snatched from the wreckage, but only for one of them. Moving forward, Clive knew he was the one.

He had never hit his father before. Now he struck him a blow on the shoulder. Most of its force went into spraining Clive's wrist, but this was a spur for him. His father gave a snorting laugh, climbed off the desk, and began to button up his pants with the same unbearable literalness—taking exactly the space and time that it took—of the whole exposed secret itself.

Clive became aware that although action was always immediate, its meaning was always fractured; with time it became a matter of interpretation. This fact was his father's only remaining cover. Clive grew impatient with it.

"Why don't you just get out of here, you old sleaze?"

"Now, Clive, don't be hasty. We've got a lot to talk about."

"What? What have we got to talk about? Blackmail? I can't think of a single other thing to talk about now, so why don't you just get out of my sight, you poisonous fucking apology?"

Mr Magister looked about the study as if checking for something. Though his father wished to conceal it, Clive was aware that, if only he thought nothing greater and more injurious could be discovered in his absence, he keenly wished to leave this scene.

Defensively—or, it seemed to Clive, *off*ensively—Mr Magister checked his watch.

"You know, I should really be getting back to work," he said, as if he had not, in fact, been planning to spend an hour or two with his new acquisition. "Clive—" the word sounded repellent in his father's mouth, "—I should really go, and we can talk later, when . . . when you've had time to think."

His father edged towards the open door, then turned and left in obvious retreat.

Clive watched him depart. He regretted the lack of violence, and feared now that there might be some reconciliation, some return to mutual cowardice. To his father's disappearing back he hissed with chiselled deliberation:

"You are a shrivelled up old phoney and if I ever talk to you again let me rot in hell."

The violence he had stopped short of venting on his father, he now channelled furiously into slamming the study door. He closed his eyes, let out a breath, and turned to the doll as if he were a medic who had been waylaid before he could reach the scene of an emergency. Turned to the doll—of course, he knew it was a doll, like Sooki, but, there was something here he didn't understand, something almost uncanny. Her lack of breath was maddening. She was so quiet. And perfect. Perfect and quiet.

He had to examine her. The lines of this face—it could not be an accident. The eyes were glassy beneath those so-delicate brows, but it was hard for him to believe they saw nothing. He reached out to stroke her cheek. Then he saw something that made him freeze. It was the freckle on the left side of her neck. He stepped back in perplexity and horror, but a sudden thought saved him. Scooping his phone from his pocket, he called Marybeth on speed-dial. The dial tone sounded. She picked up. Her voice. He hung up, relieved.

He was approaching the doll again when his phone rang. He answered. It was Marybeth.

"What's wrong?"

"Huh? Nothing."

"You just phoned and hung up."

"It was an accident. I thought you'd be in class. Didn't want to get you in trouble."

"I'm in between classes. It's okay. What's up?"

"It's good to hear your voice."

"Is something wrong? You sound different or weird or something."

"Can we talk later? I'm still . . . I can't explain. I'm not well."

"Sure. We'll talk later. Text me."

"Will do. Talk to you later."

He hung up again.

How strange it was to feel Marybeth's hair between his fingertips after he had just been speaking to her on the phone. There was no resistance in her. His fear vanished, but a new fear appeared in its place. The new fear beckoned and receded, as if leading him down a long, long corridor.

"Marybeth," he said. "So glad I stopped that old bastard before he gave you the wrong name. I guess he didn't know what he was doing. But you are, aren't you? Marybeth."

She would not disappoint; she would only accept.

He stroked her face, ran the tip of his finger along her lips. He was thinking now of that time in the woods when he had anointed the love heart with his hot seed and gasped out a prayer to any who might be able to hear.

Something—someone—had heard. He believed he knew who it was.

"Thank you, Sooki," he said in the wondering flush of conviction.

Somehow, by a twisted miracle, life had brought before him this ghost—glowing, ethereal, pink. It was a ghost of rubber and silicone, a ghost his hands could hold and his fingers could explore. The beauty of this ghost would not elude him. Now that he was a ghost of flesh, he could meet, on her frequency, this ghost of rubber. For himself, for Sooki, for Marybeth, even for his father, there was something he must do.

He bent to kiss those parted lips and his hands softly set about finishing the undressing that his father had begun.

It was then he bumped up against an unpleasant thought, like a boat against a harbour wall. His father. His father's white dragon was already coiled inside this ghost, defiling her. The white dragon was in the way, ensuring none could ever claim the treasure of the deepest caves. The ghost became, at this thought, more slimily repulsive than a maggot-slick corpse. Despair and nausea were one in Clive's gut.

But he could not give up now. The miracle was still the miracle, even if filthy with defilement. Some things could not be eaten, and for the sake of a greater duty or desire, one eats the uneatable. Both duty and desire joined forces now, and together, even against the putrid white dragon, they were irresistible. There was not only treasure to be claimed beyond the wyrm, but a true maiden fair.

The violence that had gathered, unexpressed, began to swell, heavy with desire and with pendulous joy. Words and shrieks sputtered from his lips. She accommodated him completely. Above, behind, pinned beneath, they were a revolving sphere of limbs, tangling, untangling, tangling again—two solid ghosts in a pink void.

Then he was utterly rent by the lightning ecstasy that was wrung into a trickle where his body met the silicone ghost of beauty, and through that ghost, the world.

Once, it seemed, was not enough. Lightning and cloud-burst came twice more in wet lacerations, until his cloud was empty.

He wiped her face with her underwear, careful to leave no traces, and then cleaned himself. Of what he wiped from his thighs, Clive did not know what belonged to himself and what to his father. The white dragon was slain.

Without soap and water this attempt at cleaning was unsatisfactory, but would have to do.

There was something else he had to do. He flicked the touchpad of the laptop. As he'd thought, it was a video file, in .mov format. He replayed it now. When it was finished, he bowed his head.

"Sorry, Sooki. Thank you."

Things had become clear to him. His mind was free to think unhindered.

He dressed her again, tenderly, then lifted Marybeth from the desk, carrying her the way Zak had carried Sooki.

In the garage, Clive found a mass of bubblewrap that had not been there before. The car was gone, but he guessed his father hadn't gone back to work at all. He'd probably gone to some bar to try and get some distance, to rationalise with a few shots of whiskey. There was the bicycle, though. "You're going to have to hold on tight," he said to the heavy ghost-girl in his arms.

Sorting through drawers and shelves, Clive found a few things that were useful to him. He recognised usefulness now as something rare, like water in a desert. With cord, he tied her behind him, binding her wrists in front of his stomach. Someone might see him, of course—they probably would—but that also seemed necessary somehow. He was most worried that she would unbalance him in traffic. Where possible, he would ride on the pavement.

He practised the balance a little in the driveway, then he let the bicycle wheel down to the street, and began to pedal.

School had finished by now, and as he glided on his way, he recognised people here and there. Occasionally, a head would turn. Becoming self-conscious, he tried to think of a back route to his destination that would be practical considering his unwieldy passenger. Inspiration came to him and, turning onto a quieter, narrower road, he felt calmer, almost as if he were already there.

After a couple of turnings, he came to a downward slope between houses that would take him almost the whole way. He had gone some distance down this slope when two figures emerged from a turning ahead, themselves turning left, so that their backs were towards him. It was Christie and Marybeth. They must have been on their way to Marybeth's house. As the distance between them narrowed, his mind raced through his available options. In the time it took him to consider stopping or turning around he was already nearly on them. It was too late—to stop or turn now would only catch their attention. Instead, he would pedal just a little faster.

He passed them with a whoosh, almost believing that he smelt them. It was, he decided, the best thing he could have done. And to look back would be a disaster. He felt like an umbrella turned inside-out in the wind.

It was done. The ground levelled out. He turned and turned once more. For a while he had to pedal against a gradient. At last, however, he had arrived at St Mary's Cemetery. He dismounted and fairly discarded the bike, only retrieving the bag that had dangled from the handlebars, and undoing the cords that bound him to the doll. He carried her again in his arms.

The ground was uneven, and he slipped a couple of times, but he knew what he was looking for. He had seen it on Saturday, when he had come to visit his mother's grave, the day after the party, the day after that night of confusion.

To his considerable relief, it was still there—a gaping, six-foot hole in the ground, without a headstone, as if designed to bury someone with no name or family. He paused at its edge, but not for long. He released the burden—he wanted to release it. Rubber limbs and artificial hair tumbled into the hole. From the bag he took a small can of kerosene. He shook it, upside-down, as if scattering earth. Then he set light to some gathered pages of newspaper and tossed them into the hole.

From long familiarity with this place he knew there were few visitors, but it was quite possible someone would happen along and discover this strange scene—a single mourner at a burning, stoneless grave. Somehow, he did not care.

The rubber was beginning to bubble and black smoke was rising. He rubbed his forehead and saw there was ash on his fingertips. His muscles ached from the strain of the last few hours, and he was rooted at the grave's edge by a glad exhaustion. Let them come. He was a ghost burying a ghost. Who could touch him? A strange phrase came back to him: Let the dead bury the dead. What could it mean? Lies, he decided. Lies made more lies—the dead buried the dead. Personally, he'd had enough.

He scooped out his phone again, scrolled down to Marybeth's number and tapped in a message:

MARYBETH UR STILL THE CUTEST GIRL IN CLASS. SAY HI TO CHRISTIE.

He pocketed his phone and turned to walk back to the bicycle.

Friday, 12th October, 2.21 p.m.

Zak called Thad for the thirty-sixth time, letting the dial tone drone for a monotonous minute until its recorded message played, tinny and muffled, the hollow Styrofoam sound of a displaced voice.

"Hi this is Thad, I'm not here right now," it said. "So I must be doing something important. Message me after the beep and I'll get back to you . . . or not. Stay beautiful!"

He hung up and immediately called again, repeating the process until he reached his forty-third attempt. He had heard the recording enough times to have memorised its every pause and intonation but hadn't left a message, his inner state being too volatile and formless for clear expression. Earlier he had fallen asleep in his chair and the dial tone had persisted into his dreams, which formed on the thin, anxious edge of waking and contained no contrasting elements, only that endless pulse echoing in an imageless void. Without Sooki his mind had nowhere to settle, and he felt himself crushed by the weight of his unmoored thoughts and the unmoored emotions beneath them. Something inside him spasmed like a severed limb struck by a spark. He got up and walked around the room until he realised that he was moving in ever-tightening circles. A perceptible dread shadowed each step; he felt both thoroughly abandoned and constantly watched by hidden, derisive eyes.

He put the phone down, turned on his computer and pulled up an old playlist of NYC hardcore from the mid 90s: Gorilla Biscuits, Quicksand, CIV, Orange 9MM and Youth of Today. Mixed in with it were random tracks from Rites of Spring, Sunny Day Real Estate and The Promise Ring. In the first month of his fifteenth year Zak had discovered these records in his older brother's room after the latter had left for college, and in that room's poster-shrouded seclusion he had initiated himself into an unsuspected world of bombastic purity. Four months later, after scrawling Xs on the backs of his palms with a black Sharpie marker, he vowed never to break his edge. He would not drink, smoke or

certain incidents

compromise himself for any reason. He would stay whole.

Listening to the music now, he felt a chasm opening inside him. In the end hardcore unity had not been enough, and he had never worked up the courage to attend a live show. He had broken his edge gradually, letting himself slip into the world around him; had lost control by not paying close enough attention, that ultimate sin of omission.

He opened Firefox and let the browser load its cache of tabs, the hundred or so pages he left open but never managed to read. There was nothing in his inbox, but twenty-three new messages had accumulated in the spam folder. He idly scanned them, deleting the usual

CANADIAN ULTRASOUND PHARMACY Rewards Alert Christian Credit Card Centre @ Low Rent to AT&T несовершеннолетних девочек Vodafone Homes Browse Beautiful Facebook Latin Singles For Free e-Cigarette Trial Size Matters من الكسكر للبيع في السعودية Cialis Viagra & Levitra 90% Off Major 2-4 Inches Permanently Enlarged Best Life Offers Secure

*Your Family's Future Event About to Happen Next Payday Un-
secured Small* 黒ギャルパイズリビデオ *Business Nationwide
Sexual PayPal Tax Credit Injury Lawyers ZERO APR Lasik
Miracle or Work-At-Home Dad Katy Perry Scam 3 Days Free Join
My Rachel Ray Weightloss Network on *APPROVED* Linke-
dIn Only $2500.00* 研发项目经理, 谁是你的敌人 *[Free
Pills] Deposited In Your Account Re: Foreclosed Homes In Your
Area Today Entitled to £4,764 See Results Now!*

undifferentiated ads, until a single subject line impaled
his attention:

SOOKI GETTINF UCKED

His throat constricted. It was spam, he knew; not anything he should open. There were phishing programs that
could have pulled Sooki's name from his computer. It was
not personal, not real. He would have deleted it, had it not
been sent from Thad.

He opened it.

There was no text, only a .mov video attachment, 3.23
in length. He moved the cursor to the Delete button and
paused, feeling dizzy horror overwhelm him. The ever-
tightening circles were back, but this time it was the room
moving, not him. His hand dragged the mouse down and
saved the attachment.

"Sooki . . . why couldn't I . . ."

He opened it with QuickTime and pressed play. And
saw

*Rutting man-shaped apes stroke flesh coloured plastic eros in
chains changing her face to dilation crisis*

Not personal. Not real. Her mouth and eyes open, filled
with sorrow. He watched

*cameras and chains transfixing mute sex shadows in flashlight
fluid love hung from a hook, grasping thrusting fists in mouth under*

as they reduced her

*inflamed receptacle caressed by hand spiders crawling crevices to
inner alleys forcing open flesh flower fists beating spraypaint tattoos on
the inner outer walls shaking beaten bone struts of ransacked inner
mansions*

to an object

*aflame with flashes and laughs whoops and crashes fuck fuck fuck
fuck fuck fuck fuck fuck fuck fuck fuck fuck fuck fuck fuck fuck fuck
fuck fuck fuck fuck fuck fuck fuck fuck fuck fuck fuck fuck fuck fuck
fuck fuck fuck fuck fuck fuck fuck fuck fuck fuck fuck fuck fuck fuck
fuck fuck fuck fuck fuck fuck fuck fuck fuck to uncertain glitter of
some pearly drop pushed aside to reveal the final spasm of the male
member tangled black willow hairy drooling Madonna crawling into
the sun in sorrow.*

The video ended. He stared at the screen for eight seconds and moved his head back and forth in feeble protest. He tried to smash the keyboard but banged his elbow on the table and felt himself slipping from the chair. On the floor, he crawled under the desk and held his face in his hands. He cried for twelve minutes and when he felt the emotions relenting he forced himself to cry more, as if he were squeezing not only pus, but also blood from a wound, expelling sickness and sensitivity alike.

In his fifteenth year, shortly after he had begun exploring his brother's room, Greg Richards and Joe Barrett from Linden High had dared Zak to grab the electric fence that protected the Barrett Farm's cows. Joe reassured him that the current would be non-lethal, as according to his father there was "no need to chargrill the beef—just to give it boundaries." Zak had protested, but following the discovery of

certain incidents

certain materials in his locker they had threatened to tell the rest of the school unless he complied. The fence-grabbing would be part of a stunt series pilot they would send to MTV, Greg informed him. They had already filmed themselves trampolining off the roof of Joe's house in a shopping cart, followed by Joe spiking his infant brother's baby food with Tabasco sauce; now they needed more impressive footage. They were doing him a favour, Greg emphasised as the three of them walked across the field to the fence enclosure, and if MTV accepted the pilot they would give him a regular spot on the show testing other pain-inducing devices. As he stood before the fence, Zak readied himself for a cartoon explosion, some sizzling shower of sparks to propel him through the air. There was nothing to do but get it over with. As Greg held up the camera, he dropped his hands to the fence and gripped the wire.

At first, nothing happened. For a moment he wondered whether the fence was turned on; then he felt his left foot go numb. Sensation soon returned, but he didn't notice, as a grenade had just detonated in his left shoulder, turning bone and muscle to meal and mash. He felt a crawling sensation in his scalp, and then the final, consciousness-destroying bomb exploded inside his head.

He remembered laughter next, Greg standing over him with the camera as Joe pointed and made faces. Somehow they had gotten him away from the fence, but he didn't feel right for the rest of the day and suffered from migraines for the next week. His powers of concentration, which had never been impressive, further declined.

Over the years Zak had come to think of real emotions—distinct from the graduation, wedding and funeral kind—as manifesting much like those bursts of electricity: total, localised convulsions asserting themselves too suddenly and seriously for understanding or control. You couldn't express real emotions in public or everyone would laugh; only proscribed emotions were acceptable in real life. That was why music existed: so you could feel something real and not be locked up. But finally there had to be something other than music; there had to be someone to accept it all. Sooki had done that for him, even when his emotions had overflowed, but maybe he had expected too much even from her.

He emerged from under the desk and took his phone from beside the computer. There was no one to call and nothing to do, so he would drive somewhere far away and think. He reached into his pocket for his keys, and when he brought them out he noticed a scrap of green paper caught in the keychain. There was a number scribbled on it in fading blue ink, and beneath it a name: PHIL BOUGHTON.

He remembered Jed, the solicitous Christian with the focused gaze and distant manner. For most of his life Zak had regarded religion as a joke, but at least this Jed had not threatened him with anything, had not wanted to take everything he had. And Jed had said the pastor could help. Zak doubted anyone could help him at the moment, but neither did he want to be alone; he felt like talking, even if it led nowhere. After pausing for a moment to steady his nerves, he tapped out the number on his phone and pressed call.

For a long time there was no response, and he was on the verge of hanging up when someone at last answered, a deep male voice which sounded as if it had been startled out of sleep.

"Hello?"

"Hello . . . is this Pastor Phil Boughton?"

There was a muffled coughing sound on the line.

"I'm Phil Boughton, yes, but I'm not a pastor anymore. How can I help you?"

"You're not a pastor anymore . . .?"

"No, I'm sorry, I haven't been a pastor for a few weeks. Now I'm just Phil the dental assistant."

"But Jed said . . . I mean, you know Jed, don't you?"

"I know several Jeds, but yes, I think I know the one you mean."

"My name's Zak . . . Jed said you'd be able to help me."

Another cough.

"Help you with what?"

"It's . . . well, some people have kidnapped my girl-friend."

"Call the police?"

"I did. They said they'd try to find her, but I don't think there's anything they can do. They never really help any-one."

"Ahaha . . . yes . . . isn't that the truth. Well Zeke, I guess I could give you some advice. But I'm not promising any-thing, you understand. Whereabouts you live?"

Zak told him.

"Well, that's not far from here," Boughton said. "I'm over at the Aflame Fellowship Church, that's A-F-L-A-M-E Aflame."

"The church is on fire?"

"No, it's a reference to the Holy Spirit. I can give you the address, or you can look it up on your computer or wher-ever people look things up these days."

Zak opted for the computer. Fifteen minutes later he was in his car driving down the road with his iPod nano blasting Deftones' *Around the Fur*.

"It feels good to know you're mine . . ."

As a child[1] he had been excitable and effeminate; had played with not only dolls but princess crowns and cotton dresses.

Following certain incidents

"Now drive me . . . far . . . away . . ."

You couldn't let your emotions overflow around other people—only at the right time and place. You couldn't cry any time you felt like crying.

Otherwise certain incidents

You had to stay away from drugs and alcohol and not lose control otherwise people would see. Stay away from drugs . . . except Ritalin, but that didn't count.

"I don't care where just far . . . away . . ."

Caught in the locker electric wire around my heart drooling that quick flavour turning in a hardcore kid's eye underprivileged organs

He wondered whether he could stop his emotions from overflowing; whether, like Jed, he could make the leap to God. In a faraway place.

He found himself crying again and pulled over to the side of the road. If he could pass over into God. A hideous Jesus waited for him on the other side of the fence, beyond the electricity and emotions, grinning like a statue.

"I don't care where just FAR—"

If he could just make the leap over the fence into God. Anywhere, out of the world.

Plastic virgin cadaver lively and beautiful today will tear for us this hard forgotten lake that lurks beneath the frost

He pulled back onto the road and drove with the tears dripping down his blotchy, coffee-toned cheeks. At an inter-

---

1. What's wrong with your skin faggot huh what are you Michael Jackson huh are you black or white faggot what's that come here fucking hdghajddh fucking stop moving hdhsghwydh get the hssgsg get his pants down guys hghdgdgh are you gonna cry look guys he's crying why are you crying faggot what's wrong

section, two teenage boys in a modern Volkswagen Beetle pulled next to him and began miming sex gestures through the window. He ignored them and drove on, passing a local character he recognised on the sidewalk, but who he saw now with a fresh ache of despairing compassion—an old man with a sandwich-board proclaiming, "Scarlett Johansson raped me"; beneath this indictment, the case for the prosecution was laid out in smaller letters. Eventually he pulled into a parking lot as indicated by his car's navigation system.

The Aflame Fellowship Church looked nothing like he had expected. Crammed between an art supplies store and a laundromat, it resembled a medium-sized storefront office more than a house of worship. A neon coil twisted in the shape of a dove flickered dully above the church's name, spelled out on a sign in Gothic text. Through the window Zak could see that the interior was filled with boxes, chairs and tables, giving it the look of a run-down furniture store.

Zak knocked, and after a few moments the door was opened by a tall man wearing a blue cardigan and an old pair of work trousers. He looked to be around twice Zak's age and sported a severe, military-style crewcut, along with several days' growth of salt-and-pepper beard. The contrast between the neat haircut and unkempt beard struck Zak as unusual. The man's tiny blue eyes appraised him without blinking.

"Phil Boughton," he said. "You must be Zeke."

Zak nodded, not bothering to correct him; even his own name no longer seemed to matter. "Yeah. This is your church?"

"It was, until I told everyone to leave," Boughton said. "But I think Dave Stone is starting up a new one somewhere. I'm sure it doesn't matter. Come in, if you want."

Zak followed him inside, where he saw that the church was filled not only with furniture but all manner of detritus: an acoustic guitar, two densely-packed book cases, several baseball bats and tennis rackets, a small television with a rounded glass screen and an old VCR with VHS cassettes stacked on top of it. There was a bed at the back, its sheets stained beige and wadded into a ball.

"What you see here are stage props from my marriage," Boughton said, gesturing to the piles of kipple. "I had to move out and this was the only place I had left."

"What happened?" Zak asked.

"My wife was having an affair with my grandfather," Boughton said. "Of course, that's just the short-term cause. The long-term cause . . . well, it's difficult to say. But I've changed my mind, changed it about a lot of things. Anyway, enough about me . . . you've come here for advice, if I understand right." He took a seat on a wooden stool and gestured for Zak to sit in an old leather armchair. "What's this about your girlfriend?"

Zak sat down and started to relate the events of the past few days, but as he spoke he found himself qualifying and elaborating on each incident until the account turned into a recounting of his entire life. After giving an overview of the past few years, he explained how he had met Sooki, and how the threat of dollnapping had overshadowed their happiness and eventually left him bereft. Occasionally he glanced at the Garfield clock on the wall, but Boughton listened attentively, and when Zak at last finished he saw that he had been speaking for over an hour.

"I think that's it," he concluded. "I don't know what to do now. It's like everything's finished. There's nothing left."

Boughton looked directly into Zak's eyes and thought for a moment, then spoke. "That's the stupidest story I've ever heard," he said. His voice was calm and contained no especial emotion. "You're obviously a moron. Just like me, in other words." He smiled.

Neither of them spoke for a while.

Boughton said, "I think rather than tell you what it all means, or what I think you should do now, rather than do that, which is what I would have done a few months ago, instead I'll do something else. Since you've shared so much, let me share a few things of my own. But first let me make you some coffee."

He got up and went to a small range at the back of the room. When he returned, it was with two mugs of Folger's Original. The mug he handed to Zak was embossed with a Bible verse: Romans 12:2.

"Where was I. Oh, that's right. I'm no longer a pastor, so I can't really help you. You see, I used to look at this material world around us as a kind of prison, or a training camp at best, something we could eventually escape from. That's what kept me going."

He took a sip from his coffee mug, which was embossed with Snoopy.

"But I no longer believe that to be the case." He held out his hand to Zak. "You can feel this pulse here. I think this is all there is, just this pulse going on second after second, minute after minute." He withdrew his hand and gestured to the room. "The prison is here, and it's filled with junk."

"That's not all there is," Zak said. "You can escape. There are all kinds of other things . . ."

Sooki's eyes flashed into his mind, opalescent, changing. Then he thought of Thad, but was surprised to feel no anger. All his bitterness and dread had seeped away, leaving only a nameless urgency.

"Well, maybe you can tell me about them," Boughton said. "And maybe you can take some of this junk away." He stood. "What about the VCR? Or how about a wicker chair? That one over there could be on Antiques Roadshow."

"We have to figure it out now," Zak said. "We have to figure out whether there's any meaning to anything."

"I'm going for dinner soon," Boughton said. "Do you think we can decide before then?"

"We'll ask the universe," Zak said. "We'll ask it to send us a sign."

"Then let's go outside. I'm in the mood for chicken and biscuits."

Zak followed him to the door. Outside, dusk had fallen, and the moon was already visible in a cloudless sky. Boughton had no car, so they climbed into Zak's.

"There's a good place just down the road. They serve chicken and waffles too," Boughton said.

Zak turned on the ignition, but found himself unable to drive. The urgency that had risen in him returned; he found that his hands were shaking. He thought again of making the leap to God.

Boughton reached over and turned on the radio dial. Immediately a voice blurted into life.

". . . who've just tuned in, this is the Doctor Mockjock Show, where, after the unbelievable response we had from his run on our afternoon slot, Doctor Graham Clegg, otherwise known as Uncle Reasonable, has returned for our early evening call in. He's here to answer any and all questions, so let's open up the lines again . . . callers remember, the number is 732-562-0993."

"This is it!" Zak said. "It's not an accident. We have to call."

Before Boughton could protest, Zak had taken out his phone and was dialling the number immediately after Doctor Mockjock repeated it.

"Hello?"

Now Boughton heard the voice from the radio echo the voice beside him.

"Good evening, you're on the air with Uncle Reasonable."

"This is Zak Landers. I'm here with Phil Boughton the pastor," Zak began.

"Dental assistant," Boughton said.

"Phil Boughton the dental assistant. We want to know what to do to escape from this world of junk and find love and meaning. There has to be somewhere we can go and something we can do and someone who will understand. Can you tell us how to get in touch with God so he can give me my girlfriend back?"

"And why is there evil, ask him that too," Boughton said.

"What can we do about evil and how can I find my girlfriend?" Zak asked.

Uncle Reasonable coughed.

"Zak, do you and Phil have any cocoa in the house?"

"I'll check. Phil do you have any cocoa?"

"Instant cocoa? I think so."

"He says he does."

"Marvellous," Uncle Reasonable said. "I would suggest that before turning in to bed tonight, you make yourselves two nice mugs of cocoa, listen to some relaxing music, and get a good night's rest. Sleep is the best medicine, and cures most problems, I've found."

"Uncle Reasonable, we're really trying to solve evil . . . solve it for good. Because the real heroes are the ones who know how to trust, right? And everyone I've ever trusted has fucked me over . . . so what kind of hero am I? Fear is the past, love is the future, right? So where's my future?

They took everything from me, the only love I had. All I wanted was to be left alone with her. So where is she now? WHERE THE FUCK IS SHE?"

"With any new endeavour, I think it's best to start with a nice cup of cocoa. Especially before turning in at a reasonable hour."

"WHERE THE FUCK——"

"Of course, all kinds of problems can arise. But in the end, as I said, I think the best course for now is to make yourself a nice cup of cocoa, listen to some relaxing music and get a good night's sleep. So with that, I'll wish you goodnight, and again, I hope you can turn in at a reasonable hour. Once more: Good night . . .

. . . good night . . .

. . . good night."

OTHER SNUGGLY BOOKS YOU WILL ENJOY...

BLUE ON BLUE
by Quentin S. Crisp

A SUITE IN FOUR WINDOWS
by David Rix

NIGHTMARES OF AN ETHER-DRINKER
by Jean Lorrain

DIVORCE PROCEDURES FOR
THE HAIRDRESSERS OF A METALLIC AND
INCONSTANT GODDESS
by Justin Isis

BUTTERFLY DREAM
by Kristine Ong Muslim

GONE FISHING WITH SAMY ROSENSTOCK
by Toadhouse

THE SOUL-DRINKER
AND OTHER DECADENT FANTASIES
by Jean Lorrain

MENDICANT CITY
by Yarrow Paisley

THE OUTCAST SPIRIT AND OTHER STORIES
by Lady Dilke

CLARK
by Brendan Connell

AN ARCHIVE OF HUMAN NONSENSE
by Jason Rolfe

BLUEBIRDS
by Catulle Mendès